NO
PLACE
IS
SAFE

C. L. BREES

ISBN-13: 978-0-578-65110-1 (Paperback)

Library of Congress Control Number: 2020903631

C. L. Brees

Printed and bound in the United States of America
First Printing: April 2020

Editing by Ryan Quinn
Front cover image by Book Cover Zone

www.clbreesauthor.com

To Jesse. Thanks for all you do.

"The past is never where you think you left it."

— Katherine Anne Porter

PART 1

SATURDAY

"Home is a shelter from storms-all sorts of storms."
William J. Bennett

CHAPTER 1

"I NEED YOUR HELP."

Those four words were the ones Detective Sergeant Christian Anderson forever despised—not just now, but always. Yet there he sat on the edge of his bed with his iPhone pressed against his ear. A quick glance at the clock on the nightstand: 3:45 A.M. His heavy eyes closed, and his breath slowed.

"What's wrong?"

"It's Cassidy. She's vanished."

He rubbed the crust from his eyes. "How long?"

There was a pause on the line. "Two days. I didn't want to call, but I can't trust anyone else."

Her voice cracked. In all the years he'd known her, she'd

never been this shaken before.

"I need to make a few calls, so it'll be a few hours. That okay?"

"So, you'll come?"

Christian sighed. "I'm only doing this because it's you. But, yes—I'll come."

❖

NOT ONCE DID RETURNING TO THIS derelict town filled with ghosts of his past ever cross his mind. At least that was the plan ten years ago. But then Gemma, his best friend and only real attachment left to Cedar Lake, phoned in hysterics. Without hesitation, he upended his entire world, loaded his sedan, and traipsed six hours across the vast province.

The ankle-deep snow buried the street he remembered as a kid and the vehicle sliced through like a champ. With the flick of his wrist he shook his digital watch awake. One o'clock on the dot. As he maneuvered the thoroughfare, happier memories flooded his mind, yet one thing was certain, *Same old shithole it always was.*

He crossed over Fourth Avenue, and the last house on the block dwarfed anything else on his mind.

His foot slammed against the brake pedal, and the car skidded along the unplowed pavement. Frazzled, he gripped the steering wheel, let up on the brake, and seconds later glided into an empty space along the bare-treed avenue outside a neglected, gray, split-story house.

Everything Christian remembered about Cedar Lake had changed, although none of those transformations would anyone with half a brain consider an improvement. His shaky hand pushed the gearshift forward, and after several minutes he turned his head toward the front lawn where he spent the better portion of his childhood.

His eyes remained transfixed on the exterior, which in its prime was one of the most attention-grabbing houses on the street. Now, as he scrutinized the chipped-away paint, the screen door hanging on for dear life, it was evident the pizzazz had faded and what remained was one of the worst houses he'd seen in some time.

He diverted his eyes away from the front door and rolled toward the driveway. Ten years ago, as he pulled away in a cloud of smoke, the junk collection pile had been small, but somehow in a decade the tiny pile of crap had sprouted and consumed a majority of the yard.

He twisted back the key in the ignition and the flow of warm air stopped. He clenched the steering wheel while his heart raced, and his palms grew wet. He closed his eyes and took in a deep breath. After a few repetitions, he opened them and caught sight of himself in the rearview mirror.

"Just breathe like the therapist taught you."

For all his effort, the exercise failed and soon the *what ifs* engulfed his soul. What would he say when he saw him? Would the man who raised him recognize him after so many years? Worse, would *he* even recognize his own father? Much had changed over a decade; then again, Christian was naïve if he supposed deep down anything in the Anderson household were different.

He flung the car door open and plodded his black snow boots against the packed snow. After the long car ride with no pitstops, he inhaled deeply. A hint of smoldering cedar

3

lingered in the frigid air, and the familiarity dredged up more unsolicited recollections. He shook them off and slammed the heavy door behind him.

During the six-hour drive from Regina, Christian had ample time to deliberate how he'd explain his presence. However, as each justification grew more intricate than the former, Christian questioned why he even wasted his energy concocting pointless lies. His intuition told him the moment the front door swung open, he'd find his father with his fingers wrapped around a bottle of booze. At least that's the vivid picture he remembered from the evening after his high school graduation. The day he packed his bags and bolted as fast as he could from this one-stoplight town.

He trudged along the icy walkway, unsure if his hands trembled from the cold or the anticipation of what he'd find behind the front door. A quick glance to his right and he found his father's 1980s Dodge pickup covered in a foot of snow.

Must have been a while since he was last out.

He stood at the screen door, which hung on by one hinge, and he contemplated how he'd get past without tearing it away from the doorjamb. With precision, he pulled lightly back and pressed his knuckle against the door.

Thud. Thud. Thud.

Believing a changed man would fling open the door, his optimism faded when mere stillness greeted him.

Undeterred, he banged again three times and twisted the door handle. No surprise to him, the door popped. He extended his hand and pushed against the substandard barrier between the inside and outside.

NO PLACE IS SAFE

The moment his left foot crossed the threshold, the stench of urine and body odor attacked his nostrils. He sprang back to prepare for what horrid scene awaited him. Christian turned his head, gasped his last nip of unsullied air, and forced the door inward.

"Pop?" he called out.

Only the eerie calm greeted him.

The floor creaked beneath his feet, and he took two steps into the foyer. "Pop, you home? It's Christian."

He rotated in a circle, and the mounds of garbage alarmed him. After the initial shock of surveying how his father was living (if one could call what he had a life), his hazel eyes perused upward. There was the man who from the time Christian was a child overlooked him, slouched in his beloved lounger from circa 1988, with his emaciated fingers clasped around a fifth of cheap gin. He squinted and gave a long, hard stare at the man who he shared half of his DNA with.

He had changed, all right. Now, the short hair his father had sported his entire life was scraggly and greasy. His beard was unkempt. There were holes punched in the walls, and Christian stopped counting at five. Time sure hadn't been kind to Matthias Anderson.

"Christ," Christian whispered underneath his breath. "Pop, wake up."

The house was in sadder shape than the day he left. With uneasiness, he tiptoed around the empty pizza boxes, liquor bottles, and bugs that speckled the brown Berber carpeting. With each additional step he gained, his skin crawled from the crunch of roaches underneath his feet.

He hovered over his father, yanked his pants legs up, and crouched. The stench of booze wafted, and Christian deliberated if waking him was a wise decision.

Leery, he set his hand against the older man's shoulder and shook vigorously. "Pop. Come on, wake up."

His eyes fluttered. He slurred three words. "Leave me alone."

"Pop, it's me. Please wake up."

The older man opened one bloodshot eye. "Christian? Is that you?"

Christian couldn't bring himself to confirm. All he could do was shake his head.

Matthias opened both eyes and glanced at the bottle he clutched in his hand. "I can explain."

"Here we go again; I don't need another rationalization. Face the facts, Pop, this is just who you are and have been since the day Mom disappeared."

The tattered man adjusted his body in the chair, dropped the half-drunk bottle to the ground, and rubbed his hands across his haggard mug. "Wh-why are you here? God, how long's it been?"

With a snarky tone in his voice, Christian responded. "I'm not here for you. I came for Gemma."

The name provoked an immediate, sobering response and Matthias started to panic. "Has something happened to her?"

Christian pressed against his father's chest and he fell back into the lounger. "Relax. Gemma needs my help with a family matter. I only dropped in to check on you since I'm in town."

Matthias pressed his hand against the chairback in an effort to get to his feet. With too much liquor pumping through his bloodstream, he let his equilibrium get the better of him, and he dropped back into the chair.

Christian hung his head and pinched the bridge of his nose. "Jesus, you're an absolute mess."

The father and son stared at each other in silence, and eventually, Matthias labored to stand to his feet again. With some sort of miracle, he managed this time to keep his balance, and Christian wrapped his arm around his father's back and steadily guided him to the couch.

He tossed a stained pillow against the armrest and lowered his father onto the couch. The old man plonked against the tweed cushioning. Christian squatted next to his head, and again, his father grilled him for answers.

"Tell me the truth, boy. Something's wrong with Gemma? . . . No, wait, there can't be, I saw her two days ago and she was fine."

"Gemma's good. It's Cassidy who's in trouble."

He scrunched his face at the mention of her name. "Hopeless girl's in rehab. The third time, you know. Tried to overdose on whatever brew she got her hands on this time."

Christian shook his head. "No, Pop, they released her two days ago."

His slurred speech continued. "And she's in trouble already? What'd she do now?"

"It's not what she *did*." He wiped his hands across his face. "Gemma says when she arrived to pick her up, Cassidy had vanished, and no one has seen her since she signed out of the rehab center."

Matthias strained to sustain eye contact but babbled in a judgmental manner. "Most likely ran off with her low-life, drug-dealing boyfriend. You're a cop. You should know rule number one: junkies never change."

Christian exhaled and scanned the place he once called home. "Yeah, they don't, do they?"

He crinkled his nose in disgust and refocused his attention on his father, who had once again blacked out. With a snap of his fingers, Matthias resurrected. "Pop. I'm heading out. Do us both a favor and get some rest, perhaps a shower if you sober up long enough, and I'll come back to check on you tonight."

The man smacked his dehydrated lips together and shooed him. Christian stood to his feet, turned, and walked to the door. As he reached the foyer, he rested his hand against the wall and turned his head around to catch one more glimpse of the man he previously considered his idol. With a quick tap against the wall, he continued on and stepped back into the winter white world of Cedar Lake.

Once in the car, he slid the key into the ignition and right before he turned over the engine, he stopped. The radio revived, and a sappy song from 2009 filled the hollow space. As much as he wanted to turn over the engine and head back to Regina, or anywhere far away from this godforsaken place as he could, his repressed feelings had other plans.

He arched forward, his forehead rested against the steering wheel, and the reality of everything sank in. All the guilt and resentment ambushed Christian, and soon what started out as a drip escalated into a full-fledged stream of tears that spurted from his eyes as if he'd learned his father had died.

Midway through his emotional collapse, the lively ringtone from his cell phone interrupted. Without lifting his head, his hand rummaged about for the phone. With a tap of the power button, the ringing quieted. What should have worked the first time didn't, considering seconds later the phone rang again. This time he wiped the wetness from his stained face, and through the blurriness the name on the caller ID slowly came into focus.

Gemma Williams.

His hand trembled as he clutched the phone in his hand. "H-hello?"

"Hey, handsome. You make it back to this marvelous place you *used* to call home?"

He sucked back the mucus dribbling from his nose. "Yeah. Got here about twenty minutes ago."

"Wait. Are you crying? Why the hell are you crying?"

"Don't ask."

"Oh Jesus, please tell me you didn't do what I think you did."

Christian remained silent.

"For the love of all that is holy, tell me you aren't where I think you are."

"If I said I wasn't, then I'd be lying."

"Oh honey. Why would you torture yourself?"

"I had to."

Gemma sighed. "You did not *have* to. As I told you this morning, your father is not a well man. You should have swung by here first, and we could have gone together."

"You're right. I shouldn't have gone alone," he said. "But what's done is done."

9

Even through the phone, Christian pictured her standing there, shaking her head disapprovingly. He coughed. "Where are you?"

"Where I always am: home."

Christian collected his strength and pulled himself together. "I'll be there in five minutes."

Without as much as a goodbye, he lobbed the phone in the cup holder, turned over the engine, and pulled away from the curb.

✣

THE CAR APPROACHED A MODEST HOUSE ten blocks away, and the silhouette of Gemma pacing the front porch emerged. Christian coasted into the driveway at the precise moment she lifted the butt of her cigarette to her lips and inhaled.

For as long as they had been friends, Gemma struggled to go cold turkey. For a number of reasons, Christian never harped on her (although deep down he wanted to shake the ever-living shit out of her). For most who grew up in Cedar Lake, if you didn't have at least one addiction, the locals considered you abnormal.

They exchanged waves as he stepped out and flung his tan, knee-length wool jacket over his shoulder. He bumped the door with his hip and walked to the trunk to retrieve his belongings. With one hand he first snatched a small duffle bag, followed by a suitcase, setting each of them on the curb. With one swift move, he slammed the trunk closed and shuffled along the walkway.

He continued his trek along the thin path someone had cleared, doing whatever he could to avoid any icy patches. Gemma gleamed as he advanced, sucked in her last drag, and rushed down the stairs to grab the duffle bag from his hand.

"Well, look at you, Mr. Important." She exhaled what smoke lingered in her lungs and wrapped her arms around his neck.

He pulled away and scrutinized her outfit. "When was the last time you visited the mall?"

She smirked and twirled around. "What? Not fond of the jacket?"

"Considering I was with you three years ago when you bought the thing, no, I'm not fond of it. Once we find Cassidy our first trip is to a store."

She scoffed at his bluntness. "Not all of us are as lucky to have escaped and are making hand over fists' worth of money now. Besides, the kids today would call it vintage. You know that's all the rage right now."

They traded grins and laughed. This was without a doubt the exact childish behavior from the early 1990s that built their friendship.

Gemma reached into her jacket pocket and pulled out another cigarette from the pack.

"Um, I'm going to catch my death out here," Christian said. He rubbed his hands dramatically along his arms.

"Fine," she rolled her eyes and slipped the cigarette back into the pack. "Besides, my dad's excited to see you."

He cocked his head. "Huh? If memory serves me correct, wasn't he ecstatic when I pulled away from the curb ten years ago?"

She hung her head in embarrassment. "The last few years, well, he's evolved. Suppose that's what you have to do when you have your hands full with, well, a train wreck."

He stuck out his arm and blocked the door. "You're talking about Cassidy?"

She dipped her head. "Amongst other things."

"Well, as I said earlier, I'm here to help as much as I can."

"Thanks. If I haven't repeated myself enough, thank you again for coming back here. I bet this is hard for you."

He extended his hand, grasped hers, and squeezed. "You were there during some of my worst times, so it's only right I repay the favor. Besides, that's what friends do. We help each other when the going gets tough."

She patted the top of his hand and smiled. "Yup."

The door swung open, and the warmness thawed Christian's chilled face. The house was a stark contrast to the one he'd called home for eighteen years. The living room was cheery and welcoming, no dirty dishes littered the floor, no empty booze bottles collected dust. And for once, he was jealous of Gemma for the stable life she had.

He ventured farther inside; the feminine touches everywhere brought a smile to Christian's face. Gemma and Cassidy sure had stamped their individuality on the décor.

Gemma's father, Liam, rested on the couch with his leg crossed atop the other. He jumped to his feet and immediately opened his arms and exposed his pearly white teeth. "As I live and breathe, Christian Anderson."

Christian scanned the floor, trying not to make eye contact with him. "Yup. Here I am."

A sudden movement brought Christian's eyes up, and he froze stiff in disbelief as he studied the older man's face. He'd aged, but not gracefully. Most notably were the swollen bags beneath his eyes and the significant amount of gray that overtook his unkempt whiskers. As Liam approached he extended his hand. "I can't thank you enough for agreeing to help."

"Of course. I'm here to help in any way I can."

The two men shook. "I'm worried about her, you know. The inept constable up at the station keeps saying she ran off with her boyfriend on another bender."

Still chilled from the subzero temperatures, Christian kneaded his hands together and shifted his hip. "But I gather you don't think so."

Gemma's mouth widened and, without missing a beat, words began to spew. "Hell no. This time was different."

"How so?"

"For starters, she was finally clean. And as far as that layabout Charles is concerned, well, a couple of us politely asked him to get the hell out of town."

He rolled his eyes. "You? Gemma Williams, queen of brashness, *asked* him politely?"

She grinned. "I may have made a few threats; but let's be fair, most drug dealers I've encountered aren't in the business of taking orders. But then, neither am I. Regardless, rumor has it he packed up and is crashing in some shady drug den down in Glaslyn."

"So, this Charles is out of the picture? You're sure about that?"

She shook her head and the words came out at top speed. "Who knows. Like I said, Christian, it's a rumor. You hafta

13

believe me—they were through. And for the record, I never laid a finger on him."

Christian glanced up and scanned both of their faces. "Chill, I'm not here to arrest you. But one thing is certain; I'll find out what happened to her."

"I know you will. Gemma tells me you're the best investigator the Regina Police Service has ever had."

Christian blushed and dropped the duffle bag on the floor. "I consider it a team effort. I don't have time for 'it's all about me' attitudes."

Liam scanned Christian from head to toe. "Well, I admire your attitude. We're all proud of you back here for making something of yourself."

"Yeah, but at what cost? I've sacrificed the last ten years of my life to get to where I am, and you know what?"

Liam shook his head.

"I'm not satisfied."

Liam scoffed under his breath. "Satisfaction is overrated. Be glad you got the hell out of Cedar Lake."

The telephone rang in an adjoining room, and Liam stared at Christian with a forced smile. "Excuse me a moment." A second ring came, then a third, and Liam shouted out as he stomped away, "Oh, for God's sake, I'm coming."

Liam disappeared behind the wall into what Christian remembered as the dining room. They lingered in an awkward silence while Christian's eyes darted everywhere except at Gemma. Gemma unfolded her arms and clutched the duffle bag from the floor. "What d'you say we get you settled in, hmm?"

Christian wheeled the suitcase behind him as he followed her through the modest house, where even the faintest of voices wafted. His eyes adjusted as he emerged into the windowless room, and he focused on Liam's silhouette in the corner with the receiver from a 1980s landline phone pressed against his ear.

Christian grabbed her arm. "Damn, Gemma, you guys still have that antique?"

"What?"

Christian pointed. "I thought the rotary phone faded away with the Nintendo 64."

"Don't make fun."

"You're right, sorry."

Gemma marched forward, but Christian trailed behind with his eyes never diverting from Liam. The room more resembled an obstacle course than a dining room these days. The older man's voice, which began as a whisper when Christian entered, grew stronger, gruffier the further Christian weaved through the room.

Christian lingered in the murky corner opposite the older man, eavesdropping and studying Liam's nervous movements. The rubbing of his thick fingers against his eyes, the pacing, but not once did Liam ever turn to check his surroundings. Then out came a side of Liam Williams that Christian had never witnessed.

"Yeah, I heard you the first time, and while it's a tempting offer, I have a connection with someone better who can get this situation under control."

He slammed the phone on the cradle and his head drooped.

Whatever Liam tried to quash, it instead aroused Christian's curiosity even more. Watching Liam was like witnessing a slow-motion car crash. You should help, but instead, you stand there, paralyzed out of fear, or shock, or maybe even a combination of the two. Gemma reappeared and tugged at his jacket. "Anderson . . . what's the hold-up?"

"Ah, yeah. Sorry, got distracted."

"Whatever. Come on."

Christian hustled to catch up with Gemma, and the darkness of the hallway shrouded him, just as Liam turned his head and glared down the hall.

CHAPTER 2

GEMMA'S ROOM WAS EXACTLY HOW HE
remembered it from ten years earlier. The same corkboard
from middle school remained plastered to the wall, but after
twenty years it should have seen its expiration date years ago.

Two steps in, and he couldn't take his eyes off the
overwhelming number of photos she had amassed over the
years. As he took a few more steps, one shot in particular
caught his eye and he moved closer. He ran his fingers across
the glossy, dust-covered four-by-six photo of him dressed in a
red graduation gown with a black mortarboard affixed to his
head. Just staring at how far he'd come, it provoked a soft
scoff and grin to grace his face.

He stepped back and scanned the rest of the room. One thing was evident; some people never change. Gemma was still the innocent girl who covered her walls with photos, either of friends or posters of her favorite celebrities. And for a thirty-two-year-old woman, her adolescent behavior would send out red flags to anyone; Gemma couldn't let go of the past.

Christian completed his three-sixty of the room, and as his eyes lowered, they fell on an air mattress laid out on the floor at his feet. The white linens, two pillows, and a plaid quilt covered the makeshift bed, and his eyes darted toward his best friend. Immediately, she stuttered to explain the situation.

"Sorry, short on space around here. So, guess what?"

He smiled. "Guess you and I are going to be roomies for a few days."

"Won't be any different than back in high school. And don't even get me started on those nights you used to sneak over here, and we'd stay up all night—"

"They were the best, and truly, the only thing that kept me from going insane."

She smiled and plopped on her bed.

"Well, I suppose since Cassidy's been missing for two days, we should just jump right into business," he said. The teeth of the zipper grinded together and he pulled out a thin, black notebook.

Gemma laid back and rested her head against a pile of pillows. "You're right. I get too carried away reminiscing."

The dimples in Christian's cheeks surfaced.

"I can't believe we've allowed three years to pass without seeing each other. We shouldn't let a crisis be the only reason we get together."

She twirled her kinky hair. "We shouldn't. And from this moment forward, we won't."

"For sure."

She raised her head off the pillow and clapped her hands together. "All right. Let's get down to why you're here. Is there a point you'd like me to lead off with?"

"Why don't we start with giving me a little more insight into who Cassidy, the person, is. We've been friends for over twenty-five years, and yet, I know so little about her."

Gemma muttered under her breath. "Count your blessings."

His eyebrows raised. "Come again?"

"Oh, nothing. You would have seen her last, what, ten years ago?"

"Right."

"That was her freshmen year of college."

Christian jotted against the cream pages of his notebook. "If I recall, she showed up for my graduation dinner and was back on the road before I even packed my last bag."

Gemma uncrossed her arms. "It was her first time away from home. I suppose she had better things to do and people to see."

"I know what you mean. She always had better things to do than to hang with us. That night, she spoke maybe two words to me."

She let out a nervous giggle. "Like you said, you two weren't tight."

Christian clenched the pen in his hand and doodled against the page. "Was she using back then?"

Her body immediately tensed. "Not then, no."

"Do you remember when things changed?"

Gemma drooped her head and took a second to reflect. "Six years ago—no, wait, seven."

"Seven years ago? You sure?"

"Not totally. Christian, let's face it, I have difficulty tracking my own mellow life, so to follow her action-packed one, well, that's like asking me to part the sea."

"I hear you. Tell me a little more about her boyfriend . . . umm . . . Charles."

Her eye twitched. "What's there to tell?"

"Oh, I don't know. Does he have a criminal record? When did they start dating? Why does this inept constable believe she's run off with him? Which brings me to another point—this constable have a name?"

"Cassidy and Charles met at a party in college. He's the asshole who got her hooked on those damn methamphetamines."

"I see."

"As far as I know he's been arrested a few times."

"He served any time?"

She pursed her lips. "Nah. Charges were always dropped because, as the courts would say, the police lacked hard evidence. If you want my opinion, it's because of these lazy constables up here who can't be bothered to do any *actual* police work. And that inept bastard, Constable Lucas Pearson, sits at the top of the food pyramid."

Christian ignored her slam against the police and continued with his questions. "Pearson. Got it. When did she drop out of school and move back here?"

"2014. The Mounties busted her with meth, and you know we can't afford any fancy lawyers."

"And let me guess, this was the beginning of the downward spiral?"

"You got it. The court ordered her to thirty days in rehab. She fell behind in classes, quit, and Dad drove down to Lloydminster and dragged her from another drug den."

"Damn," Christian said.

"Exactly. My dad thought bringing her home would help clean her up."

"But it didn't, huh?"

"Nope. Asshole followed her back."

"It's a shame but it happens more than you think."

She nodded again. "It shouldn't, though. He destroyed her, and I was helpless to stop it."

"What could you do? From what you've said she had her mind made up."

Her lips curled into a frown. "I suppose, doesn't make my guilt sting any less."

"Hey, you have nothing to feel guilty about. Okay?"

Her shoulders slumped forward. "If you say so."

"Let's fast-forward to the present. When did you last see Cassidy?"

"Thursday evening. It was her final night in the rehab center."

"What'd you guys talk about?"

"A little of this, and a little of that. We were practically strangers getting reacquainted."

21

"Can you elaborate? What do you mean by a little of this and that?"

"We kept the conversation low key. We talked about how therapy was going, she asked a lot about Dad, and she had reservations about what she would do with her life once she got out."

"I assume you finalized the pickup arrangements too?"

She nodded.

"Where is this place at again?"

"Down in North Battleford."

Christian jotted in the notebook. "That's what, two hours away?"

She validated his question with a simple nod.

"During your visit, did you note anything out of the ordinary?"

Gemma mulled over his question, and her eyes rolled upward. "No, nothing stands out. She kept saying how nervous she was to come home, but things would be different, and—"

A few seconds passed and Gemma left her thought hanging. Christian stepped in. "And . . . what?"

"Something she mentioned left me with more questions than answers. Eh, it's probably nothing."

Christian's hand stopped scribbling and he glanced up. "Gemma, every minor detail could be relevant in missing persons cases. Right now, time is working against us. Even if you think it was nothing, it could be the missing piece we need."

"Right. She mumbled about something from twenty years ago."

"What was it?"

Her eyes rolled to the side. "Too many prying ears around."

"Did she give any more details?"

"Only that she wasn't sure if it, in fact, happened or if it was a false memory she concocted in her fractured mind. I told her we'd discuss it on the drive home, you know, where we had a little more privacy."

Before Christian could get out another question, Liam appeared in the doorframe. "You get settled in all right?"

"I have, thanks."

"Now, no hanky-panky under my roof. Okay?"

Gemma clutched at her chest, appalled by his offensive comment. "Dad. We don't have *that* sort of friendship."

Liam snickered and bowed his head. "I'm only teasing, for heaven's sake. You two have had many chances to hook up. If it hasn't happened by now, it'll never happen."

"Charming, Dad."

"Anyway, I dropped by to let you know I'm running out to the store. Anything you need while I'm out?"

Christian closed the notepad. "Oh, don't worry about me. The only thing I need is coffee to get going. In fact, I should head out myself."

"You need a ride?" Liam asked.

"Thanks, but I doubt you want to see that constable. What was his name again? Pearson?"

The smile on Liam's face curled into a frown. "He's the last person I want to see right now. He's a piece of work, as I'm sure you'll find out soon enough. I'll be more shocked if you even get your foot in the door."

"How encouraging, but rest assured I'll do my best."

Liam tapped his fingers against the doorframe, and once again he disappeared into the shadows of the hallway.

"Sorry about my father. He's—he's special."

"Ah, he still doesn't know about . . . the thing?"

"Oh, if by 'the thing' do you mean about liking dudes?"

"Yeah, that."

She pointed her chin upward. "Nope, I've never told a soul. You made me swear on that Bible you dug up I'd never say a word until you were ready."

"How can you remember something from sixteen years ago?"

Her hands rested on her hips and she tilted her head. "When have you ever known me to hold a Bible in my hand?"

His eyes darted upward, and he tapped his finger against his cheek. "Only once."

"Exactly. Hey, seeing as I've answered a lot of questions, I have a personal one for you."

"Shoot."

"Were you planning on coming out of the closet while you're back?"

He cringed inwardly at the thought of using his visit to spill his secret. "This may not be the most appropriate time to blow down those closet doors."

Gemma frowned. "He has a right to know. He *is* your father, whether you choose to claim him or not. And wouldn't things be better between you two if he knew?"

"Life isn't *that* easy."

Gemma ignored his hint and carried on. "How's what's his name doing?"

"Who?"

"You know, the tall nurse you were dating when I visited last."

Christian scanned his brain for a name. "Are you talking about Andrew?"

She snapped her fingers. "That's him."

"Jesus, Gemma, we've been old news for ages now."

"A shame, I thought he was a keeper."

"No. He was a pain, that's what he was."

"Why'd you break up?"

"Same sad story I hear time and time again: you work odd hours, you might die. Ah, the love life of a cop."

"You win some and lose some. His loss."
Christian straightened his shirt. "Well, I'm gonna head over to visit this Pearson fella."

"Need an escort?" she asked.

"Might be better if I go this one alone. From the impression you and your father have painted, I might get further than you two have. No offense."

She scanned the floor. "None taken."

"I'm just saying he might be more open with me as fellow law enforcement."

"Or . . . maybe he'll tell you the same repetitive thing he's said for the last two days: she's a junkie and, sorry, want to help, but I can't."

"While she and I weren't close, she's been in my life for damn near twenty-six years. And the Cassidy I knew isn't the type who just up and vanishes."

"That's what I said."

"And given you both finalized the pickup arrangement, something tells me someone got to her before you did."

25

Gemma made hand motions and her voice raised an octave. "Finally. Someone understands what I'm saying."

"I totally get it."

She gripped his hand and squeezed. "Please, do whatever you need to, just make sure you persuade Pearson to take this more serious."

"I won't make promises I can't keep, Gemma. But I'll lay out the evidence and my own personal interactions with her. Ultimately, the decision to pursue or not is up to him."

Her eyes drooped, and she held her tongue.

He covered her hand with his free one. "Listen, if I get the vibe he's unwilling to help, then you and I, we'll take matters into our own hands. Deal?"

She lifted her head, and a glimmer of optimism returned to her eyes. "Yeah?"

"Of course. I didn't spend all these years as a cop to stand by and do nothing when it's clear something is what needs to be done."

Christian pulled her into a hug, and she nestled her head in the crevice between his shoulder and chest. Immediately the tears streamed down the golden skin of her face.

This wasn't the first episode in their lengthy friendship when Gemma teetered on the verge of a nervous breakdown, and it probably wasn't the last. Then again, as Christian would soon discover, this wasn't the first time Cassidy had used the victim card to her advantage.

CHAPTER 3

CHRISTIAN PRESSED AGAINST THE METAL DOOR of the one-story, red brick building. Once inside, a frosted glass window with a small hole greeted him, and as he looked around the tiny vestibule, a flood of vivid memories returned to those countless summer days he spent at this RCMP detachment.

Since as early as he could remember, Christian had been fascinated with law enforcement and dedicated his entire adolescence to doing whatever he had to do to make his dream come true.

He grew closer to the window and reached into the back pocket of his dark indigo jeans for his badge. He didn't want to be like all those people he dealt with daily—unprepared.

A quick tap against the window and a hostile man with the voice of a two-pack-a-day smoker barked, "What?"

"Uh, yes. I'm DS Anderson with the Regina Police Service. I'm here to speak with Constable Lucas Pearson. Is he—?"

"Is he expecting you?"

"No. Can you let him know I need to speak with him urgently?"

"What about?"

"Cassidy Williams."

The man groaned, as if Christian wasn't the first one to request information about Cassidy over the past few days and he was getting tired of hearing the name. The man poked his finger through the hole in the glass and pointed at the row of chairs lining a wood-paneled wall. "Take a seat and let me track him down."

Christian did as the man instructed. Before sitting in the chair, Christian swept his hand across the scratchy, red fabric and brushed a few cookie crumbs to the floor from whatever unlucky soul last waited. He slid into the uncomfortable chair, and his butt shifted several times until he found the one position he could relax in. He slouched back, but not before crossing his arms across his chest to give an unsociable vibe.

This place sure has gone downhill since I was here last.

Ten minutes passed, and he fidgeted with his jacket and bobbed his leg. *It doesn't take this much time to track down a constable in this small of a detachment.*

Christian tapped his foot against the tile floor, and when another two minutes passed with no signs of urgency on anyone's part, he peeled himself from the tweed seat. He managed four steps toward the window before the squad room door flew open. Christian stepped back and the short man in his early forties who filled the doorway with his broad shoulders was a far cry from what he expected.

Each of the men scanned the other from top to bottom. Two immediate things drew Christian's interest: first, the man's eyes. Even from afar the Aegean blueness sparkled. As his eyes scanned down, the scowl scribed across his face destroyed the constable's otherwise flawless Romanesque features.

If this man toned down the macho exterior and smiled, he'd certainly be more attractive.

"DS Anderson, I presume?"

"Yes." Christian's eyes continued scanning downward and his eyes focused on the monogrammed strip of cloth that read "Pearson."

"Constable Smith says you needed to speak with me. Was there something in particular I can help with?"

Christian leaped to his feet. "I'm here on behalf of the Williams family."

The constable smacked his lips. "Ah, I see. Suppose good ole Liam sent you, didn't he?"

"Not quite. You see, Gemma and I have been best friends for over twenty-five years, and naturally, she called me."

Pearson cocked his head to the side. "She called you. Why?"

"For starters, she's desperate for someone, anyone, to help find her sister." His eyes locked with Pearson's. "And I don't get the impression your station is too eager to offer its assistance."

Pearson's eyes darted away, and he nodded his head toward the door. "Let's talk more at my desk."

Pearson extended his forearm out and motioned Christian inside the core of the station. The constable's broad shoulders and barrel chest obstructed half of the doorframe, and Christian squeezed through the narrow gap, hoping every second he didn't accidentally brush the unwelcoming man.

Once in the large room, Christian lingered while he awaited further direction from the constable. Pearson grabbed the handle, slammed the door closed, and without a word aimed his index finger toward the back of the room. Christian walked, all while he scanned the room in search of anything that resembled a desk. The intimidating presence of Pearson on his heels propelled him forward, and soon, under a heap of folders and papers, the outline of the desk began to emerge.

Christian rested his hands on yet another identical chair to the one he endured in the lobby, except this time the fabric was neon green instead of red.

"Take a seat," the constable said.

He yanked out the cheap chair, once again checking for more crumbs, but to his surprise, the chair was the cleanest thing in the vicinity.

Pearson pulled out an oversized leather desk chair, one that appeared more comfortable than the one Christian occupied, and sat. He slid aside a stack of manila folders and clasped his hands together. And while the two men exchange no words, Pearson's eyes did most of the talking.

After a moment, Pearson adjusted his posture and dove headfirst into a barrage of questioning. "While you waited, I looked into your background."

Terror overtook Christian's face. "You what?"

Without missing a beat, Pearson reached for the top folder in the stack. "Born and raised here, took part in our RCMP volunteer program from 2008–2009. Your father is Matthias Anderson, and no offence, he's seen better days."

Christian gave a half shrug. "And your point?"

Pearson closed the cover. "My point is this: you escaped from this place ten years ago and never looked back. I guess I'm a bit confused on why you'd come back to look for a junkie?"

"I—" Christian strained to sputter out a coherent sentence.

"Look, you seem like a stable young man. More so than Liam or Gemma."

"They just want—"

"I know what they want. Information. I'll level with you and tell you exactly what I told Liam this morning. Cassidy is a screwed-up girl."

Christian tried to get a word in. "But—"

"The truth is, she most likely ran off with her boyfriend to get high. I'm sorry Gemma manipulated you into returning, but trust me, she'll turn up in a few days—like she always does."

Christian chewed at his lower lip while the fury bottled up inside him. Immediately, all he wanted to do was drop-kick the constable to the ground and pummel the assclown until he promised to do more than just spew theories. Soon the amusing image faded, and he acknowledged bloodshed might leave an execrable first impression, so he pumped his brakes.

Christian drowned out Pearson's baseless position about Cassidy, and out of nowhere, he curled his hand into a fist and slammed it against the one empty spot on the cluttered desk. "Cut the bull. With all due respect, Constable Pearson, I beg to differ."

Pearson chuckled. "You? Mr. 'I fled town a decade ago' begs to differ. Tell me this: When was the last time you saw Cassidy? Hmm? How about Gemma? Even better, when was the last time you checked in on your father?"

Christian jumped to his feet. The rage boiled over, and the brake line that barely held together snapped. His suppressed wrath overtook his rationale, and by the time reasoning kicked in, he found one hand in the middle of the desk, while the other wagged in Pearson's face. And then all hell broke loose.

"Now, you listen, and you listen good. My father has nothing to do with why I returned. You think I don't have better things to do then step foot back in this cesspool? I could go two lifetimes without being reminded of this place."

Pearson smirked. "You talk a good game, Anderson. But, look, here you are, back in the one place you hate. All because Gemma spun some tale about her sister being in trouble."

"You're right, here I am. And do you want to know why?"

"I'm sure you're about to enlighten me, so go ahead."

"I care about my friends, I care about doing the right thing, no matter what. Now, the real question here is simple: Are you going to help us . . . or not?"

Pearson looked away and slid a few folders aside. The shuffling stopped when he found the one he needed, and without reestablishing eye contact, he leaned back in the chair and flipped open the cover. Christian grabbed his bag from the floor when it became evident his passionate plea would get him nowhere.

In one last-ditch effort, Christian threw his hands up and advanced for the door, but the booming voice of the constable startled him, and he paused. "For Christ's sake, take a seat, and tone down the overdramatic bullshit."

Hesitant, Christian reverted to the chair and clasped his hands together before resting them on the desk. He glared while the constable sifted through the file in his hand. After a minute, he tossed the folder atop the desk and a five-by-seven mug shot caught Christian's attention.

"Cassidy Williams. A thirty-six-year-old Caucasian female. Arrests in 2013, 2016, twice in 2017, and most recently she was admitted to Cedar Lake Memorial after an alleged drug overdose."

"Alleged?"

"We believe it might have been a suicide attempt."

Christian shook his head. "I don't buy it."

Pearson continued reading from the folder. "At the wishes of her father, she was admitted to Battlefords Rehabilitation Center on the twenty-sixth of December last year and released on the thirtieth of January."

"I didn't drive six hours to be spoon-fed something I already know. Give me something new. Like, were there witnesses who saw her leave? And if so, did they catch a glimpse of who picked her up? Have you even been in touch with the Battlefords detachment?"

Pearson closed the file, and he glanced up and his eyes locked with Christian's. "Nobody saw her leave. And, yes, of course, I've spoken with the local constables who are scouring

33

any and all available CCTV footage they can get their hands on."

Christian scooted out the chair and slammed his hands on the desk. "You've wasted two days to get this. Come on, man, you gotta do better. Has anyone there made *any* progress? Aren't there search teams out looking for her?"

The constable shrugged. "Don't know. None of my contacts have reached out."

"You aren't taking any of this serious, are you?"

"In case you forgot, Detective Sergeant, this is Cedar Lake. And here, the criminals far outweigh the constables. I just don't have the manpower to send someone to search for her."

"When I was a volunteer, we did one search and rescue operation. Have you or anyone made a plea for volunteers?"

Constable Pearson returned to whatever the manila folder contained, which Christian took as more important.

"Have you even set anything up?"

Pearson's eyes glanced up from the pages. "I haven't. But then again, neither has Liam. No pleas to the media, and all he asks us is if we're searching for her while he sits comfortably at home."

Christian plonked down in the uncomfortable chair and composed himself. "Well, I'm here. And with your permission, I'd like to help set something up."

"DS Anderson, while I appreciate your loyalty to not only Gemma but to doing the right thing, need I remind you you're far from your jurisdiction. As I'm sure you're aware, you can't just show up uninvited and insert yourself into an open investigation. No, I'd prefer if you left everything to me."

He murmured under his breath. "Yeah, that's what I'm afraid of."

The constable rose to his feet and hovered over the desk. "I know you don't believe it, but I am taking this seriously. You're aware this vanishing act isn't her first, right?"

Christian's eyes widened. "I was not. How many times has this happened before?"

The constable held up his index and middle fingers. "Twice in the last two years. And if memory serves me right, I don't recall you swooping in to save the day back then."

"I—I had no idea."

"Right, because it was me who brought her back unscathed. And now suddenly, Liam acts as if she's been murdered or something."

"I didn't come all this way to step on your toes. But one thing you have to understand is I've always been there for Gemma through the tough times. I don't know anything about the last two times, but one thing I can be certain of is if Gemma thought there was something wrong, my phone would have rung."

Pearson's knuckle cracked as he balled his hands into fists.

"And another thing—"

Pearson gnashed his teeth and stopped Christian from annoying him any further. "Look, let's both cut the crap. I understand you're trying to do your friend a solid by being here, but when I tell you things are under control, then they're under control."

"And what if they're not?"

"Then I'll reach out. Now, until then, do us both a favor."

Christian shifted his weight to his left leg. "And what sort of favor are we talking?"

Pearson unclenched his fists and leaned across his desk. "For the love of God, man, go spend a little time with your broken father. In five years, and a handful of encounters, you're the only thing he ever talks about."

Christian's mouth dropped. "I am?"

Pearson relaxed his chauvinist attitude. "He misses you. And while I don't know you, I suspect you miss him too."

"You suspect wrong."

"You know what your problem is?"

Christian raised his shoulders.

"You're a stubborn bastard."

Christian scoffed. "Thanks, I suppose. Never been psychoanalyzed by the RCMP before. No offense, but your evaluation could use work."

Pearson shrugged. "Just my opinion. Anyway, go spend the remainder of your time with him, and then get back to Regina."

What could Christian have uttered to convince the pig-headed man to change his mind? The longer Christian loitered in the chair, gazing at Pearson's face, he thought back to those Aegean blue eyes and noted how as his aura soured, so did those radiant eyes. At some point as the tempers flared, the blue dulled into a carbon gray.

Maybe it's the dim lighting?

Despite what Christian believed, one thing became evident in their ten-minute interaction: Christian's return to Cedar Lake ruffled the locals, and one, in particular, stood between doing some police work and hindering justice.

Instead of launching into another spat, Christian smirked and extended his shaky hand. "While we've reached an impasse, I do appreciate your time."

The constable grabbed Christian's hand, and they shook a few seconds lengthier than usual. "Safe journey back to Regina."

"Thanks. Good luck with the case, and all I ask is you keep the Williams family in the loop. Okay?"

Pearson grinned, but his lips never separated to utter a single word. The only thing he did was bob his head.

Christian turned and bolted for the exit. All he wanted was to get back to Gemma and accomplish what he swore he would: determine the backstory that led up to Cassidy's disappearance.

CHAPTER 4

THE SEDAN PLOWED THROUGH THE SNOWY streets of Cedar Lake. As the car crept through the intersection, the house came into view. There stood Gemma, perched on the front porch, with yet another cigarette between her lips. As the car pulled up out front, she took a drag and through the dimness the cherry burned a hot red.

Her destructive behavior was nothing new, and when the stress got ahold of her like a dog gnawing on a bone, it only got worse. Christian realized a long time ago the best course of action was to stay out of her way and keep his mouth shut.

During high school, she was the queen of bad choices. If Christian had more time in the day, he certainly could rattle off a list. But if this were a countdown of "Gemma's worst habits in high school," they'd be as follows: skipping classes, gnashing her nails until they bled, and drinking alcohol under the bleachers. Regardless, Gemma's past inclinations were insignificant to the here and now.

Her nail-biting, Jameson-guzzling days ended twelve years ago when she walked across the same stage that Christian would cross two years later. But now, she had swapped out several of those habits for the worst of all—smoking.

She had yet to notice him pull up to the curb. Back and forth, in a tight circular pattern, she crisscrossed the front porch, but as he killed the engine, her head spun around and her eyes lit up immediately.

Guilt. It's an ugliness no one ever wants to experience. Yet, even worse is returning with unwelcome news. Christian sat with his hands gripped to the steering wheel, and all he wanted was for those swirling emotions to go away.

She looks so happy to see me. Wish I had better news to deliver.

He stepped out of the car and slammed the door closed behind him. Halfway up the walkway, with only feet left until he'd find warmth, the tiny ice balls that spat from the sky, now switched over to flecks of soft snow. He turned his nose upward and internally cursed Mother Nature. Yet, she wasn't taking his criticism lightly on this night.

Suddenly, a gust of wind blew across the landscape. He pulled the faux-fur-lined hood of his jacket over his head and mumbled under his breath. "Well played, ma'am, well played indeed."

Gemma shouted from the porch. "How'd things go?"

39

He stepped onto the first step of the porch, gritted his teeth, and then gave his famous head shake. "As you and your father expected, I suppose. The man's the cockiest asshole I've come across in a long time."

Christian ascended two steps, and Gemma extinguished her cigarette butt against the railing and chucked it into the snow-filled front yard. "He won't help . . . will he?"

Considering the choice of looking his best friend in the eyes or hanging his head in defeat, he chose the latter.

"Come on, Christian. What'd he say?"

"Exact words?"

"Are there any other words?"

"I quote, 'She'll show up like she always does, and I've got everything under control here.' It's clear he is in way over his head."

She slammed her palm against the rail and the snowdrift tumbled to the ground. "The hell he does."

Christian raised his hands in front of him. "Calm down, Rambo, remember, I'm the guy in your corner."

She dusted the flakes of snow from her hand. "I know you are, and I appreciate it. From the bottom of my heart, I do. What I'm having trouble with is how this idiot makes everything sound peachy keen when it's not."

"No, it's certainly not."

"Did he elaborate?"

Christian nodded. "The only new information I gained was this isn't her first time. How could you not mention that to me?"

Her head lowered. "I should have mentioned it earlier, and I'm sorry. But this time isn't like the last two times."

"Okay, okay . . . I believe you. Still, a heads-up would have been nice. Anyway, you should have seen this man's face, so smug and sarcastic about everything. Who says stuff like that?"

"He does."

"Well, it's not right."

"Come on, he must have said something else?"

Christian shook his head. What good would it serve to upset Gemma more than she already was?

Gemma crossed her arms across her chest and stomped. "I'm telling you, Christian, I've combed through every crack den within a hundred klicks and grilled more addicts over the past two days than ever before. Not a single soul has seen her since before December. No, this time, it's different than before."

Christian's eyes homed in on her hands as she hammered the unsoiled butt of a fresh cigarette against her lighter.

"Seriously? You just finished one."

Her nostrils flared and she pointed in his face. "Don't even go there with me right now. It's this or I whoop someone's ass. Which one's it going to be?"

"Is there a third option?"

She rolled her eyes and with a flick of the lighter, the vivid red cherry burned as she pulled in a long breath. She turned away and exhaled, and as she brought it to her lips a second time, she resumed pacing.

"Guess that's a no. Listen, has Cassidy ever bailed on you like this before? You know, has she ever said she'll see you the next day and then gone rouge?"

Gemma leaned forward as a billow of smoke escaped her nostrils. "No."

41

"What about the last two times? Was she using then?"

"She was. It's just the night I saw her at the clinic, something had her nervous. Pure speculation, but I believe she had dirt on someone, and whatever it is either has her running for her life . . . or the person caught up with her."

"And you have no idea what it could be? Come on, Gemma, think."

She sighed. "I've mulled over this for two days, and the only person who keeps coming to mind is Charles."

His back fell against the wooden rail, and he closed his eyes. "It can't always be the boyfriend."

"Ex. Ex-boyfriend."

His eyes sprung open. "Irrelevant. We have to dig around for some clues or we'll keep running in circles."

"Wait," she blurted out. "She writes in a journal. I walked in on her once, and she acted nervously and tried to hide it under the covers."

"This journal, do you think it's here? Somewhere in the house?"

She shrugged. "Maybe. She didn't take any of her belongings with her when they transported her to the clinic. But I don't even know where to begin our search."

"Her bedroom?"

"If there's one thing I've learned about addicts is they are the most skillful people at hiding crap."

"Exactly. Do you think your father would object if I searched her room?"

Her head tilted up and she drummed her fingers against her cheek. "I don't know. It feels like we're prying into her private life."

NO PLACE IS SAFE

"You can't look at it that way. This might be the opportunity to uncover where she went, or better yet, maybe we'll figure out who she's running from. Isn't that why you asked me to return to this place?"

No response. All Gemma managed was a few more puffs, but she kept her face turned away. As she took her final drag, she turned and locked eyes with Christian.

"You're right, I'm being overprotective. And for what?"

"This journal might have some answers."

"Right again. I need answers, I need to know what had her so paranoid the past few weeks."

Christian clasped his hands together and rubbed hard to warm them. "So, why are we still standing out here in the arctic?"

"Beats me. Come on, I can't stand to see you shiver like a baby."

CHAPTER 5

GEMMA PRESSED AGAINST THE OAK DOOR to Cassidy's room, and as it opened, the hinges belted out a creak. She peeked her head inside, and her hand searched in the darkness for the switch. The room came to life underneath the fluorescent light, and she took a deep breath before entering.

"This is it," she said as Christian followed close behind.

"Hasn't changed much in the last decade. And to be honest, I don't know why I expected it to be drastically different."

"I mean, Cassidy isn't one for frills. Any cash she gets her hands on goes toward, well, you know."

"Yeah, a cheap high."

She positioned both hands on her hips and loudly exhaled. "You're the expert. Any place in particular we should start?"

Christian took a moment and scanned the room. Just like any random bedroom in the world, it had a bed—nothing entirely up to Christian's standards, but then again, it wasn't the worst he'd ever seen either. Flanking the bed sat two matching nightstands, a cheap desk, dresser, and one lonely halogen lamp towered in the corner. From Christian's perspective, the room cried for a makeover, but then he already forgot the mentality of the people of Cedar Lake. This wasn't the town where people drank from the "keeping up with the Joneses" Kool-Aid jug he'd grown accustomed to in Regina. People here were raw, blunt, and real.

He crept toward the desk, which contained the ordinary items one would find: several tawdry, ragged romance novels heaped in a careless stack, mail slung in a fan pattern, and several photos, which gave Christian a brief glimpse into her life.

Gemma interrupted his analysis. "Hello? Earth to Christian. Can I get a hint where to look first?"

"Well, the first place I'd check—nightstand drawers."

A baffled look adorned her face. "Seriously?"

"Yeah. Most people tape things to the underside of the drawer and the more elaborate ones have false bottoms."

"You're joking."

His left eyebrow raised. "Of course not. Knowing you, that's probably where you hid your weed in high school."

Her jaw dropped. "How'd you know?"

He exposed his pearly white teeth and carried on. "Next, I'd check any of the air vents in the room."

45

"How do you know all of these things?" she asked.

"You don't think they promoted me to DS based on my boyish good looks, do you?"

She paused and let out a long, "Um."

"Just a joke, relax."

She made a wiping motion against her forehead as Christian continued. "I earned my promotion by working hard and refusing to confine myself within the norms of what society expects."

"Sort of like go big, or go home?"

"Yeah, exactly. I put myself in either a criminal's or victim's head. What would they do? You get me?"

Her distinctive laugh breathed life into a room that otherwise sat barren of any emotional warmth. "This is exactly why I called you to help. Even though there's so much going on around me, I can still count on you to keep my spirits lifted."

He stepped closer and with one swoop his arms surrounded her petite frame. He lifted her from the ground as he hugged her tighter. "I know this entire situation sucks, but we'll pick apart the secrets and get her back."

He squeezed her bony shoulders one final time before he pulled away. "Now, I'll check this one, and you check the other. Yeah?"

With a nod, the two split off on opposite sides of the bed.

Moments passed, and with the contents of the drawers scattered across the floor, Gemma peeked her head over the bed. "Anything?"

"Nope. You?"

"Zilch. You said the air vents next, yeah?"

"That'd be the next best place to stash something."

Without a word, she walked across the room, pulled the wooden chair from the desk, and planted it directly beneath the vent in the wall. She slid her fingernails behind the metal and popped off the screen. Her feet arched upward, and her body fell against the wall.

"Ouch. You okay? You want some help?"

"Nah, almost got it," she said as the cover popped off. She slid her hand into the hole in the wall. "Ah-ha."

The heels of her feet lowered on the chair, and he exhaled the breath he had held in. As she turned, in her hand she clutched the sought-after red leather journal.

"It does exist," he said.

She jumped from the chair, and as her feet slammed to the floor, it shook. Not wanting to be the one who snooped into her sister's private life, Gemma extended both hands, as if she were presenting a gift.

"You sure you're ready to find out what she knows?"

Gemma brushed her hand against a crinkle in the quilt and plopped on the bed. Her mood shifted and her face instantly dropped, and while holding back tears, she came apart at the seams. "I just want her back where I know she's safe and sober."

Immediately, Christian raced to her side, and she burrowed her face into his chest. They exchange no words; only the sobs from Gemma bounced from the walls. Being emotionally vapid himself, whenever people got teary eyed, he tensed.

And for someone who worked in the major crime's unit, human emotions were a daily reality. Over the last two years, he'd grown detached to death and the outbursts of emotions that they entailed. Yet, this time, things were closer to home, and a single tear fell down his cheek.

Five minutes elapsed, and a glimmer of hope appeared in her red, tear-stained face. Her eyes locked with his. "Sorry, I thought I'd gotten all those out."

"Don't be."

Her hand shook as she held tight to the journal. "Well, I suppose this book holds all the secrets. But you do it, I can't."

She laid the book in his lap and looked away. Christian wiped his bony hand across the tattered exterior and, without much ado, flipped open the cover and bypassed numerous older entries in search of more current ones.

November 18, 2019

Dear Journal,
Everything in my life has gone off the rails . . . again. Here I sit, at 3:15 in the morning, scared to fall back asleep since no matter what I do, the ghosts of my past terrorize me every day.

I've tried hard to stay clean, believe me, I have. I've even tried to be more affectionate with Charles, but it's hard being the girlfriend of someone who so clearly doesn't want to give up his life of crime. We can't have a moment's peace without Jason, Thomas, or Lee showing up and destroying our special moments together.

I want an escape from Cedar Lake. I just want to leave all of this behind. But how? How can I when mustering up the courage to fall asleep brings me angst. I just want her lifeless face to disappear from my memory.

But it never will. Not until I tell someone what happened that night. But who? Who in this town full of unruly beings can I trust?

Yours,

Cassidy

Christian flipped to the next page. And the first sentence immediately raised the hairs on his arms.

November 20, 2019

Dear Journal,

I know the truth, and being the guardian of the truth kills my soul each and every day. How can something that occurred so many years ago still haunt not only my dreams but my waking body each day? I need a sign, something, anything to guide me on what I'm supposed to do. If it never comes, if I don't do what's right, this is the moment I'll regret for the rest of my life.

God, just give me the strength to let go of this pain. If you can't, I don't know if I can go on with this thing called life anymore.

Yours,

Cassidy

Christian shut the book and glanced at Gemma, who sat with her head still turned away. "When I say this, don't take any offense. But Cassidy had some pretty dark demons."

She faced him, still wiping away tears. "She had lots, far too many for me to ever wrap my head around. How troubling is it?"

"You remember that time someone photocopied Lindsay Ross's diary and shoved a page or two into the entire school's lockers?"

"*That* dark?"

His drew out his "eh". "Darker. I know this is going to come across as harsh, but did Cassidy ever give off the suicidal vibe?"

She nibbled her lower lip. "Yeah, maybe a few times. But I don't know how many different ways I can put this: she was stronger when we talked the other night. And yeah, she had reservations about coming home, but she also said she was ready to face everything headfirst."

He squeezed her hand. "Maybe she wasn't quite ready to face whatever it was just yet. She mentioned not being able to get a woman's lifeless face out of her memory. Could it be something to do with an aunt, cousin . . . perhaps your mother?"

"Did she give more information?"

"Whoever it was, it happened twenty years ago."

She rolled her eyes upward and immediately her eyes widened. "Not my mother—yours."

"Mine?"

"I mean, didn't she disappear twenty-four years ago?"

"Yeah, but, come on, Gem . . . it can't be her. Pop told me she skipped town for greener pastures. It has to be someone else. Think . . . what else happened in town around that time? Any murders? Did anyone else go missing?"

"The only major event back then was when your mother vanished. Wait. What if she had information on what *really* happened to her?"

Christian waved his hand in doubt. Besides, what could Cassidy know about what happened to his mother?

He reopened the book and skipped ahead and read a few more pages. Gemma slid closer and peeked over his shoulder at the words her sister had inscribed on the pages.

Sixteen pages in and the entries grew more intricate. Near the end, though, the entries transformed, and numbers replaced letters, there were plus and minus signs dotting the pages. Then, by the time they reached the twelfth of December, the night before her overdose, gibberish lined the page.

December 12, 2019

Dear Journal,

K yedpqtgyeu elw hhcv zj ljl mlchwtld nzqsp saje raiot zy qq fyerx. Ml yhs twist hs ulc.

Zqd cffpv uvmvzrw K'ce bysop moi xc wpaiip pahl cfxqav hn lyjgtnimlfdg hck? Sso yplc T ingy lfzo sv ahzd twtzoe tr ljl frni sihie?

T wzqblu rs lq ahv lyljvrzemwu, iuk hlg yvuco ingy bvwmwxl a afrckl lzvi eg?

I loved you so much, Charles. You're the only one who ever fully understood me.

Cassidy

Christian dabbed the tip of his finger against his tongue and turned to the next page, but to his shock, it was blank. His head cocked to the side, but soon, Gemma chimed in and provided him an explanation.

"She overdosed the next day. Dad found her unresponsive right here," she said, pointing to the rug on the floor. "She hasn't been back since."

"I know I'm beating a dead horse, but level with me. Do you believe it was an overdose or a suicide attempt?"

"I couldn't say. All I know is the ambulance rushed her to the hospital, and for three weeks, I couldn't visit. Why?"

"It's this last sentence. It's written in past tense, as if she didn't expect to be around."

Gemma stared off into space.

Christian continued, whether she paid attention or not. "This code. I once dealt with something similar on a case a few years back, but don't ask me to break it."

"Wait, can we go back a minute?"

He nodded.

"I want to change my answer. I don't think she tried to take her own life. She never said anything during our visits, and she tells me everything."

"People hide things they're ashamed of. And while I don't have any siblings myself, surely they don't tell each other *everything*."

She shrugged. "You could be right. Lord knows I've kept a lot from her."

"We always think we know those close to us, but when you dig a little deeper, you realize we're just naïve fools."

Gemma moaned. "After reading her words, the one thing I can say for sure is, I never knew my own sister at all."

"Everyone has secrets, Gemma. Some of us even share secrets that we'd never want anyone to know."

The color drained from her face. "And no one will ever know."

"Right."

"Hey, let's rewind again, okay?"

"Sure."

"Why are you so certain your mother left on her own accord? Do you remember anything about the day she left?"

"Do we really have to do this now?"

"I know, I know. It's a touchy subject. I just have to know."

"I just do . . . okay?"

"Maybe we could ask your father some questions?"

He jumped to his feet. "Absolutely not. Have you been inside the house?"

"In fact, I have. I dropped off groceries and a pizza just last week."

He stood with his mouth wide open. "And you weren't appalled at the condition of the place?"

"Of course. I'm not his maid though, Christian. I check in on him a few times a month and make sure he's eating. You don't truly believe he looks after himself? Do you?"

With a quiver in his voice, Christian spoke. "You? You've been checking on him? How come I'm always the last to hear these things?"

"Not to hurt your feelings, but you ghosted years ago. Sorry, but I can't stand by and allow him to waste away all by himself."

"Look, after my senses were attacked earlier with an overload of piss, booze, and body odor, I have to decline another visit."

"I get it. You loathe your father for your messed-up childhood. But guess what? He's still family to me. And family looks out for one another."

A roaring engine outside the window interrupted Christian's comeback. He pulled back the lacy curtain and watched as the headlights cut off and Liam's stocky figure exited into the light snowfall that swirled about the air.

"Your dad's back. Listen, I'd prefer we not tell him about the journal. Okay?" She nodded, and Christian let the curtain slip from his fingers. "Because, at this point, there's no telling who we can trust."

"But it's my dad. Come on, we should at least let him know something's up."

Christian hovered above and folded his arms across his chest. "Not even your father. I said you and I were dealing with this. Sorry, but this excludes your father as well."

"Deal. It stays between us." And without missing a cue, she returned their conversation back to where it was before the interruption. "I'm thinking we pick up dinner for your pop and swing by around seven."

"You *really* want to go down that ugly road? Not even three hours ago the man was drunker than a frat boy during pledge week."

"And? We don't have a choice in the matter. While I realize Cassidy wasn't your pop's favorite person, I believe there's some connection to the circumstances surrounding your mother's disappearance and Cassidy's."

"Gemma, I—"

"Zip it. I'm tired of listening to your habitual excuses. You can't evade this for the rest of your life, Christian. Can you sit there and tell me you aren't even a little curious to know what happened *that* night in 1995?"

He covered his face with his hands and remained silent. After twenty-four years, what difference would it make to have the truth now? The only thing he remembered about his mother from that April night in 1995 was that she tucked him into bed, read him his typical bedtime story, and kissed him on the forehead.

Expecting to find her cooking away when he awoke, he tossed off the blanket and raced into the kitchen. He rounded the corner and the room sat empty. There was no breakfast on the table, no Dad, no Mom, just a four-year-old boy in his flannel pajamas, alone and scared.

On that early spring morning, something inside of him died, and his capacity to attain solace dwindled away, never to surface again. If ever asked to pinpoint the reason why he never allowed himself to get close to anyone, then it boiled down to the abandonment he felt when she vanished. Or was it all the years he watched his father seek comfort in the bottom of a bottle of whatever bargain booze he could get his hands on? Whatever the reason, Christian vowed at four years old never to allow himself to get close to anyone, for all they ever did was crush your heart into a million pieces.

Gemma snapped her fingers. "Hey. Are you listening to me?"

"What? Um, yeah, I was."

"So, why are you still sitting there? Get your jacket on and let's go."

He groaned and his feet planted on the carpet. Gemma watched as he shuffled across the room, and with each step he took, his pace grew slower and slower.

"Oh, for the love of God. Is doing this *that* unpleasant?"

A simple shake of the head was all he could muster. "Being there today—I don't know. I blame myself for how his life turned out. I'm a terrible son, aren't I?"

"His poor life decisions were his and his alone. You—you were just smarter and got the hell out of here the first chance you could. No one around here blames you for taking the opportunity to better yourself."

"I don't need another pep talk. Can we just go and get this over with before I lose my nerve?"

Gemma extended out her hand, and Christian walked through the doorway and into the hallway. As he emerged into the dining room, he passed by Liam, who bent forward, shoving groceries from his earlier trip into the cabinet. Their attempt of going unnoticed failed, and Liam swung his head.

"And where are you two off to in this weather?"

Christian froze at the man's booming tone.

"Down the street. Suppose Matthias should see his son since it's been damn near ten years."

Liam shook his head disapprovingly. "That's a long time."

"Eh, I had my reasons."

"I'm sure you did, son. Now, promise me you'll be careful. Roads are a death trap."

Gemma and Christian exchanged a smirk and in unison replied. "We promise."

CHAPTER 6

CHRISTIAN FOLLOWED BEHIND AND CRADLED
A cardboard box filled with what at one time he'd considered fresh pizza from the local gas station. The sun had set hours ago, and Gemma pulled against the screen door while rummaging through her pockets for the key.

"Ah, gotcha."

"It's probably still unlocked from earlier."

She ignored his comment, slammed the storm door against the railing, and inserted the thin piece of metal into the keyhole.

The door flew open, and she stepped into the darkened foyer like she owned the place. Christian hovered on the front steps, his eyes scanning the street for anyone who might see him entering.

"What's the delay?"

His head spun around. "Uh, yeah, I'm coming. Chill."

He stepped inside and closed the door behind him. The storm door swayed in the gentle breeze, and Christian knew it was only a matter of time before the next blizzard blew it away. He loitered near the door, afraid to delve farther into the wasteland he once called home. Gemma knew her way around and ventured deeper into the belly of the house in search of Matthias.

"Mr. Anderson, it's me, Gemma. Are you here?"

A raspy voice called out. "In the kitchen, dear."

Gemma motioned for Christian to follow, and he reluctantly waded through the piles of junk, which only grew more unpleasant beyond the entryway. Unsure where to step, he took off blindly. Closing in on the kitchen, he made one wrong move and stepped into something that squished beneath his shoe. Christian jumped back, and in the process of freaking out, nearly dropped the box. He cringed and scraped the sole onto a cleared patch of carpet while Gemma disappeared into the kitchen. He peeked around the corner just as Gemma reached out her arms and hugged the haggard man.

"What's going on here?"

Matthias propped the broom against the kitchen island. "I cleared a path."

"Well, look at you, getting your life together. Any special reason why?"

"Christian."

"Christian? Your Christian?"

59

Matthias nodded and grinned. "He was here earlier, ya know. My baby boy came home. Wait. Have you seen him? Did he make it over safely?"

Christian groaned under his breath and stepped out from the shadows. "She has, Pop. And I made it safe and sound."

Matthias politely brushed Gemma aside and crept toward his son. For the first time in a long time, Christian noticed the old man's balance was steady, and his voice was remarkably less slurred than earlier too. Was it conceivable that perhaps his father was sober for a change? And if so, why? Why after countless years of drinking himself into a stupor had he chosen tonight, of all nights, to do a one-eighty?

The father-son duo stood at the edge of the kitchen where the tile met the soiled carpet, with a few inches separating them. Matthias took another step and Christian's hands trembled harder. Then it materialized—the man swooped in, wrapped his arms around his son, and squeezed. "My boy. You have no idea how much I've missed you."

Christian stood, paralyzed, while Gemma leaned against the counter and monitored as the awkward interaction continued for several minutes. After getting the side eye from her best friend, she broke up their reunion.

"Mr. Anderson, we've—"

"Now, Gemma, I've told you a hundred times; call me Matthias."

"Okay—Matthias. We'd like to ask you some questions."

"What about?"

"As you've probably heard, Cassidy has gone missing. And today we uncovered some information, which has left us with more questions than answers. You don't mind sitting with us for a few minutes, do you? I even brought your favorite pizza."

"Child, I don't know anything about where your sister is."

"There's a little more to it than just her. What'd you say? Can you spare a few minutes for us?"

"Well, yeah, anything I can do to help. I uncluttered most of the table earlier. You two make yourselves comfortable."

Christian rolled his eyes and followed behind Gemma and his father into what used to be the dining room, but now resembled a swap meet more than anything else.

Gemma and Matthias pulled out chairs and sat immediately, but Christian hesitated to sit.

"Boy, sit down. It ain't gonna bite you," Matthias barked.

Reluctant, Christian wiped his bare hand across the tabletop and brushed a few crumbs onto the floor. "Fine."

With everyone seated, Matthias had a few questions of his own for Gemma. "So, how are you holding up?"

"Hanging in there. I just want the police to dedicate more time to finding her, you know?"

"It's frustrating, I'm sure. You said you had some questions for me. I'm all ears."

"How do I put this delicately?" she began before Christian cut her off.

"Gemma has this crazy notion that Mom didn't just vanish, but that she might have met with foul play. And the information we stumbled upon implies that Cassidy may have witnessed her murder."

The color drained from the older man's face as he fell hard against the back of the chair.

"I, um, what exactly did she say?"

Gemma kicked Christian under the table as retribution for his impolite utterance and quickly regained control over the conversation. "We located a cryptic journal from her bedroom this afternoon."

"Okay . . . was there something in there that is proof she was murdered?"

"Cassidy never mentioned names, but she alludes to seeing the face of a lifeless woman and that this has haunted her for over twenty years. Logically, the only person who came to mind was your wife," Gemma said.

Matthias leaned forward. "Nah, it can't be her. I sat on the edge of the bed and watched her pack up her things; hell, I even carried one of her suitcases to the car. She gave me one final kiss on the cheek, got in her car, and I watched her back out of the driveway."

"So, she left on her own accord?"

"She did. It's no secret our marriage was far from perfect. Although, everyone in town would have you believe otherwise. I won't lie, there was turmoil, and on that night, everything reached a tipping point."

"I hate to solicit personal details about you and Mom's marriage, but was she having an affair?"

He crossed his arms over his chest and hung his head. "I knew about the other men in her life." He paused. "I suppose you're old enough to learn the truth."

"The truth is critical, Pop."

"That night after she tucked you in, we waited right here in this spot until we were sure you'd fallen asleep. Our number-one rule was: never fight in front of you and never inside the house."

Christian rested his elbows on the table and leaned in closer.

"We always took our arguments outside, and this night was no different. As soon as the door shuts, she lays in on me, and let's just say we swapped some heated words, which to this day I wish I could take back."

"Did you hit her?" he asked.

Gemma gasped. "Christian."

"Jesus, no. I gave her an ultimatum; it was either her family or the party life. I think it's clear what took more priority. Boy, I loved your mother more than words could ever express, but the drugs, the sex, and the lies had a hold on her tighter than the devil himself. Not even I could break her free from the grip."

"And, what, you just let her walk out the door?" Christian asked.

He scoffed. "Yeah. What else *would* you have me do? Force her to stay here against her will? I know life's been rough for you all these years, but trust me, son, if she had stayed . . . things would have probably been far worse."

Christian's eyes shifted down. "I suppose letting her go was the right thing to do. I just always got the impression you and Mom were happy together. At least that's what she always said."

"Well, she lied, and that's the God-honest truth. Now, back to your question, Gemma, I can't tell you *whom* she's referring to, but it certainly isn't my Sarah."

"Okay, not to overstep my boundaries, but how can you be so sure? I mean, has she ever reached out to you once over the last twenty-four years?"

The man itched his head. "In fact, she did. I got a letter from her a few weeks after she left. Said she ran off to Calgary to make a fresh start for herself."

"And by chance did you keep this letter?"

"Nah, I tossed it away the same day."

"Do you remember if there was a return address on it?" Christian asked.

"God, Christian, that was over two decades ago. Hell, I barely remember what I did last week."

Christian sighed. "Maybe if you set the bottle down every so often you'd remember things like that."

"Don't even go—"

"Go there with you? Pop, you're a depressed alcoholic. I get it, life handed you the shit end of the stick."

Matthias interrupted his son before he dug a deeper hole. "Christian, you're my son, and I love you. And I applaud you kids for looking out for Cassidy, but your mother has nothing to do with it."

"What if she was just the beginning of everything?"

"Trust me, I bet if you do more digging, I guarantee you'll find Sarah living happily in Calgary."

Gemma exchanged a glance with Christian, who fidgeted in the outdated chair. "I think that's great advice, Pop. I'll run a search tonight. Even better, I could get a few friends who owe me favors from Calgary to look into it for me."

Matthias smiled and quickly shifted the subject. "You do what you gotta do, son. Now, how long are you staying in town?"

"A couple of days. I took emergency leave; told them you were in poor health, and I needed to come back to check on you."

"Uh-huh. Well, since you've already used me as an excuse, it'd be great if you and I could spend a little time catching up."

Christian shifted his eye contact away from his father. "All depends on how things go with locating Cassidy and bringing her home safely."

Matthias's lips curled into a frown.

Guilt sunk in and Christian cleared his throat. "On the other hand, if time permits, I'll swing by and perhaps we can talk and clean?"

Matthias leaned in across the table. "Promise?"

Still avoiding eye contact, Christian replied. "Yes. Of course. I promise."

The room fell silent, and Gemma reached her hands across the table and gripped Matthias's. "Well, thank you for taking the time to talk to us. You've given us an excellent starting-off point to run with. If we find either Sarah or Cassidy, you'll be the first to know."

Gemma scooted away from the table as Matthias locked eyes with her. "And if you don't? What then?"

"Well, if we don't find the answers, we'll be back with more questions."

Immediately Christian bolted for the door. After spending so much time in the house already, the stench was less "in your face," but regardless, it didn't stop Christian from scratching at his arm any chance he had.

Matthias followed behind as they crunched their way through the garbage on the path to the door. In the foyer,

Gemma turned and hugged Matthias, and as she pulled away she gripped his face with both hands. "You take care of yourself, old man."

"I will. Thank you for always being there for me."

She smiled and stepped aside. Christian, however, stuck to his stubbornness and extended out his hand. "Pop, nice to see you."

Disappointed, Matthias played along and extended his hand.

Matthias stood guard and watched as they shuffled down the driveway to Christian's car. The friends traded no words on their short walk, but once inside the insulated vehicle, and Matthias had closed the front door, Gemma let Christian know exactly how she was feeling.

"Is this how you run all of your investigations?" she asked.

"What are you talking about?"

"You were so—blunt."

He grinned. "It's a component of the method I have in place for extracting truthful information I need from people."

With each fancy word that cut across his lips, it only drew her attention more rooted in the conversation.

"When you want the truth, you have to blindside people. You throw them off their game. Gives them zero time to make stuff up."

"He's your father, whether or not you like it. I think just this once you could have shown a little restraint."

Christian buckled his seat belt and slipped the car into reverse, but just as quickly slammed it back into park. "I'm not this coldhearted asshole like you want to make me out to be. It's—"

"It's *what?*"

"Our recollections of the evening in question differ, that's all. Come on, I know you saw the color drain from his face when we told him Cassidy might have witnessed her murder."

Her smug grin drooped into a frown. "It was odd."

"I'm telling you, he knows more than he's saying."

She scoffed. "Why have you always been so distrustful of others?"

His eyes shifted.

She continued badgering him. "You want my opinion?"

"Awe, you're giving me a choice for a change? If so, I'll pass."

"Christian, you don't trust anyone because you've never forgiven your father."

"Forgiveness for what?"

"For letting your mother walk out the door, for caring more about staying loaded than taking care of you. Do you want me to go down the list?"

His head raised, and their eyes locked. "I didn't request a full psychoanalysis, thank you."

Christian slammed the car into reverse again and rolled down the driveway and out onto Third Street. The remainder of the short drive back to Gemma's was a silent one. Christian returned the car to the spot it had departed an hour earlier and killed the engine.

"Gemma?"

"Yeah?"

"If you and I are going to work together to locate your sister, we need to set some boundaries."

She shifted in the seat so she could face him. "Like what?"

"Like, follow my lead. Your approach is, how do I say this, too naïve to get any truth out of anyone."

"Okay. That's the boundary you want to set?"

"No. Not even close. You're my best friend, and having that title bestowed on you has granted you an inside look into my personal life. But you're only aware of what *I've* chosen to share with you."

"So, tell me everything. Isn't that why I had that titled bestowed?"

"Gemma, please. Not everything I've experienced in my crazy life is worth uttering again."

Gemma flung open the car door and immediately lit up a cigarette. "So, what you're saying is, there're tons I don't know about you?"

"Exactly. Anyway, it's getting late, and I'm running on fumes. What I need is sleep."

"And tomorrow?"

Christian plodded his feet against the fresh snow. "I'd like to track down this Charles guy. If I let you tag along can you *not* show your ass?"

She considered his proposition. "Yeah. For you, I'll keep it together. All bets are off should he start anything."

Christian smirked. This was Gemma's lying ways, all for the chance to say what she had to say to her sister's deadbeat boyfriend without any of the fear she usually faced. Regardless, he also recognized that unless he took her along, she'd figure out a way to interject herself at the most inopportune time.

"As long as you can keep yourself in check, then we'll do it."

She clapped her hands together like a little kid whose parents guiltily broke down and bought that toy she'd been eyeing for a while. "You're the best."

"Yeah, yeah. Don't suck up . . . it's not cute."

Gemma shivered, and Christian took the subtle suggestion. "Why are we always hanging outside instead of inside? Oh, right, it's you and your damn nasty habit."

She pushed the limit with her overdramatic chattering of her teeth before exhaling the smoke. "You love it. Admit it. You miss the biting cold."

"What I miss is sitting next to the heater."

She tossed her cigarette and linked arms with Christian. "Fine. Tomorrow we'll start early, and I know just the spot to start our search for Charles."

"You do?"

She nodded. "I do. And if memory serves correct, you love rednecks, don't you?"

"Love's a strong word."

"It is, isn't it? Well, you're in for an adventure you won't soon forget."

Christian shook his head. "Yeah, that's what I'm afraid of."

PART 2

SUNDAY

"Question everything. Trust no one."
Nishan A. Kumaraperu

CHAPTER 7

A JINGLE FROM HIS IPHONE AWOKE Christian from his short-lived slumber. His hand rummaged across the air mattress, and with the phone in his grip, he pressed his skinny finger against the snooze button. With one eye open he lifted the phone and glanced at the time. A soft groan escaped, and he tossed it into the void next to him.

His heavy eyes refused to open, not until a whispering voice pierced through the stillness. "What time is it?"

Christian rolled over again. "It's six. Sorry, I forgot to turn off my alarm last night. Go back to sleep."

In a panic-stricken voice she clicked the bedside lamp on. "Cassidy's been missing for three days; we can't waste any more time."

Christian groaned, rubbed at the crustiness that had accumulated in his eyes, and propped his hand against the partially deflated bed. "Right. Forgive me; I'm irritable when I first wake up."

Gemma flung the duvet aside and wriggled to the edge of the bed. "I know what you mean. On any other day, you'd never see me rearing to go this early. Then again, I haven't slept much these last few days."

"Same. Sleep is the enemy," Christian replied. "You know what we need?"

In unison they screeched. "Coffee."

Her raspy laugh emerged. "Come on, grumpy, I got generic. Hope that's up to *your* standards."

"Beggars can't be choosers . . . now, can they?"

They tiptoed along the hallway, trying their best to not disturb Liam. The faint glow of Christian's phone's flashlight guided the way.

Christian pulled out a chair at the table in the kitchen while Gemma struggled with the machine. A few minutes later, she approached the table with two steamy, sought-after cups of joe.

The coffee mug clanked against the table and Christian glanced up from his phone. "Ah, you're the best."

She pulled out the chair next to him. "I know. So whatcha doing? Browsing through Tinder on the hunt for the next Mr. Anderson?"

He dropped the phone onto the table, and the corners of his mouth turned upward. "Why? All guys do is bring misery with them."

She imitated swiping her imaginary long hair away from her face. "Don't I know it. All jokes aside, I've never seen someone type and swipe so much in my entire life. Something must have your attention."

He took a sip from the mug. "If you must know, I've been searching the internet for dirt on Cassidy's boyfriend."

"Ex. You seem to keep missing that little word."

"Fine, ex-boyfriend. Do either of them use Facebook or Instagram? Perhaps Snapchat?"

Gemma snorted. "I don't even think either of them know how to turn on a computer, let alone use a smartphone."

"That's a shame."

Gemma wrinkled her nose and added a heap of sugar to her coffee. "Why?"

"I've just found people divulge more about their personal lives to complete strangers than to the people closest to them. Thought maybe we'd find clues buried in her social media, or better yet, I'd learn more about Charles before I come face-to-face with him."

"If it's information on Charles and his entire trashy family you're looking for, you've come to the right place."

While tempting to let her run her mouth about hearsay, he immediately diverted the topic to another angle. "I've also been scouring for stuff like criminal histories, land ownership, maybe even a few mug shots."

She sipped her sugar water with a splash of coffee before returning back to spilling every detail Christian needed to know. "News flash: I can do you one better than any internet search can. First thing you should know about Charles is he's the son of Lee White."

Christian stared at her as he bit at his lower lip. "Is he famous around here or something?"

"He's only the renowned leader of the local drug market. And I'm not talking about pills or weed either."

"What are we talking about, then?"

"Heroin, but mainly meth; you know, the shit dirty, old white men cook up in their basements."

"Oh, goody. They sound like a quality family. You know what they say: the family that cooks together, stays together."

She leaned inward and ignored his botched stab at humor. "He owns a farm about three klicks east of town; out on the 905."

"And you assume we'll find Charles there?"

"As I told you yesterday, I overheard whisperings he was laying low in some crack den over in Glaslyn. But, given the strong ties with his father *and* Cedar Lake, it wouldn't surprise me if he's slinked back to the farm."

"Anyone else caught up in this local drug ring?"

Her eyes squinted. "There are two other guys. Lee calls them 'farmhands,' but I call them thugs."

"They got names?"

"Thomas Campbell and Jason Nelson."

"Anybody packing?"

"Packing? As in guns?" she asked.

"Exactly."

She ran her fingers through her bedhead. "Never seen any, but then again, I try to keep my interactions with them as brief as possible."

He flashed a nervous grin. "I don't know about this, Gemma. Something about this doesn't seem safe."

She shrugged. "They won't dare mess with me if they know what's good for them. I mean, look at you, you *are* the police and even *you're* scared of them. Imagine what the local cops feel every day."

Christian's eyes widened at her audacity. *What the hell does that mean?*

"We could always let Constable Pearson know we're heading out—"

His hand hit the table and the mugs shook. "Oh no, he's the last person we want involved in this. For Christ's sake, Gemma, he flat-out told me yesterday to leave the police work to them."

She pushed herself away from the table and rushed to the sink. "Then it's settled, we're going," she declared as she lifted her arm and deeply inhaled. "But first, we both could use a shower."

"Speak for yourself. You reek of someone who passed out on a barstool. I, on the other hand, still catch a whiff of rosemary and mint."

"It's that cheap cologne you wear screwing with your mind. I'll be back in a bit."

She disappeared down the hallway and Christian chugged the last drops of coffee while mulling over whether maintaining secrecy was in their best interest. All of his training told him to inform somebody where they'd be; then again, perhaps Gemma's plan had merit.

You have to trust she knows what she's doing. There's no way she'd lead us to the slaughter. Right?

He set the mug and spoon into the sink and gazed through the double-pane window into the darkened backyard. The mission did have one positive element to it: the sooner he eliminated suspects, the sooner he could find

Cassidy and bring her home. But doubts continued to swirl in the back of his mind.

How did I allow myself to wind up in this mess? I'd give anything to be back in Regina, doing the same ole boring things I always do.

He turned from the window, and standing at the end of the hallway was Liam.

"Everything okay, Christian?" he asked.

Christian's eyes squinted to bring the man's face into focus. "Oh yeah, sorry we woke you. We wanted to get an early start."

"You didn't wake me; I never sleep these days."

"I feel your pain. Well, I suppose I should get myself ready."

Liam blocked the hallway. "What's she coerced you into today? Checking more crack dens?"

Christian stepped back and the counter prevented him from moving any more, and he released a nervous laugh. "You could say that."

Liam walked closer to Christian. "I love that girl, but some days, eh, I don't know."

"I'm confused."

"Keep an eye on her for me, okay. She has this nasty tendency to speak before she thinks. One of these days, she's going to cross the wrong person and—"

Christian didn't need him to continue on. Without saying the words, he knew exactly where the conversation was heading, and it wasn't what he needed to hear right before they departed for the White farm.

"Don't worry, I'll keep her in line. She'll be safe with me."

NO PLACE IS SAFE

"I knew there was a reason your name popped into my head when we needed someone to help," Liam said. The older man muscled in and poured a cup of coffee, and Christian inched forward toward the hallway.

"Well, suppose I should get ready. Good talking to you, Mr. Williams."

CHAPTER 8

THE SUN CRESTED THE HORIZON AS they zipped down the deserted two-lane highway away from any signs of life. With nothing obstructing their view, Christian gazed in awe and reminisced about those unforgettable mornings as a kid watching the sunrise in this sleepy town.

A small part of him missed these simple days more than others, but soon he snapped out of his daze and the reality of here and now stepped in: getting the hell out of Cedar Lake was the best decision he ever made.

Coming up fast in the distance was the first intersection he'd encountered in two kilometers, and Christian assumed, without asking, this was his turn.

Gemma chimed in, "Take a left ahead."

His inner voice laughed since he anticipated those exact words. As the intersection loomed, Christian decelerated and hung a sharp left onto the dirt road the locals referred to as "the 905."

Covered in a blanket of snow and ice, the untouched road bounced the car every few feet as it plowed through the elements. A few hundred yards ahead, Christian caught a visual of the large farmhouse, and he gulped down the little bit of saliva that had accumulated. What awaited them the moment they pulled into the driveway remained a mystery, and it was the unknown that concerned him.

Christian could sense Gemma's intense stare and he wiped away a bead of sweat that had lined his hairline.

"Everything okay?" she asked.

"Never better. Why d'you ask?"

"Well, given our conversation earlier, you had some reservations about doing this . . . and you're sweating like a hog."

He wiped harder against his forehead while struggling to maintain control on the icy road. "I'm not going to lie. Me and rednecks—not a good combo. Plus, these aren't your average rednecks. Oh no, these guys cook up meth for a living."

"It'll be fine if you let me do all the talking. And if anyone asks, you're not a cop. Got it?"

He hesitated before responding. "Uh, sure. Why am I not a cop?"

"You seriously have to ask that?"

He shrugged. "Just curious."

"We'll get more out of them. If you go in there and start waving a badge around, it's goodbye, intel. Besides, you know damn well Pearson won't save your scrawny behind, and your 'buddies' are hours away in Regina."

She had a valid point, but regardless, the knot in Christian's stomach tightened. Misrepresenting himself was uncharted territory; nonetheless, he trusted Gemma to make the right call. Besides, he hadn't come back to involve himself in the day-to-day Cedar Lake drama. He'd returned to locate Cassidy and nothing more.

Christian braked and allowed the car to glide along toward the edge of the driveway. The car stopped just shy of the drive, and he cocked his head to the right, staring hard up the long, winding lane at the camouflaged farmhouse. The area was still, and Christian seized one final deep breath before he stepped on the gas pedal and turned into the driveway.

He pulled behind a large, white-trashy pickup with the slogan "100% Asshole" embellished on the back window.

"Charming," Christian blurted out.

"Oh, just wait until you meet him."

Christian kept his seat belt fastened and turned to Gemma. "I question how they'll take it when my preppy ass rolls up next to you."

She pulled at his tan wool jacket and shook her head. "Yeah, we should have gotten one of my dad's jackets for you. Too late now."

He gripped the steering wheel.

"It'll be fine as long as you remember my only rule."

"I know, let you do the talking."

"Exactly. You just listen, and no matter what these guys do to get you riled up, do not say or do anything to draw suspicion to yourself."

"You want me to act ignorant?"

She grinned.

"I'll do my best. No promises, though."

Christian killed the engine, unbuckled himself, and they flung open the doors. Having not even taken three steps, the front door swung open, and a scraggy guy with a mullet emerged in the frame of the door.

Christian muttered quietly under his breath. "This must be the father?"

Under her breath, she replied. "In the flesh."

Gemma took the lead and Christian shadowed close behind. Lee eyeballed their every move with a shit-eating smirk smeared across his face.

"Well, well. Who do we have here? It couldn't be Gemma Williams gracing us with her presence, could it?"

"Cut the crap, Lee. I got some questions."

He leaned his body against the frame and crossed his arms across his chest. "Where are your manners, young lady? You can't even start out with a simple hello? I thought we were closer than that?"

She clenched her jaw and didn't give in to his snide remark.

"No? Straight to business, I see."

"Yup."

He scanned Christian from top to bottom and pointed. "Who's your friend?"

"Don't worry about him. He's with me, and that's all you need to know."

"Damn, sweetheart, chill. What's on your mind?"

She treaded imprudently onto the porch, but Christian hung back. "As I'm sure you've heard through the chatter about town, Cassidy disappeared three days ago."

"Yeah, I heard. Awful thing, that is. So, why call on me?"

"I was hoping Charles was around."

Christian's eyes stayed transfixed on the toothpick in the old man's mouth as it shifted from one corner to the other. "Charles? He ain't been around in a few days. Not since you and your friends ran him out of town."

Gemma planted her hand on her hip and leaned forward. "I didn't chase him out of town. I politely asked him to go sell his drugs someplace else."

"Well, darlin', I'm sorry you drove all the way out here, but I got nothing for ya."

Her eyes darted to the barn behind the house. "Well, if that's the case, then you won't mind if I take a peek around for myself?"

He shrugged his shoulders. "Knock yourself out. Ah, can you do me a favor while you're snooping around?"

"Depends."

"If you see Jason, let him know I need to see him in the house."

"Yeah, *if* I see him, I'll be sure he knows. Now, if you'll excuse us."

Gemma smirked, and as she turned to leave, Lee delivered her an unsettling remark. "You know, your sister isn't a well young lady."

Her head spun around faster than Christian ever witnessed in all the years they'd known one another. "Excuse me?"

The man thrust his frail body away from the doorframe and scuffled to the edge of the porch. "She'll never get better until she fights those demons that haunt her. You can only suppress them so long before they find a way to escape."

"And how in the hell would you know anything about her demons?"

He planted his foot onto the top stair tread and leaned forward. "We all got 'em, don't we? Secrets? Those things we wish we could forget."

Gemma remained dumbfounded.

"Look like you saw a ghost, darlin'."

She wanted to reach out her hands and strangle the life from him, but instead, she bit her tongue and pushed his unfounded comment aside. "I'll let Jason know you're looking for him."

She whizzed past Christian and yanked the arm of his jacket. Once out of earshot, Christian leaned toward Gemma. "He's just trying to get under your skin, but I'm impressed . . . you kept your cool. Maybe I'm rubbing off?"

"Shh. Let's get to the barn, take a quick peek around, and then get out of here. This place creeps me out, and these people, well, I don't need to tell you."

Gemma jerked at the handle of the heavy timber door and heaved it sideways. A cloud of hay rained down from the rafters, and as Gemma's head spun upward, a scruff voice accosted them from afar.

"Can I help you?" The man stepped closer, but not enough to make out who it was.

"Looking for Jason?"

At first the man paused but then took a few steps forward. The rays from the morning sun caught the side of his face, and one infuriated word passed over his lips. "Gemma."

"Yeah, it's me. Lee needs you in the house."

"Why, why are you here? You come to buy something?"

"You wish. Look, I'm looking for my sister. You haven't by chance seen her within the past few days . . . have you?"

"Cassidy? She ain't here."

Unfazed, Gemma advanced. "You realize we've reported her as a missing person, yeah?"

"I might have heard talk. What's it to you?"

"What's it to me? What's it to me? Listen, you shit-for-brains idiot, she's my sister, and anything involving her involves me."

He backed up. "Whoa. Listen, psycho chick, you need to take a breath."

"I'll breathe when I find her. Now, has she been around here or not?"

Jason pursed his lips and ran his fingers through his hair. "Nope. Last I saw her was right before Liam locked her away in that hellhole rehab center."

"What about Charles? You see him lately?"

"Maybe. You sure are asking lots of questions. You work for the pigs now?"

"If you mean police, hell no. They don't want to help bring my sister home safely, so, as usual, it's up to me to save her ass."

"Nah, something's up. I mean, you've always been a nosy wench, but you're being extra nosy."

She rubbed her hands across her face. "It's too early to argue."

Jason stepped closer to Gemma, and the wrath, not to mention the two tear drops tattooed next to each eye, alarmed Christian. He stuck his hands in his pockets and abided by Gemma's strict orders: remain silent and analyze every word they spoke. Even so, if things escalated into violence, he'd have no choice but to step in to protect her from herself. And with the overconfidence she flung around, that moment to plunge in headfirst drew closer with each additional exchange.

She huffed. "Jason, I'm done arguing with you. Go find Lee and let me satisfy my curiosity."

Jason stepped aside, and Gemma passed by with no problem. Christian remained hot on her tail, but Jason had other plans. He stepped in front of him and pressed his hand against Christian's chest.

"Not so fast, buddy. Who are you?"

Blindsided, Christian scanned his brain for a name. "I'm, um, Tim."

Christian courteously extended his hand, but Jason swatted it aside. "Tim who?"

"Tim Peterson, from Saskatoon."

Jason twirled around but his brawny hand remained affixed to Christian's chest. "Gemma, who the eff is this guy?"

She turned and got up in Jason's face. "Sounds like he already said. Now, if you don't mind, I need to find my sister." She shewed him away with the flick of her wrist.

Jason scanned Christian from head to toe and whispered in his ear. "I'm watching you."

Christian stepped back and the annoyance bubbled over. "And? Tell you what, if you're so uncomfortable with me escorting her, come follow us around. Right, Gemma?"

She belted out a half grin. "Yeah. We got nothing to hide."

Jason scoffed. He wasn't accustomed to his intimidation tactics backfiring. "Think I'll pass."

Jason fled and Christian breathed a sigh of relief. He opened his eyes, and Gemma had already set off fulfilling her mission.

"What exactly are we looking for?" he asked.

"Any evidence to prove she was here. You check over there, and I'll be over here," she said as her index finger pointed to the west side of the barn.

They split up, and Christian tiptoed towards the unlit southeast corner where a workbench filled the entire wall. With his iPhone in hand, he clicked on the flashlight. It didn't take long before he stumbled across a suspicious rusty-brown stain concealed behind a few tools hanging from hooks.

"Gemma, get over here."

She rushed through the barn, and her stride slowed the closer she got to the dark corner. She proceeded carefully, and Christian held the light near the spot.

"What'd you find?" she asked.

"Might be blood, but I'm not sure."

"How can we tell?"

Christian patted the lower parts of his jacket—nothing. Then, as luck would have it, he recalled having a collection swab in his inner pocket from a crime scene he worked just the night before he arrived.

He fished it out and Gemma lurched back.

"What the hell?"

He snorted. "Don't you watch TV?"

"Yeah, of course. What I meant was why do you have one of those readily available?"

"Long story. Do you want to know if it's human or not?"

She nodded as he snapped the plastic cover open and smeared the sterile cotton tip through the stain.

"Shouldn't you be wearing gloves or something?"

"What's with all the questions? Take a good, hard look around; would me wearing gloves even matter?"

"Suppose not."

"Besides, I left them in the glove box. Not sure how you'd explain *that* to those two idiots."

"Would be a bit suspicious, huh?"

"Exactly. So, quit questioning my every move and be grateful I even had this on me."

"You're right. I suppose I'm worried you'll taint the DNA or something."

"Taint? DNA? Honey, I'm only checking to see if it's human or animal blood."

Christian pulled the wooden stick down and recovered it with the plastic flap. He slid it into his jacket pocket. "We'll test it once we're far away from here."

"If it's human blood, what then?"

"Then we'll hand it over to Constable Pearson and let him get a search warrant for the property."

"Might be paint. After all, this is a workshop."

"Could be."

"Yeah, it's too high off the ground for human blood," she said.

He punctured a hole in her inflated confidence. "Not necessarily. I once responded to a scene where this guy used a chainsaw to sever some guy's limbs. Trust me, when the struggle is violent, blood flies all over."

Gemma cringed. Her stomach churned at all the blood and grotesque murder scene chatter. "Okay, I've heard enough."

Outside the barn, the raucous voices of Jason and Lee echoed off the grubby, wooden-plank walls. Christian quickly extinguished the light and they nervously darted away from the corner.

The door slid sideways, and the sun flooded the darkened corners of the barn. The two men stormed inside, and this time Jason clutched a pump-action shotgun, which thankfully he aimed toward the ground.

"All right, young lady. I've given you plenty of time to search. Satisfied?" Lee asked.

Gemma used her Academy Award–winning skills. "For now. I have one last favor to ask of you."

Lee wrinkled his nose. "You never stop. Do you?"

"What can I say—I'm persistent. But, here goes: If you happen to see Cassidy, will you let her know all of Cedar Lake is looking for her and to please come home and at least check in with us?"

His top lip curled upward. "Ah, what the hell. Sure. If I see your sister I'll drive her to your doorstep myself."

"Cool, thanks. Come on, Tim, let's get out of here."

Gemma grabbed Christian's forearm and dragged him between the two men who obstructed the exit. Before his head stopped spinning, he found himself only feet from the car.

"That was too close," he whispered.

Gemma glanced over her shoulder. "No talking until we're in the car."

The doors slammed closed, and Christian cranked over the still-warm engine. Before he receded to the dirt road, he shot a glance at the two men loitering at the fringe of the barn. By now, the shotgun rested on Jason's shoulder.

Not only did their physical appearance send out the creepy vibe, but it was obvious by their body language that the two men were on different wavelengths. Even from a distance, it didn't take a rocket scientist to see something shifted in the short two minutes it took to reach the car.

The most significant shift came from Lee, who now flailed his arms about and on a couple of occasions stuck his finger squarely in Jason's face.

But then there was Jason, who acted collected, the same guy who took a second to rest his burly hand on the old man's shoulder in some sort of failed effort to pacify the tension.

Whatever was transpiring, it didn't quell Christian's nerves. One thing was certain: they were dumb, but they also had more information than they led on. However, lacking tangible evidence, the only proof Christian possessed was two junkies acting like, well, junkies and a cotton swab of what may or may not be blood.

Christian rested his elbow on the center console and tilted his head toward Gemma, who tapped away at her old-school phone. "You don't think they suspected anything . . . do you?"

The tapping ceased mid-text, and her eyes shot up. "What? No. You did amazing. You impressed me how you stood up to Jason when he had you cornered."

"But you're certain?"

"Trust me. Those idiots have no clue."

A chill of apprehension crawled down his spine. Not wanting to alarm Gemma further, he staved off his concern and snagged one final glance at the local ruffians before he backed the car down the driveway.

I sure hope she's right.

CHAPTER 9

CHRISTIAN AND GEMMA SQUEEZED INTO A
booth at the only local diner worth a damn in town.
Christian stirred his coffee and glanced out at the sunny
surroundings, which made the town seem surprisingly less
awful. Gemma sat across the booth with her nose buried in
her phone. Tapping away, their conversation trailed off and it
gave Christian an opportunity to brainstorm his next moves.

On the one hand, getting the swab processed was crucial,
but he lacked one thing to make it happen—leucocrystal
reagent. The last thing he wanted to do was turn up at the
detachment with an illegally collected piece of evidence.
Constable Pearson had already made it perfectly clear he was
not to insert himself into the investigation.

Then the most off-the-wall comment he'd made yet blurted from his mouth. "We need to drive to The Battlefords."

She sighed and her eyes shifted from the screen toward his. "What for?"

"Could help if I can see firsthand her last known whereabouts."

She vigorously shook her head. "That's damn near a four-hour round trip, and a complete waste of our time."

"But," he began before she cut him off.

"Cassidy had no ties except to that second-rate facility. Trust me, she's nearby—I have this gut feeling."

Christian grinned and stirred faster. "Too bad your *gut feeling* would never stand up in court."

She crossed her arms over her chest. "Can I be blunt?"

"Better than anyone I know."

"I'm serious."

"With me, you can always be blunt. I prefer your straight-no-shooter attitude over fakeness."

"I'm get a sneaking feeling Lee and Jason know more than they'd have us believe. Now, whether they planned something, I couldn't say."

He stopped swirling the spoon and tapped it against the rim of the mug. After a quick sip, he responded. "What I hear you saying is you don't believe Cassidy would have gone freely with any of them?"

Devoid of words, she only motioned with diffidence.

Christian's efforts to continue to delve deeper into her hunch faced a roadblock as the waitress appeared with a plate in each hand.

"All right, who ordered the Belgian waffles?" Gemma eagerly raised her hand. "Here ya go, sweetie," she said as the plate hit the table. The older woman took one look at Christian and wrinkled her nose. "Suppose you must be the vegetarian omelet, then?"

Christian smiled. "You know, watching my figure."

The woman wrinkled her nose again and, as she sashayed away, she called out, "Enjoy."

They devoured their first meal of the day in silence, with a few *ahh*s and *ooh*s sprinkled in here and there.

Christian's phone dinged, and he dropped his knife and fork onto the ceramic plate and grabbed the device from his coat. It was a text from back home.

Angela: *Dug up those records like you asked. Check your e-mail.*
Christian: *You're the best. I owe you dinner when I get back.*

Christian flicked away the text message screen and clicked the power button, and the screen faded to black. Gemma drew another sip of her coffee before she grilled him.

"A hot date?"

"You wish. Just a colleague who did me a little favor."

Gemma blew across the top of the mug. "Do tell."

"What's to tell? I asked them to dig up some information and they did. End of story."

"Digging? Oh, you mean he did a background check for you?"

Christian smirked, rubbed his hands together, and evaded divulging too much information. "Well, she did, but that's beside the point."

"Come on, man, who are you stalking?"

He huffed and gave in as he always did when she begged. "Who do you think? Lee and his merry band of thugs."

"And? Did he find anything?"

"Again, *he* is a she, and I don't know yet. Confidential records are the sort of thing you check someplace a little less open to looky-loos."

"Ah, right. I guess we should get the check and hide out back at my place?"

He nodded.

Within ten minutes they rushed out the door and found themselves speeding off to Gemma's. Christian's eyes scanned each side of the street he once wasted hours hanging on. Things now were a stark image of what they used to be in the late '90s. Back in those days, there was no White family running around town hooking people on their homemade drugs. Nobody locked their doors, and people said hello in passing. Now, the locals oozed a distrusting tone. It was the sort of vibe where it wasn't a matter of *would* something happen, it was more like *when* would it happen.

Christian had to think long and hard to even remember when the last murder was.

That all changed four years ago when the largest supplier of jobs shuttered their factory doors, and the mass layoffs caused a ripple effect so massive there was nothing anyone could do to stop it.

Those same hardworking, neighbor-loving, trusting souls turned to alcohol, then drugs to cope with the depression. Welfare recipients soared, and soon after, the illicit world of drug manufacturing engulfed the once quaint town.

Christian propped the screen door open while Gemma fumbled through her jacket for her house keys. The once sunshiny day faded as looming charcoal-gray clouds gathered throughout the morning. Christian jumped in place and tilted his head back to gaze at the angry sky.

"Snow's coming again," he said.

Gemma slid in the key and twisted the door handle. "What's new? For once, I just wish it would stay sunny. Bet your winters are as nasty down there, huh?"

"Not like here."

"Good to know. Might just be the motivation I need to pull a Christian Anderson and move on with my life."

"Should I take offense to that?"

She ignored him and pushed against the door. Once inside, the house sat eerily still and dark. Gemma called out. "Dad? Are you home?"

No response.

The jog down memory lane reminded Christian of something. "I forgot to ask, what's your dad doing for work these days since the factory closed?"

"A little bit of this, and a little bit of that. I have been working part-time delivering pizzas on the weekends, but it's not enough to sustain a livable household."

"Sorry to hear. It's a shame how the factory up and closed like they did," Christian said.

Gemma chucked her keys on the dining room table. Deep down he was right; what they had done caused irreversible damage to the town but slinging snide comments wouldn't do a damn thing to change any of it.

"We're allowing the day to pass us by."

Christian glanced at his watch. It was nearly one in the afternoon. "We need to set a plan."

"What we need to do is get that sample to Pearson who can run the test."

Christian shook his head. "Not yet."

"And why the hell not?"

"We can't go until we have something more concrete."

"Like what, her body shows up on my doorstep?"

"What I mean is, what I did was not only highly unethical, it's downright illegal. We need to have a well-spun story or reason why we suddenly have a blood sample in our possession from the White farm."

"Okay. Well, then we better spin a web."

Then he remembered the cryptic message. "Right. I still haven't figured out how we'll crack that one entry."

"Well, that needs to be our top priority before we do anything else," she said.

"One thing at a time. I want to read through these files first and then I'll either decrypt the message myself or find someone who can."

Then came the dreaded question Christian had hoped would never cross her lips. "I've heard the more hours someone is missing, the lower the chance of finding them alive becomes. Is that true?"

Christian hung his head. She had to go there. She had to remind him of something he was fully aware of when it came to these types of situations. "Hey, instead of focusing on the negatives, let's focus on remaining positive and finding Cassidy. Now, do you have Wi-Fi?"

She leaned toward him. "We don't live in the Stone Age. Of course we have the internet."

NO PLACE IS SAFE

They set up shop in Cassidy's room, and while Gemma retrieved the hidden journal from its new home, Christian unzipped his bag and pulled out his laptop.

He crouched down to the floor and rested his back against the bed, and soon, Gemma joined him. The monitor came to life, and he tapped the keyboard and rested his index finger above the fingerprint scanner.

"Damn. Look at you, Mr. High Tech."

"What? It's standard these days."

Her head bobbed and eyes fluttered. "Uh huh, sure."

"Whatever. What's your Wi-Fi password?"

"Nope, it's top secret. I can sign you in, though."

He handed over the laptop, and after a few clicks, she handed it back over.

"Good to go. Where should we start?"

"Now that the looky-loos aren't around I'll get started on reading the dirt my colleague dug up on Lee White."

"And what about me? What should I do?"

"You? Flip to that page in question."

"Check."

She flicked the pages of the journal while Christian logged in to his e-mail, and there sat the information he'd requested. He double-clicked on the attachment, and the first page of the document was a recent mug shot.

Yup, there's his ugly mug.

He scanned down through the lengthy rap sheet.

Drunk and Disorderly in 2019
Breaking and Entering in 2017
Possession of Drug Paraphernalia in 2016

The list was lengthy, stretching all the way back to 1984. And as he scrolled down, one heading popped out.

Interview in the disappearance of Sarah Anderson

"Um, Gemma."

Her fingers stopped flipping, and she glanced over at him. "Yeah?"

"Didn't my father confirm my mom up and left for Calgary?"

"He sure did. Why?"

"Says here the RCMP interviewed Lee White about her 'disappearance' five days after my father says she left."

She inched closer and glanced over his shoulder at the screen. She skimmed a few sentences, and her body jerked back. "I'm starting to get the vibe she didn't leave town on her own accord."

"No, I get the same vibe. What if you're right, and there's a connection?"

"Christian, I love you, and I get you want to reinvestigate your mother's case. But can we find Cassidy first?"

"Right. Sorry. Have you found the entry yet?"

"Getting there. I got this nasty habit of allowing other stuff to distract me. Maybe I have adult ADHD or something?"

"When it comes to you, anything's possible."

She flipped to the last page of the journal and stopped. "We're missing something, but what?"

He shrugged. "I don't know. What I do know is that I'm going to snap a photo and shoot it off to a close friend of mine in cyber. I've never been any good at this cyber stuff."

"You? Christian Anderson, the smartest guy I know, can't decipher this?"

Christian arched his lips. "I'm not as smart as you think I am, but it means the world to me that you think I am."

She chuckled softly to herself.

"What's so funny?"

"How you're a byproduct of this town blows my mind."

Christian snapped a quick photo of the page and opened his e-mail. He typed in A-D, and immediately a familiar name populated in the list of choices: DC Adam Prescott.

While this wasn't his case, and everything he was about to do was against agency policy, he knew for certain Prescott was in his corner and would keep everything on the downlow. He attached the photo to the e-mail and pressed send.

He waited for a few seconds and then dove immediately back into the lengthy file about Lee White and his associates that Angela, the DC in his department back in Regina sent earlier.

Hours ticked by, but Christian couldn't set down the laptop. The droves of data his colleague unearthed was far too engrossing. Of the four men—Lee, Jason, Charles, and Thomas—there were two who could pull off a kidnapping, and they rose directly to the top of his list. Thomas Campbell and Charles White.

"Gemma. Thomas Campbell—how well do you know him?"

"You should know him too. He graduated the year before you did."

Christian wracked his brain trying to place the name, but after so many years and his inclination to forget anything he ever knew about this town, he came up with a blank.

99

"Sorry, I can't place him. What's his character like? Where does he hang out?"

"He loves McGinty's Pub. You know, the one downtown on First Street. If I were you, that's where I'd start."

"You know this guy, right?"

"I know of him. We're not close."

"So, you wouldn't mind coming along with me, then?"

"Yeah, but it's still way too early. He typically gets there around nine o'clock or so."

"Brilliant. You'll go with me then?"

"Where you go, I go. But first, I need a smoke, so how about we make our way to the front porch?"

He scoffed as she flipped open the top of her cigarette box to find it empty. "Shit."

"Something the matter?" he asked.

"Fresh out. You be okay here for a few minutes while I run down to the corner market?"

"In this weather? No, I'll drive you over there. Just let me get my shoes—"

She didn't even let his final words come out before her hands waved in front of her. "Nah, it's two blocks away. I'm fully capable of going myself."

"I'm sure you are, but—"

She stood to her feet. "But nothing. Christ, you think I'm going to get abducted too?"

"I doubt they'd keep you too long, given your mouth."

"Exactly."

"All right, go. I'll stay here and read a little more. But, the moment you get back, we're forging our plan of attack."

She smiled, walked toward the door, and the darkness of the hallway shrouded her. Little did Christian understand in the moment, as he watched her smiling face trek out into the world, things from here forward were about to get more complicated in the search for Cassidy.

CHAPTER 10

THE GLOOMY GLOW THAT ONCE FLOODED the
room had faded twenty minutes earlier. Christian pinched the
bridge of his nose to dull the stabbing throb behind his eyes.
As usual, he immersed himself in a computer monitor longer
than necessary and lost track of time. He flicked his wrist, and
immediately it dawned on him: *Where in the hell could she be?*

He slammed the lid of the laptop and hoisted himself up
off the floor. With one numb leg, he limped to the bedroom
door, jutted his head into the hallway, and hollered.
"Gemma? You back yet?"

His voice echoed off the empty walls. Christian cocked
his head and tapped his hand against the doorframe before
returning to the spot he'd occupied for the better part of three

hours. He bent down and snatched his phone from the floor. The screen illuminated, but to his shock, no new notifications accosted him.

Then a tingly sensation bubbled up from within, which he quickly dismissed and unlocked his phone.

"Jesus, Gemma, you should have just let me take you to the damn store."

He searched through his recent calls, and there her name showed in the number-one slot. With a simple tap, the phone dialed. Without even half a ring, voicemail intercepted. "You've reached Gemma. You know what to do next."

He pressed end without leaving a message and dialed again. The same outcome. He lobbed the phone against the paisley quilt and jumped to conclusions. "Shit. Whoever they are, they got her, and now they'll probably come for me next."

His hands trembled, and the jerkiness interfered to the point he needed to stop and collect himself. He shoved his hands into the pockets of his jeans, crouched to the floor, and followed the spot-on advice his therapist taught him. He closed his eyes and wiped his mind clear of any negative voices. Right now, the only thing he needed was to focus on the vibrations of his breath.

With his mind a blank canvas, he inhaled and exhaled in rhythmic fashion. After a few minutes elapsed, he opened his eyes. *I'm worthless to her if I can't stay calm and focused.*

He quashed the dreadful images that tried to permeate, because should he allow them to overrun his mind, he'd dwell. And the moment he permitted negative energy to settle in, he'd snowball past the point of no return, and there was no time for any of that.

He scooped up the laptop and journal from their comfortable spot on the floor, but just then, the trembling resumed, and he lost his grip on the items and watched helplessly as they tumbled to the floor. He knelt and scrambled to recapture control—yet anything he did was useless.

He exhaled forcefully and did what he always did when he was alone—he coached himself off the ledge. "You need to stop worrying when you don't have all the facts. You got to stop letting your mind run this show. You are the one in control. If there was ever a time to keep it together, this is it."

For whatever reason, he snapped free from the grips of his overactive mind and snatched the items. Without allowing himself to think, he chucked them into the duffle bag and flung it over his shoulder. It thumped against his back, and as he marched for the door, his inner voice of reason stopped him in his tracks.

Who was on to them? Was Lee behind Cassidy's disappearance? Or was this one of Gemma's many tricks she liked to play? Plenty of scenarios played out in his mind, but one thing seemed off.

If I just abducted someone, would I go out and do a repeat so close together?

Without answering his own question, he gave the room a final once-over—and after he ensured no sensitive information remained strewn about, he flipped the light switch and headed for the front door.

✳

THE CAR PULLED UP ALONG THE side of the nearest corner market he was certain Gemma had alluded to when she walked out of the door forty minutes earlier. He killed the headlights and stared forward. An enormous faded advertisement of two kids enjoying an ice cream cone plastered to the brick façade transported him back to a simpler time. This was the exact hangout spot for him and Gemma back when they were kids.

Back then, the place was bright, cheery—a place where he experienced his first heartbreak, the same spot he met Gemma and Cassidy for the first time, and the last place he stopped as he sped out of town.

When he flashed forward to the present, the place he fondly remembered had seen better days. Blame it on the economy, hell, blame it on the rampant neglect the entire town experienced over the past couple of years. Regardless, the place needed a good pressure wash and an updated advertisement.

His boots stamped against the freshly plowed asphalt, and a bitter blast of cold wind tickled the back of his neck. He locked the doors and raced for the front doors.

His hand gripped the grimy door handle, and his skin crawled at what mystery substance his fingers touched. He gave a quick tug and wiped the goo stuck to his hand against his jeans. One step inside and the warmth was a welcome sensation to the alternative outside.

His eyes swept down each and every aisle in the tiny store. They sat barren, and the lone body that occupied the space was an older, gray-haired woman who hunched over the counter, too absorbed in the newest issue of *Vogue* to glance up. As Christian advanced, his wet boots squeaked against the linoleum floor, and the plain-featured woman jolted.

"Scare the Jesus out of me. Can I help you with something, sir?" she asked.

"Maybe. Gemma Williams hasn't been in this evening by chance, has she?"

"Oh, Gemma, sure. She was in here about thirty minutes ago for her usual, two packs of smokes and a coffee."

He wrung his hands and continued. "And, let me guess, she struck up a lengthy conversation like she does with everyone, huh?"

A smile formed on the woman's face. "She's a sociable girl. And when you know someone as long as we have, well, you're bound to gossip now and then."

"Her favorite pastime. Speaking of, did she have anything new to share?"

The woman shook her head. "No, cheerful as always. Oh, but she mentioned she had an old friend in town; I assume that's you."

"Indeed," he began before extending his hand. "Christian Anderson."

"Anderson? You're Matthias's boy, aren't you?"

His head plunged. "Damn. Everyone in this town knows him."

"It's a small town, dear. Or have you been gone so long you forgot?"

"I suppose some things never change."

"My God, I can't believe how much you've grown."

"Happens, ya know."

"I remember the last time I saw you. It was the week before your graduation, and you and Gemma sat right out there on that picnic table." Her bony finger pointed outside

106

the plate-glass window. "I tell ya, I never seen two people as close as the two of you were."

Christian remembered the day clearly, and he arched his lips at her kind words bringing back some happy memories of his life in Cedar Lake.

"You don't remember me, do you?"

Christian gazed into her eyes, and an image of a much younger woman flashed before him. "Debbie. Debbie Armstrong, right?"

She clasped her hands together and flashed her teeth. "Oh, you do remember. You just made my night."

His head lifted, and another forced smile adorned his windburned face. "Of course. Still have the warmhearted personality you always had. And to a misplaced child like myself, it meant the world."

She reached out her hand and squeezed his.

Christian placed his hand atop hers and hated to break up the happy moment. "What I'm about to say may come across as odd, but how did Gemma act when she was here? You know, what was her demeanor like? Did she happen to mention where she was heading?"

She rubbed her chin. "I see your high-priced education paid off, using big words I have no clue what they mean."

"Oh, sorry. Did she give off a good or bad vibe?"

Debbie scanned the countertop. "As I said, she was fine. She seemed a little rushed, but she said she had to get home. I guess the two of you are out searching for Cassidy."

"We are."

"Why so many questions, then? Are you certain everything is okay? Gemma in some sort of trouble?"

He pursed his lips. "I don't know. She hadn't returned, and it's surprising considering we have so much to do."

"Should we call the police?"

The last person he wanted to see was Constable Pearson, and he waved his hands feverishly. "Let's not get ahead of ourselves. Do you know of any other places she'd go?"

She shrugged. "Maybe McGinty's Pub?"

"Yeah, she mentioned something about that place earlier. I'll check it out, thanks."

Christian backed away from the counter and out the door. As he stood in the parking lot, he did a full three-sixty and studied his semi-familiar surroundings. A mere three-minute walk separated her house from the corner market, and it was clear to Christian that whatever had happened, it happened quick.

He marched back inside and eyeballed the store again. "How long ago did she leave?"

Debbie glanced up from the magazine she had quickly returned to as if nothing was wrong. "Twenty minutes ago, or so."

"And has anyone else been in since she left?"

"Nope. Just you."

"Okay. I guess I'm off to McGinty's, then. Mind if I leave my car in the parking lot?"

She smiled and nodded.

"Well, wish me luck."

CHAPTER 11

THE NASTY CHILL IN THE AIR aggravated Christian's already sore face as he inspected the sticker-ridden door, full of biker and anarchy symbols, of the shadiest pub in town. Without a doubt, it wasn't the family-friendly place you'd take your mother, or a first date, for that matter.

As he reached his hand out for the handle, two drunken men stumbled out onto the sidewalk, and one of them crashed into his left shoulder. "Hey, watch where you're standing, asshole," one man shouted as he rushed for the gutter to throw up.

Christian ignored his comment and propped himself against the brick wall. *Ugh, I sure as hell don't miss this place.*

He drowned out the gagging coming from the curbside and sucked in a deep breath before he waltzed into the dark bar. The rock music thumped, and a few heads turned as he strolled to the bar. Sitting next to his left was a biker couple, who barely came up for air from their public make-out session, but off to his right sat four empty barstools. He picked the one closest to the wall and pulled out the stool.

For a Sunday, the place was full of life. In truth, what did anyone in town have to look forward to on Monday morning other than another day of collecting welfare checks and nursing a hangover?

He scanned the room and studied the faces of the patrons. Some appeared happy, but many sat alone, swirling their glasses with the hopes that the answers to all of their problems awaited them at the bottom of the glass.

Christian spotted the barkeep at the opposite end of the mahogany counter and motioned. Within a matter of seconds, the man wiped down the counter in front of his spot and grinned. "A fresh face. Where ya from, outsider?"

Christian drummed his fingers against the bar top. "The truth, here. Just getting reintroduced."

"Right on. So, Mr. Reintroduced, what can I get you?"

With Cassidy still missing, and Gemma in the wind, alcohol was the last thing he needed. Then again, with all the shady characters of Cedar Lake scrutinizing his every move, he had to play along.

"A double bourbon on the rocks."

The bartender flung the towel over his shoulder and pounded his hand against the wooden counter. "My kind of guy. Be back in two seconds."

The tall, hipster-like man dashed to the middle of the bar and Christian pulled out his phone to check if by chance he'd received any text messages or missed calls since he last looked.

Nothing.

He unlocked the screen and tapped on the e-mail icon. Immediately, a message popped up.

To: DS Christian Anderson
From: DC Adam Prescott
Date: Sunday, February 2, 2020 19:55:33 CST
Subject: Re: Cryptic Message

Christian,
How are you holding up being back home? If it's as bad as half the things you've told me during our late-night calls, I imagine you're weirded out and stressed to the max.

But I have some great news! After wracking my brain for hours, I cracked the code for the message you sent me. Oh, those Vigenère ciphers. I hate 'em, but love 'em at the same time.

Anyhow, here's what your friend wrote in her journal:

'I remembered the face of the murdered woman last night in my dream. It was clear as day.
How could someone I've known for my entire life commit an unforgivable act? How will I ever look at this person in the face again?

I should go to the authorities, but who would ever believe a junkie like me?'

Dude, you got your hands full with this one. Best of luck and call me if you need me.

Stay safe,

Adam

Christian grinned from ear to ear before he closed the e-mail and set the phone, screen side down, on the bar. Before he finished blinking his eyes, the overly friendly man pouring the drinks threw out a cocktail napkin and planted the half-filled glass within reach.

"So, tell me, why would you want to reacquaint yourself with Cedar Lake?"

Christian took a sip and it burned as it trickled down. "A friend's sister went missing a few days back."

He fumbled with his backward snapback hat. "Let me guess: Gemma?"

"Yup. I take it you know what's going on."

"Word around town is Cassidy wandered away from that rehab center. But trust me, fella, this isn't the first nor the last time this will happen."

Christian lifted the lowball glass to his lips and took another sip. "Wh-what makes you say that?"

He leaned in. "She's pretty messed up in the head."

"Is she?"

"Yeah. Biggest train wreck I've met in a *long* time."

"What else can you tell me about her?"

He leaped back. "Why you want to know? You the police or something?"

The loud conversations converted to low murmurs at even the mention of police, and Christian took another drink and released a nervous chuckle. "God no. I'm just a good friend doing Gemma a solid. Stupid cops—hell, even the local constable here doesn't even think anything's wrong."

"And there's a simple reason for his belief: ain't nothing wrong around these parts. What's your name, outsider?"

"Anderson. Christian Anderson."

He yanked off his hat and scratched his head. His face shuddered at the name as if he needed every last brain cell to figure out why he recognized it.

"Wait. Wait a minute. You ain't related to Matthias, are you?"

Christian hung his head in embarrassment. "I want to say no—but if I did, I'd be lying."

The bartender scrunched his face. "Come again?"

"He's my father."

"Damn, dude. He's yet another soul that Cedar Lake chewed up and spat out. How long's it been since you were here last?"

"Ten years ago."

"What year did you graduate?"

"2010. You?"

"2014. We might have crossed paths back then."

"It's possible."

"And you, what, up and left right after you graduated?"

"Yup. Packed all my belongings and was out of here the next day."

"Lucky you. By the way, I'm Linus," he said as he extended out his hand.

Christian countered the stranger's kindhearted gesture. "Nice to meet you."

The man kept quiet but grinned.

"So, Linus, can I ask about a few of the locals? Gemma worries a few of them might know something about Cassidy's whereabouts. I assume as the bartender of such a lively spot, you're the right guy to get the lowdown from."

A man at the opposite end of the bar hollered, and Linus turned his back, motioned with his index finger, and returned to face Christian. "Tell you what, let me grab this impatient asshole, and I'll be right back."

Christian sympathetically nodded, and Linus dashed away. With a bit of privacy for a moment, he picked his cell off the counter and opened the e-mail from his colleague.

He tapped "Reply" and sent a simple response.

To: DC Adam Prescott
From: DS Christian Anderson
Date: Sunday, February 2, 2020 20:26:13 CST
Subject: Re: Cryptic Message

Thanks for going out of your way getting this to me. You're truly a lifesaver.

I don't know what else I can say except I'm doing the best I can to stay safe. However, the local constable here told me to stay out of their affairs and get back to Regina.

It's a damn shame there isn't trust anymore between fellow officers.

Will you be around if I need more information?

Shoot me a text if you can, this e-mail is too burdensome.

Christian

Christian pressed "Send" and then his eyes caught a flash of Linus returning. He switched off the screen and flipped the phone facedown once again. His head lifted, and he shot a grin just before Linus returned.

"So, where were we?" he asked.

"I hoped you might be able to fill me in on a few people. I want to help Gemma find her sister, but I sort of need to visualize what I'm up against here."

"Let me guess. You want to know about Lee White?"

His voice trembled as he attempted to reply. "How-how did you know that?"

"I mean, Cassidy spends much of her time out on the farm with Charles. Call it a lucky guess."

"Is he dangerous? Do you think he's capable of hurting anyone?"

Linus stepped back, and his eyes shifted from side to side as if he were sure someone would listen in on what he was about to say. "You sure you're not a cop?"

Christian sighed. He had to be honest with him because all it took was one quick Google search and his name would appear in hundreds of news stories from the *Regina Leader-Post.*

Look, I'll come clean with you because you seem like a stand-up guy. I'm a detective with the Regina Police Service, but before you totally flip out, I have no jurisdiction in Cedar Lake and anything you say couldn't be used against you."

Linus fiddled with the towel in his hand. "Just talking to you could get me killed, ya know?"

"I'm strictly here as a friend to the family, and all I need is to bring Cassidy back, unharmed. Once that happens, I'm out of here. You get me?"

Linus hesitated. Eventually he leaned against the counter and tilted his head closer to Christian's. "I'll help, but we can't talk here. Meet me at the swing set at the elementary school in about an hour?"

Linus pulled away, and Christian answered with an outlandish request. "You heard me right; another double bourbon."

"Coming up."

Christian hung around the bar, sipping at his second, even stronger drink in less than an hour. His phone vibrated, and he plucked it from the sticky counter. It was a text from Adam.

> **Adam:** *You okay?*
> **Christian:** *Yeah, just making friends with the locals.*
> **Adam:** *I'm worried about you. Do you need me to drive up?*
> **Christian:** *Nah, I got everything under control. Wait . . . why are you worried about me?*
> **Adam:** *How's Gemma?*

He didn't know how to reply. More curious, why was Adam so worried about him? He drummed the fingers of his right hand against the counter while he stared at the screen.

How could everything be under control when he wasn't even sure where in the hell his best friend was?

Just lie.

> **Christian:** *She's good, she's around here somewhere . . .*
> **Adam:** *Where are you?*
> **Christian:** *At McGinty's Pub.*
> **Adam:** *WTF? You're at the bar while Gemma's sister is missing?*
> **Christian:** *Yeah. I'm trying to get some leads.*
> **Adam:** *I don't know about you sometimes. Anyway, you'll text me if you change your mind about needing my help, yeah?*
> **Christian:** *Don't I always?*
> **Adam:** *Don't be a smartass. It's not fitting, even for you.*
> **Christian:** *But you didn't answer my question. Why are you worried about me?*
> **Adam:** *Didn't think it required a reply. Figured the fact that we're sleeping together was reason enough.*

Christian scoffed and dug into the inside pocket of his jacket for his wallet. Maybe Adam was right. Why was he hanging out in a trashy place like McGinty's when his sole purpose for being here was to find Cassidy? Besides, he felt confident Linus would follow through and he'd get some answers he needed to move forward with locating Cassidy—and now, perhaps, Gemma too.

He flagged Linus down, and he rushed over. "You can't be ready for your third already?"

"Nah. I'm going to settle up and head out," Christian said. "Fifty minutes at the playground. Right?"

Linus discreetly nodded, and Christian handed him a twenty.

He slid off the barstool, and when his feet landed on the floor, a dizziness washed over him and the room spun.

Whoa. Way too much liquor.

He struggled along, like so many people he'd seen over the years, as he gained ground toward the exit. With each step he took, the vertigo intensified, and his vision grew blurrier. The words from the thumping rock music morphed into something indecipherable, just like the haunting voices did in all the nightmares he'd ever experienced over a lifetime.

He rubbed his hands against the door and threw all of his body weight into it. The optimism that maybe the fresh, bone-chilling air would sober him up faded, and when the dizziness got the better of him, he crashed against the brick wall. He rubbed his eyes, but no matter how hard he kneaded, it didn't stop the neon signs and orange fluorescent streetlights from blending together into a kaleidoscope of psychedelic colors.

What the hell is wrong with me?

Christian mustered through and staggered along the sidewalk, keeping his body as close to the wall as he could.

Five minutes passed and Christian had barely made it a block from the pub, and then an incapacitating blow to the back of his head tossed him nose-first into the snow-covered sidewalk.

He rolled over in a daze, as the silhouettes of two shadowy figures hovered over his lifeless body. Their identities masked by hoods over their heads, they conversed openly while Christian fought to get back on his feet. All it took was one swift kick to his chest, and Christian fell back to earth, and then all hell broke loose.

While one kicked, the other pummeled his face with his bare fist. The attack seemed to go on and on, and even if he wasn't in this impaired state, Christian still would have been no match against these two thugs. He cried out. All he wanted was for it to end, and by some miracle, it did.

Christian rolled his head and the blood-soaked snow caught his attention. He coughed hard, and from the depths of his throat, he spit up a viscous, iron-laced fluid and spit it out.

Christian whimpered and writhed, but the aggressors still had unfinished business to address with him.

The mysterious assailant who delivered the face punches kowtowed at his side and jerked him from the ground by his jacket. "Take this as a warning to get the hell out of here. We run this town now, not you, and certainly not Gemma anymore."

Before he released his grip, the man rummaged through the inner pocket of Christian's jacket before tossing his limp body back against the cold, wet sidewalk.

With one final blow to Christian's rib cage, the second assailant had his own terrifying, unsolicited warning. "If you aren't gone by sunrise, I guarantee you, the next beating will be your last, and trust me when I tell you no one will find your body."

Through his swollen eyes, Christian watched as the two foes bolted. As he lay there, every memorable experience of his life flashed before his eyes. Some good, others he wished he had forgotten long ago. The montage lasted only a few seconds, and when it was over, Christian rolled onto his side.

I have to find some help.

Instead of summoning the inner strength, he collapsed to the ground, and as he tried to cry out for help, nothing intelligible escaped his throat.

Minutes passed and while the party carried on inside McGinty's, the sidewalk remained a desolate wasteland. If he didn't want to bleed out and die in the place he fought so hard to escape, his only choice remaining was to crawl to the side of the main street through town and pray a passerby found him.

Images of Gemma, his father, and Adam flashed before his eyes, and somewhere amongst those faces, he found the vigor to roll onto his stomach, and like an Olympic swimmer, he dug his bare hands into the freezing snow and pulled himself a few inches closer to the street. He tested himself again and pushed himself up, but his battered body rejected his attempt, and he crashed face-first into the snow.

This is it. Not exactly the way I pictured my life ending, but here we are.

Drained, his eyelids closed, and everything around him faded to black.

CHAPTER 12

HIS EYES FLUTTERED OPEN, AND THE bright overhead lights blinded him. He squinted in pain as he massaged his head. He turned away and gripped the bedrail to hoist himself up. The sensation of a hand pressing against his chest startled him and he pulled away.

"What the h—"

"Hey, hey . . . relax. You're safe."

Christian winched. "Where am I?"

"Cedar Lake Memorial."

His head pressed into the pillow and he opened his eyes to see the last person he wanted to: Constable Pearson.

"Why am I here? Did you find Gemma?"

Pearson leaned in toward him. "Find Gemma? Isn't she home, where you should have been?"

Christian defied the constable's order and propped himself up. "No. She's not. I went out looking for her after she failed to return from a cigarette run."

Pearson's eyes widened. "When was this?"

"Maybe around seven-ish. What time is it?"

"It's a little after eleven. What do you mean by *maybe*?"

"It's not like I had my eyes glued to my watch the entire time, ya know."

"And you know which store she visited?"

He nodded. "Corner market two blocks from her house. You know it, the one catty-corner from McGinty's."

"Oh, I know it."

"I stopped in, hoping I'd find her there. Instead, I spent a few minutes speaking with Debbie. She mentioned Gemma had been there about twenty minutes before I arrived."

"Uh-huh. And so, what, in between finding Gemma and landing yourself here, you thought tying one on at McGinty's was the right call . . . because . . . ?"

Annoyance flashed in Christian's eyes. "Debbie said to check there. She and I had discussed—"

The room fell silent.

Pearson cocked his head to one side. "Discussed what?"

"Never mind."

Pearson scooted the chair closer to the bedside. "This isn't the time to keep secrets. Secrets and lies are what dragged us into this mess to begin with."

Christian exhaled audibly. "Fine. We were supposed to go—together—and look for Thomas Campbell."

The legs of the chair scraped against the floor, and Pearson flew up from the seat. His arms flailed like a madman. "What the hell? Do you even know who this guy is?"

Christian flinched at his harshness. "I, uh, Gemma let it slip that he worked for Lee and how she was acquainted with him."

"Yes, of course she is."

"What's that supposed to mean?"

"It implies Gemma is constantly coming to her sister's rescue. She knows that clan like the back of her hand, and I'm not one to compliment others, but I've never met someone who can switch between sweet and innocent to psycho so flawlessly."

"Psycho? I've never known her to be *that* crazy. Then again, people change, don't they?"

"Hate to break it to you, but nothing or no one ever stays the same. People evolve, grow more bitter as years pass them by. It sucks, but it's the truth."

Not giving in to his rhetoric, Christian tried to stay on the constable's good side. "She made me believe she'd get Thomas to talk. I should have known it was a fairytale, especially after meeting those losers Lee and Jason this morning."

"You what?"

"Don't freak out. I brought you a gift."

"Dare I ask?"

"It's inside the inner pocket of my jacket."

Pearson walked toward the cabinet against the wall and opened the doors. Inside was a large plastic bag filled with

Christian's bloodied clothes from the assault. He dug through and pulled out a wool jacket.

"This jacket?"

Christian squinted. "Yup."

Pearson flipped the jacket around and rifled through the pockets. "Is this a joke?"

"Huh?"

"There's nothing in here."

"No, no, it can't be," Christian said. "They must have—"

"Must have what?"

"I found what I thought might be blood, so I took a swab. I wanted to—"

Pearson interrupted. "Jesus, this keeps getting better. Indulge me while I catch up. You've been out to the White farm, you've spoken with Lee White and Jason Nelson, you collected evidence without a warrant, and for some kooky reason you and Gemma cooked up the insane idea of ambushing Thomas Campbell at McGinty's."

Christian sighed.

"Uh-huh, just another fun-packed Sunday evening. Anything else I should know?"

Christian's eyes diverted away.

"You gotta be joking! There's more?"

"I *may* have requested rap sheets on each of them."

"May have? Stop talking in riddles. Either you did or you didn't—this isn't a multiple-choice test here. Did you request the files, yes or no?"

His head bobbed up and down, but he kept his mouth shut.

Constable Pearson clenched his jaw. "I should punch you in the face, but someone already beat me to it. Do you realize how bad I want to scream right now?"

"So do it. I know I would. I went behind your back and investigated even after you told me not to. I'm nothing but a low-life, stubborn man and I apologize for my actions."

Pearson's lower jaw quivered as he slid back into the chair. "But I won't. If we're making confessions, here's mine: I went behind your back too."

Christian's jugular vein throbbed, and he glared at Pearson.

"I made a call to a couple of connections in Regina after our visit yesterday."

"You what?"

"Chill out and let me finish. They had nothing but positive things to say about you, and it got me thinking: Why would I turn away someone as devoted and bright as you when I can't even get my own colleagues to get me a surveillance tape?"

"Ah, I'm happy to hear I'm not a total pariah yet."

"However, my friend mentioned he was under the impression you returned for a family emergency. Why not just tell the truth?"

Christian eased and propped the pillows behind his back. "I didn't want to raise any alarms. Gemma is like family and it is an emergency, so it's not as if I lied to them. I just omitted some key points. Besides, I can take care of myself."

Pearson stood and paced while he nibbled at his fingernails. "Yeah? And how's that working out for you? Hmm?"

Christian gazed at the IV in his hand. "Not too well."

Pearson scanned the floor as his head rocked from side to side. There was a soft knock at the door and Pearson turned his head to see a familiar face staring in. "Looks like you have a visitor."

Christian squinted, believing by some miracle his life had transported to an alternate reality. He blinked. And blinked once again. The same haggard mug pressed against the window, and Christian released a groan. "You called my dad? Why would you do that?"

"Who else was I going to call?"

Christian mumbled under his breath. "Anybody but him."

Pearson stepped away from the bed and Christian stretched out his hand and grasped his forearm. "Do me a favor."

Pearson glanced down at Christian's hand. "Um, maybe."

"Wait."

"For?"

"I know my dad."

"Uh, okay? Do you have a point?"

"Yeah, I do. You brought a man, who for all I know is three sheets to the wind, to the hospital to stare at his beat-up son in a hospital bed. I'm certain he'll need a ride home."

"You're so far off base. Actually, he's sober for once. Suppose there's a first for everything."

Christian's eyes narrowed. "No, for real, he's sloshed . . . isn't he?"

Pearson crouched at Christian's side. "I'm not lying. Trust me, not once in three years has he ever been sober." Pearson stood. "I'll be just outside the door. I'll be back in less than ten minutes. We don't need your blood pressure to spike again."

The door opened and Christian watched as Pearson slipped out and his father slipped in. He closed his eyes, hoping this was all a bad dream. As the heavy door clanked closed, he realized it wasn't. His eyes opened and he did a double take. There was something different about the man standing at the foot of the bed.

He studied his face. His father had trimmed his scraggly beard, he had on fresh clothes, and the stench of body odor was a distant memory. For the first time in a long time, was it even possible his return somehow triggered his father to come to his senses?

"Pop, don't linger. Have a seat."

Matthias shuffled nearer, and Christian's bruised face became noticeable. Matthias muzzled his gasp with his hand, yet somehow the noise still escaped between his fingers.

"Who did this?"

"I don't know, Pop. I was having a drink down at McGinty's, and I can't be certain, but I'll bet that bartender drugged me. Then after I left he probably set his thugs loose on me."

"You were sticking your nose into other people's business again—weren't you?"

Christian sighed. "That *is* my job, Pop."

Matthias drew a few deep breaths, and his bloodshot eyes lowered toward the floor. "I hate this life you've chosen for yourself."

Christian scoffed. "A bit late to be offering up some father-son advice."

"So it is."

Matthias wrung his hands together and shifted in the chair. His eyes scanned everywhere except in his son's eyes.

"Pop. You okay?"

He hesitated and choked on his words. "I. Oh, man. How do I say this?"

Christian resituated his back against the pillows. "I don't like where this is going."

"I need to confess something."

"Okay. What'd you do?"

"I sort of, kind of, left out a few details about your mother. Now, you gotta understand, boy, none of this has been easy for me to talk about."

"I imagine it's been hard on you. What changed your mind?"

"Given everything with Cassidy, I can't keep these secrets locked up anymore. You're here to help. Right?"

"I am. Tell you what, why don't I shut up and you talk."

He glanced up. "You remember the letter? You know, the one I said your mom sent from Calgary."

Christian frowned. "Yeah? You're about to say you never got a letter, huh?"

Matthias shook his head. "Don't put words in my mouth, boy. I did get a letter, with one small detail I left out; it wasn't your mother's handwriting."

"What? And you didn't report it?"

"I took it as a prank, nothing more."

"Pop, you should have kept the letter, or at least turned it over to the police."

"Can't change the past, boy. I held out hope she'd come back. A year passed, and I knew those chances were slim to none at that point."

NO PLACE IS SAFE

Christian debated dropping another bombshell on the old man, but when he caught a glimpse of his heartbroken face, he changed his mind. As usual, when Christian spoke before giving himself ample time to compose a diplomatic response, trouble and insensitivity spilled out. "Pop, I know it was hard for you to tell me that. And we do need to tackle Mom's case, but I have to point out one thing: Cassidy is still missing and until we find her, everything else is on hold. You do understand, yeah?"

"I do. But she'll show up, Christian. You just wait and see."

"I hope you're right. But from what I've learned these past two days, not to mention having a bartender drug me then getting the crap kicked out of me, it's looking more like she is in danger, if not already dead."

"Christian." Matthias gasped at his callousness.

"Pop, let's face the truth for once . . . together. Do I want her to be dead? Absolutely not. But we also can't ignore the probability. She's been missing for three days, it's below freezing, so unless she is holed up somewhere with Charles, she'd never survive the elements."

The older man hung his head and struggled to speak.

"Was there something else, Pop? You look like you need some rest, as do I."

"There is. While I stood in the mirror this morning, it dawned on me there are a few similarities between the circumstances surrounding your mother's and Cassidy's disappearances."

Christian shifted on the bed. "I thought we said we'd find—"

"For once in your life, will you just shut up and let me talk. I know you want to find Cassidy, but maybe this could be a clue."

"Go on," Christian replied. His face drooped at his father's snappy tone.

"For starters, you remember how I told you that your mother and I had a fight outside?"

"Yeah?"

"I left out a few details."

Christian leaned forward and winced in pain. "Like what?"

"I knew she was having affairs."

"As in more than one?"

He nodded.

"Do you know with whom?"

"No idea. And they aren't important to this anyhow. What is, though, is she blurted out she had some damaging evidence on some local guy, and she was going to the police the next morning."

"Interesting twist. Any idea what she meant?"

Matthias's lower lip quivered. "I pressed her to let me help, but she wouldn't give anything up. Said it was between her and the police."

"And this is what makes you believe there's a connection between Mom and Cassidy?"

"No. It was something Gemma mentioned to me when she brought me pizza the night before she was to pick up her sister."

"Care to share?"

"She was worried about Cassidy."

"She told you that?"

He nodded. "Said she was paranoid, whispering a lot. What if she, too, had information on someone and was about to go to the police?"

"I-I don't know, Pop. It's a stretch. Besides, why would Gemma not tell me about that?"

"Boy, wake up. You're too smart to not connect the dots here."

"All right. For argument's sake, let's say your hunch is spot on, and there *is* a connection. You got a name of someone I should be looking a little closer at?"

Matthias leaned forward, rested his elbows on the gurney, and with a dead-straight face blurted out a name that he'd grown tired of hearing since he arrived in town. "Lee White."

Christian rubbed his chin and looked away. Twenty-four years was a long time ago, and times had changed since then.

"Why him?" Christian asked.

"Ever since the day that asshole rode into Cedar Lake, he's had his grubby little hands in everything and on every attractive woman within a fifty-klick radius."

"Including Mom?"

Matthias scoffed. "I don't have any proof, if that's what you mean, but my gut tells me something was going on between those two. I hate to say, but your mother had turned into a wild woman toward the end of the marriage."

Their eyes locked, and Christian stared into his serious face. The old man truly believed what he was spouting. "All right, Pop. I'll see what I can dig up, but I need some time to heal."

Matthias looked him over from head to toe. "You're right. Do you need anything before I go?"

Christian's face scrunched at the disgusting thought of his mother sleeping with Lee White. Still, he needed to get the duffle bag back, and his father was his only hope. "Pop, wait, I do need one more thing."

Matthias beamed. "From me?"

"Yeah, scary thought, I know. Listen, I parked my car outside the convenience store on First. Can you persuade Constable Pearson to drive you over there?"

"Your car will be safe there overnight."

"It's not the car I'm worried about. Inside the trunk is a black bag. It's valuable and I won't be able to relax until I know it's safe here with me."

"Sure, yeah, whatever you need," Matthias said and stood from the chair.

"The keys are in the cabinet over there, somewhere." Christian pointed and Matthias walked over.

With the keys in hand, Matthias smiled and moved for the door. "And, Pop, one more thing."

"Sure."

"I'm proud of you. Never did I think I'd see the day when you'd clean yourself up. This won't be easy, but if you and I are going to have any sort of future together, I need you to stay sober."

Matthias beamed. Not once had the words *I'm proud* passed Christian's lips. He released his grip on the gurney and walked toward the door. Matthias turned once more, and this time his eyes filled with tears.

"I-I'll be back as soon as I can."

Matthias propped open the door to the room, and Christian called out. "Pop?"

"Yeah?"

Christian laid there, paralyzed. He had to tell his father the truth about who he was, but his mind scanned back through the past two days. He understood dredging up something so personal now was in poor taste.

"Never mind. Be safe."

Matthias chuckled. "I'm with a constable, don't think I can get any safer."

"True."

Matthias flashed a broad smile and slipped through the door, which closed slowly behind him. Once his father was out of earshot, Christian sighed. At that moment the thing on his mind was not Gemma, nor Cassidy, nor even the fact that he was lying in a hospital bed. It was trying to find a way to overcome his fear of being his authentic self with his father.

He needed to rebuild the relationship that had collapsed so many years ago, but if he couldn't be himself around his father, then what was the point of trying to make any of it work?

The door latched closed and Christian closed his eyes and dozed off.

PART 3

MONDAY

"Lies are convenient when the truth is unfathomable."
Courtney M. Privett

CHAPTER 13

THE LATCH ON THE DOOR CLANKED and Christian jerked awake from the first deep sleep he'd had in weeks. He opened the one good eye he could see from, and to his surprise, it wasn't his father who had returned; instead he found Pearson. In covert fashion, Christian stared as the constable waited next to the door and helped guide it closed.

He had ditched the uniform for street clothes at some point. *He's less intimidating without the uniform.*

Pearson tiptoed across the room, and Christian spotted something flung over the man's shoulder. *My bag.*

He rustled around the bed, pretending not to have noticed him walk in seconds earlier. "Constable Pearson?"

"Christian, I didn't mean to wake you. I just wanted to—"

He waved his hands. "It's okay. Let's be honest, if it wasn't you, it would have been one of those nurses coming around to check on me. What time is it?"

Pearson swung his wrist out. "Two fifteen."

Christian's eyes widened. "And my dad?"

"Safe at home. He mentioned this was something you needed," he said and dangled the bag in the air. "You got medication in here or something?"

His voice trembled. "Nah. It's just my laptop and some confidential documents."

"Good thing I grabbed them, then."

An awkward silence persisted for a few moments, until Christian spoke up. "Well, I won't keep you since I know you have a town full of ruffians to protect. Thanks again for dropping this off."

Expecting the constable to turn on his heels and leave, Pearson surprised him as he approached the bed, scooted the chair across the floor, and plopped down next to him.

Christian bowed his head. He didn't need another lecture, but instead, he got something he never expected—compassion.

"My shift's been over for a couple of hours."

"Wait. You did this all on your own time?"

The constable leaned inward. "Yeah, why wouldn't I?"

"I'm confused."

"By?"

"For starters, why would you go out of your way for someone you so clearly dislike?" Christian asked.

"I never said I didn't like you. What I didn't love was you popping in unannounced and barking orders like you ran the place."

Christian smirked. "I suppose that would be annoying, eh?"

"Might? You're a smart guy, Christian, but there's something you should understand about me."

"And that is?"

"I don't work well with others. I'm just like you, a loner."

"What gave you the impression I'm a loner?"

Pearson shot him the side eye. "Your colleagues, that's how. Everyone says you do your best work when you're alone."

Still clinging to his damn pride, Christian folded his arms across his chest. "And what? Now we're buddies because of our shared gratification for being loners?"

"I'm going to need you to take it down a notch. And for the love of God, uncross your arms. I'm trying to make a point here, one that might benefit us both, but if you're going to put up barriers, I'll walk."

Christian hesitated but relaxed his arms and rested them in his lap. "I'm listening."

"We both want the same thing—to find Cassidy. I realize I may not have given that impression yesterday, but too much time has passed, and I'm warming up to your theory she may be in grave danger."

"Good. Now, how do we make this happen?"

"First, if we're going to team up and bring this drama to an end, let's be on a first-name basis. Yeah?"

137

Christian nodded. "All right . . . Luke. You mentioned you've been here five years. Where were you before this?"

"Moose Jaw."

Christian smirked. "Well, that solves the mystery on why we have some mutual connections."

He grinned. "Perhaps. I'll never divulge my secrets, though."

Christian eased the tension in his shoulders and pressed his back against the pillows. Was Constable Pearson trying to pave the way toward a fresh start? He'd dropped the macho-man façade and exposed a vulnerability about him. And for Christian, that was a good start.

"How do you like living up here?"

"It's okay. Certainly not the cosmopolitan life you're accustomed to in Regina."

Christian let out a small laugh. "You hate it that much, eh?"

"With a passion. In all my years in law enforcement, this little town is the worst I've ever served. Dealing with cretins, suckers, and chumps who think they can invade the whole town and the laws don't apply to them. It's exhausting."

"Wasn't always this way."

"I've heard."

Pearson slouched in the chair and kneaded his hands together. Neither of them exchanged words, just glances, and then, out of nowhere, Pearson stopped rubbing and his mouth opened. "Enough about me, let's get back to my proposition."

Intrigued, Christian locked eyes with him for the second time in two days. "Go on."

"If we're going to find Cassidy, and now Gemma, then we must work in harmony. We have to be transparent in sharing what we've learned so far. As visitor, I'm giving you the floor. Who should we look into further?"

Christian pointed at the bag on the floor. "It's all on the laptop."

Pearson grabbed the bag and set it in Christian's lap. He rummaged through one-handed and slid out the laptop. The metal casing was cold to the touch, and for a brief moment, Christian worried about the battery level.

The power button sank inward and the monitor roared to life. Christian exhaled with relief. While it booted up, Christian dug a little further and pulled out the red leather journal. He shook it in the air.

Constable Pearson cocked his head to the side. "What's that?"

"This? Just a gold mine of information."

"Huh?"

"It's Cassidy's. Gemma and I found it while we snooped around her bedroom."

"Wait, wait, wait a second. Liam let you rifle around her room?"

Christian rubbed the base of his tender neck. "Why wouldn't he?"

"When I asked, he shot me down. I probably didn't make things better when I threatened to return with a warrant."

"Yeah, Liam doesn't take too kind to threats. But, since he considers me the son he never had, I suppose nepotism factors in. Besides, I don't think he actually knows I searched her room."

Christian's phone dinged from the nightstand, but he ignored it while Constable Pearson continued asking questions. "This journal . . . you garner any fresh background on Cassidy?"

"It was, er, eye-opening to say the least. Tell you what, have a quick read. I should probably reply to that message."

"Girlfriend?"

"Girlfriend, yeah, something like that."

Pearson slouched in the chair, and Christian opened the text messages from who else but his boyfriend, Adam.

> *Adam: Where are you?*
> *Adam: Seriously, Christian. This isn't funny anymore. Answer me.*
> *Adam: Fine. You want to play games? I'm driving up! Cedar Lake is small enough I should have no trouble finding you.*

He checked the time stamp of the texts. 22:03, 22:27, and 23:00. It was now 02:30, a difference of three and a half hours. If he were true to his word (which he always was), then he'd be hauling ass along the Yellowhead Highway a little north of Saskatoon.

> *Christian: Sorry. Terrible cell service. Where are you?*
> *Christian: I hope you aren't driving clear across Saskatchewan in the middle of the night. I'm fine.*

While he awaited a reply, Christian tossed the phone onto the thin blanket that covered his body. He grunted while he ran his scratched hands across this face. Pearson glanced up from the journal. "Trouble in paradise?"

NO PLACE IS SAFE

Christian shrugged. "Who knows, you know how they get. Enough about that drama. What do you think? Something's going on, huh?"

"She buried a traumatic memory, but what it is, couldn't tell you."

Christian blinked in rapid succession. "I can."

Pearson was all ears now and closed the cover of the book. "You know something—don't you?"

"Don't get too excited, but I have a hunch."

Pearson leaned over the railing. "Spill it."

"Gemma believes the woman she refers to is my mom."

Pearson's body jerked back. "This is deep, but it's an angle we should consider. Your mother vanished twenty-four years ago?"

Christian nodded.

"Let's do some quick math. Cassidy is thirty-six now, so she would have been twelve when your mother disappeared."

"Oh, then she'd be old enough to remember. Now she's vanished. If we're right, and whoever hurt my mother is still amongst us, they'd—"

Pearson swooped in and finished his thought. "Do whatever it took to keep their crime a secret."

Christian nodded and his cell phone chimed again. This time he immediately grabbed it.

Adam: I'm nearly there, just passed Saskatoon. Where are you? And don't lie.

Christian: I suppose this is going to warrant a phone call instead of this seesaw text session.

Christian shook his phone in the air. "Hey, uh, my girlfriend wants to FaceTime. You won't mind if I have a couple of minutes alone?"

"Yeah. Of course. I assume I can take the journal with me, right?"

"Have at it. I've read it three times. Oh, and the final page is encrypted."

"Encrypted? Seems out of Cassidy's league."

"Surprised me too. It's so advanced I had to bring in the big guns from our cyber division."

"And they cracked it?"

"They did. I'll share the e-mail after I wrap up this call."

"Best of luck. Girlfriends are over the top and needy."

Pearson pulled the door open and Christian held off until his lingering shadow disappeared from the wall. Two rings and Adam's scruffy face filled the screen.

He gasped and struggled to find words.

"It looks worse than it is," Christian said.

"Babe, what the hell? Who did this to you? Are you wearing a hospital gown?"

Christian hesitated and as he went to raise his shoulders, he winced in paid. "Kinda, sort of a prolonged yet funny story."

The weight of Adam's piercing eyes traveled across the airwaves. "I knew letting you go back to that hellhole was a terrible idea. You should have jumped when I offered to come with you."

A semi whizzed by in the background and Christian defended his decision. "Babe. Don't be *that* way. Don't try to make me feel guilty. You act as if I came here on some holiday retreat. This is the last place I'd spend a vacation."

"You're right. I shouldn't have said that."

"You're damn right you shouldn't have. I'm not up here chilling with the phantoms of my past, sipping on tea or anything. I'm here with a purpose, and that's to help Gemma and find Cassidy."

"Where is she, by the way?"

"Who?"

"Gemma. Is she there keeping you company?"

"She's . . . well . . ." he stuttered.

"She's getting you a snack?"

"Not quite."

"Why are you being so secretive?"

Christian sighed. "She's gone AWOL."

Even in the dim light, Christian could see Adam's head wag from side to side. "Message received. Listen, I'm being honest. GPS says I'll arrive in two and a half hours. Under no circumstances do you leave that hospital bed."

Christian panned the camera along his body, certain he got every IV line protruding from his body in the shot. "You're in luck, I won't be going anywhere anytime soon."

"Christian. Swear you'll wait."

"I swear. On my grandmother's grave, I won't leave this hospital bed. Now get off the phone and hurry up."

"So damn bossy. I'll see your stubborn ass soon."

Just as they were about to wrap up their call, Christian broke in with one final stipulation. "Hey, before you go, there's something you need to know."

"Okay?"

"If anyone asks, we're colleagues and nothing more."

"Who's going to question us about our dating status?"

143

"There's a constable from the RCMP. I sort of gave him the impression I was calling my girlfriend. So, now when I hang up, I'm going to tell him my girlfriend called you and that's why you drove up."

Adam's jaw opened wide. "Wait. You're *not* out back home?"

"Only with Gemma, but no one else."

"How could I not know this?"

"We've been dating for a few months. I suppose we hadn't gotten that far. But, please, I need to come out on my terms. Say you can respect that."

Adam paused and took a deep breath. "Completely makes sense why you didn't invite me on your excursion now."

"Adam . . . don't be mad."

"Mad? Nah, I get it, and of course I'll keep things on the down low."

"You're the best. Now, get back on the road so you can be here at my side."

"How I ever let you wrap me around your finger is beyond my comprehension. Get some rest and I'll see you soon. And, Christian?"

"Yeah?"

"I love you."

Outside the door, Pearson lurked near the door and Christian rushed to get off the phone. "I love you too. Got to go."

Christian hung up and motioned for Pearson to return. "Everything okay back home?"

"As you'd expect, she's a tad pissed I got myself into this. So, what did she do when I didn't reply earlier? Phoned a colleague and ordered him to drive up here to find me."

"Women. Can't live with 'em, can't live without 'em. This colleague, you trust him?"

"DC Prescott? Yeah. I'd give up my life for him, and I know he'd do the same in return. He's the guy who broke the cipher."

"Sounds like a smart guy."

"The smartest. Listen, before I share the decoded message, I need to ask you a serious question."

"Shoot."

"When we spoke yesterday, you mentioned the local detachment was still sifting through CCTV footage from the morning Cassidy disappeared. Has anyone gotten back with you?"

"Ah, I forgot to mention it, but, yes, the rehab center got their asses in gear and turned over the video. Although, the constable up there said her behavior was a bit strange."

"How so?"

"He didn't elaborate."

"And you, you haven't seen the video firsthand—have you?"

"Not yet. But my source says Cassidy exited the main doors at eight thirty on the dot. Walked to a bench just outside the main door and sat. Less than a minute later, she was up, pacing back and forth."

Christian's eyes widened as an indicator to keep going. "Doesn't sound out of the ordinary. People pace when they get antsy."

"I'll give you that. Then she lit up a cigarette, glanced around like she was paranoid, and then casually strolled down the sidewalk for the main road."

"And then what?"

"Don't know. No cameras down there, but she turned left and disappeared from sight."

"What time was that?"

Pearson pulled out his notepad from his pocket. "At 8:37."

"And Gemma arrived there around 8:50. A thirteen-minute gap. How does a person vanish in thirteen minutes?"

He shrugged. "That's a great question, and unfortunately I don't have the answer you're looking for . . . not now, at least."

"How soon can your buddy get a copy of the video over to you?"

"If I met him halfway, I could have it in my hands in a couple of hours." Pearson glanced at his watch. "Knowing that old geezer, he's wide awake. Let me get him on the phone."

Pearson pulled out his cell phone. "It's just strange, isn't it?"

"What is?"

"I mean, when you ask your sister to pick you up, why wander off?"

Christian's forehead wrinkled. "Doesn't make any sense."

"Where in the world could she have been going? Does she know anyone there?"

"Not that I know of, but then again, she isn't the same girl I grew up with. Drugs controlled her life for so long, she could have a dealer there, for all I know."

146

"Could be, but unlikely she'd drive that far for drugs. Let me go get Constable Nichols on the line. You—you should rest up. I'll come back in a few hours. Okay?"

Christian yawned. "Sleep—it's a beautiful thing. If I'm lucky they may let me out of here at some point today."

"Ah, you're one of those optimists, aren't you?"

"What other choice do I have?"

"Well, don't overexert yourself."

Christian grinned.

"I'll handle the grunt work. Okay?"

"Whatever you say."

"And when your colleague arrives, *and* if they let you out of here, you two can work the video evidence. No reason to take on any more damage than they've already inflicted."

Christian yawned again and covered his mouth. "Sounds like an excellent plan, Constable."

Pearson patted Christian's shoulder then moseyed for the door. As the Mountie turned and gave Christian one final look, he chuckled under his breath to find him already passed out.

CHAPTER 14

THE HOSPITAL ROOM DOOR CREAKED OPEN and in tiptoed a handsome, towering, brunette who stopped people in their tracks. Any time Christian stared at him, it always made him wonder why someone fresh off the cover of GQ would have ever given him the time of day.

A black North Face backpack slung over his shoulder and he ran his fingers through his wispy hair. He lingered at the door while his eyes adjusted to the dim, unfamiliar surroundings. His pupils dilated, and soon, the outline of his once happy boyfriend's body grew sharper.

As a constable himself, Adam understood the risks associated with dating a colleague. All it took was a split second for entire lives to shatter; however, Adam never expected the day when he'd hover over Christian's body would come so soon.

His vacant gaze watched Christian sleep peacefully from across the room. His shoulder leaned against the doorframe, and Adam hung his head as he fought back the impending anger. They soon came, and as he choked back the mucus, he lifted his head and wiped away the wetness from his stinging eyes.

His hand still firmly gripped the door handle, and a sliver of light still peeked in from the overhead fluorescent lights in the hallway. He released his hold and tried his best to not awaken Christian, but his shaky hand failed him, and the door slammed closed.

"Shit," he muttered aloud.

Adam planted his head against the door, but through the darkness, a familiar voice echoed and startled him.

"Adam? Is that you?"

He twisted his head around. "I'm here."

Not holding back, Adam charged to his boyfriend's side. Inches from comforting him, he paused and left a gap between him and the side of the bed.

"I know I look broken, but I'm not. Can I at least get a kiss?"

At first Adam hesitated but edged closer. Christian reached out his hand and pulled his face into his. A brief kiss was all Christian needed, and he perked up. "I'm so sorry I had you worried."

Adam lowered the guardrail and sat on the bed. "Who did this to you?"

"Typical story—wrong place, wrong time. Guess my questions ruffled someone's feathers."

Adam stroked the unbruised side of Christian's face. He flinched, and Adam immediately pulled his hand away. "Oh, babe, did I hurt you?"

"No, no, I'm fine."

"Don't lie. You are not fine."

"It's a bit sensitive. Trust me, I'm better now that you're here."

Adam hung his head. "I phoned Chief Hudson an hour ago and explained everything to him."

Christian scoffed. "What? Damn, I bet he was pissed."

"Eh, not pissed—more concerned. But good news."

"What?"

"Chief granted us permission to assist the RCMP with anything they need."

"How'd you manage to convince him?"

"Like I'd give away my trade secrets. Never gonna happen. But seeing as how I did you a favor, now it's your turn to do me one."

"Like?"

"Can you catch me up on what you know, other than the cryptic message I decoded for you?"

"Cassidy is still in the wind. Constable Pearson was here a few hours ago and said the constable from The Battlefords got his hands on the video footage from the rehab center."

"Anything significant?"

Christian nodded. "Cassidy wandered off about thirteen minutes before Gemma arrived to pick her up."

"Uh-huh. And have you seen this video?"

"Not yet. Pearson mentioned he would get his hands on a copy before he came back. What time is it?"

"A little after four."

"I assume he'll be rolling in any minute, then."

"And Gemma?"

"She went to the corner store for smokes and never came back. I'm telling you, whoever took her, they did it quick and left behind no evidence whatsoever."

Adam changed the subject. "I talked to Angela earlier this evening."

"Oh? About what?"

"You."

"And?"

"And she filled me in on the list of suspects you had her dig up records for. I can't believe you thought you could handle this on your own."

"Suppose I did bite off more than I could handle. But I got the local constable and now you in my corner."

"Out of these guys, who do *you* suspect has the greatest motive to kidnap the sisters?"

"Hard to say. There's more to the story that you *don't* know."

"All right, we got all night—fill me in."

"There's possibly a personal link to all of this."

"Personal? How?"

"It may involve the disappearance of my mother."

Adam leaned closer. "You don't think that's who she's referring to in the journal, do you?"

Christian exhaled loudly. "As much as I don't want to, all roads are leading that way."

"I didn't see this curveball coming."

"Me neither. When Gemma called I figured this would be a two-day trip, tops. We'd locate Cassidy, bring her home safely, and I'd return to the comfort of my apartment. Now, I don't know. Everything's so screwed up."

Adam leaned closer and kissed Christian's hand. "I realize we haven't been dating long, and there's so much we haven't discovered about one another yet. One thing I need from you is to trust me enough to tell me anything."

"I do trust you."

"Good. Whoever you were back then, he isn't the same guy I know today."

Christian couldn't help but grin. Adam was right. Gone was the poverty-stricken boy who grew up amongst the roughest country folks. All he ever wanted was a better life than his parents had, and the only way to achieve that was to escape the hopelessness that surrounded him.

And he found a way out and set off for his new life in Regina. From that day forward, he never looked back at what he left behind. He only set his focus on the things he could achieve.

"Thanks," Christian muttered.

"For what?"

"The encouragement. I needed to hear those words right about now."

"There's plenty more where that came from. All right, where do we start?"

Christian sat up and fluffed the pillows behind his back. "We can wait for Constable Pearson to get back to divvy out tasks. For now, you and I should try to get a little rest."

"Does he know I'm coming?"

"Of course. I told him right after we hung up earlier."

Adam wiped his forehead and pretended to wipe away sweat. "And before you even remind me, we're just colleagues . . . at least for now."

He nodded his head. "For now, yes."

Adam eyed the bench along the wall, where a pillow and blanket sat folded neatly at the bottom edge. He kicked off his shoes, laid his head against the pillow, and closed his eyes.

"Adam?"

"Thank you again. Now that you're here, I know we'll find them."

⁜

ADAM SAT IN THE DARKNESS NEXT to the bed and watched him sleep. After a quick nap, the initial shock wore off, but outrage filled in as a replacement, and all Adam wanted now was to uncover the truth.

The door clicked open and interrupted Adam's concentration on the next moves. Carrying three large paper cups of coffee, Constable Pearson quietly entered, and Adam rushed to help him with the door.

"You must be Pearson," he whispered.

"Yeah, but just call me Luke. And you must be Prescott?"

He nodded and extended his hand. "Adam."

"How long has he been out?"

"Couple of hours now. You mind if we chat in the hallway? You know, let him get a little more rest."

"Sure. Ah, wait. I brought him coffee. This place isn't famous for having the best brew in town."

"Ah, he'll appreciate that when he wakes up."

"I'll leave it next to the bed."

Pearson tiptoed across the room and leaned over to set the paper cup on the nightstand. Before the bottom touched down, Christian rustled around. Pearson froze and waited.

From the doorway, Adam motioned his approval and he slid the cup next to the telephone and backed away slowly for the exit, where Adam waited with the door propped against his back.

Once the door closed and they took a few steps away, Adam's deep voice returned to a normal tone. "Man, I have to say, you've got your hands full with this one."

"The case . . . or your colleague?"

A soft snicker escaped Adam's throat. "I suppose both. Christian is one of the most stubborn and nosy people I've ever met. But I also know he means well."

"Has he filled you in?"

"A little, but perhaps there's more to learn."

"Since I hear you're the best digital forensics person that the Regina Police Service has, perhaps we can start with this?" Pearson slid out a DVD jewel case from his jacket.

"He embellishes. I'm certainly not the *best*, but if I can be frank, I'm up there as far as skills go. What's on the DVD?"

"The video footage from the rehab center. I wanted to save this for when he was awake, but I sense you're the right guy to do the analysis instead."

"Why me?"

"You don't have a stake in these people's lives. And besides, you've seen his condition; he needs rest and less excitement."

Adam peeked through the rectangular window into the room. "That he does. Besides, he doesn't have the video-enhancing software that I have. Any place we should get set up?"

"Cafeteria? I'm starving, and I bet you are after your long journey."

Adam peeked inside the room again. "Sure. Let's let him sleep as much as he can. I just need to grab my pack and we can go."

Ten minutes later, the two men found themselves commandeering a large table in the empty dining hall. While Adam prepared the laptop, Pearson dug through his bag and tossed several thick folders across the table.

Pearson arranged everything in a strategic order, and after Adam lifted his finger from the reader, his eyes scanned the files laid out in front of him.

"What's all this?"

"The biography of every single person on our suspect list."

Adam scanned the thick stack. "Whoever they are, their lives have been more active than mine."

"You think?"

The two men bantered back and forth while the computer loaded. It was as if they'd known each other longer than twenty minutes. The software was up and running, and Pearson handed over the jewel case.

"You ready?" Adam asked.

"Hit it."

The video loaded and their eyes remained glued to the black-and-white, grainy footage for the entire duration of the fifteen-minute clip.

As noted in Pearson's notepad, at eight thirty, a petite, long-haired woman exited the main doors of the rehab center.

"That's her," Pearson indicated as he tapped the screen.

They observed as she approached the bench, wiped her bare hand across to clear the snow, and sat. For a few seconds she rummaged through her purse and pulled out a pack of cigarettes.

The video skipped a few seconds, and suddenly there she was, puffing away.

"Strange place for a skip," Pearson noted.
"Shoddy video equipment. I see it all the time. Don't worry, five seconds won't hurt us."

Thirty seconds later, she stood and paced around in circles as her drags grew more frequent. At 8:36:00, she tossed the cigarette butt to the ground, stomped it out, and glanced up at the camera.

"Wait. She looked directly at the camera. Why?" Pearson asked.

"Could be nothing. Let's wait before we jump to conclusions."

At 8:37:26 Cassidy clutched the purse tight against her body and wandered along the sidewalk in the direction of the main road. Her journey took three minutes, and they both watched as she reached the road and turned left toward town.

Adam fast-forwarded the video, hoping she would reappear. Yet after reaching 8:46, there was no sign of her, or anyone for that matter. Four minutes later, Gemma's green Honda pulled up to the door.

He fast-forwarded again. Gemma waited fifteen minutes and entered the facility and didn't return to her car for twenty minutes.

Adam paused the video, and the two traded baffled glances.

"Okay. We have both Cassidy's and Gemma's timelines now, but do we have our suspect's?" Adam asked.

"No."

"I just wish we could get our hands on a few more angles of this video. Better yet, some CCTV footage from the road would be the best."

Pearson drummed his fingers on the tabletop. "Tried, no luck."

"No traffic cameras?"

Pearson's nervous hand motions continued. "Do they even have those in The Battlefords?"

Adam cocked his head. "Maybe?"

"I'll ask, but I'm confident that in a small town that gets little traffic, it'll more than likely be a no."

He tapped his hand against his head. "I keep forgetting we're not in Regina."

Pearson stood and scooted the chair back under the table. "Tell you what, I trust you, and I get the vibe you're a guy who gets stuff done."

"Appreciate the compliment."

"You go check on Christian and we can resume work on this later."

"What about you?"

"Me? I got timelines to get out of our suspects. The longer we wait, the better chance they have to synchronize their stories."

"Good plan."

"Let's reconvene around one, or sooner if something damning develops. Cool?"

Adam handed over his business card. "Cool. Take this. My cell number is on the back.

Pearson flipped the card over several times and then pulled his cell phone from his pocket. He tapped the screen a few times and walked away. Even before Pearson exited the room, Adam's phone chimed.

The constable turned and smiled. "And now you've got mine. See you in a bit."

CHAPTER 15

ADAM REVIEWED THE VIDEO AT CHRISTIAN'S side for hours, until he stirred awake around eleven thirty.

"Hey, you're still here," Christian said.

"You're in the hospital. Where else would I be?"

"Figured you'd be out with Pearson looking for Cassidy and Gemma. How long was I out for?"

"A while. Your body is trying to tell you something."

"Suppose so. Did you meet Constable Pearson?"

"Yeah, Luke dropped by a few hours ago. We discussed the case and, even better, he brought the CCTV footage from the rehab center."

"You two are already on a first-name basis now? I'm impressed."

"Don't start."

Christian stuck out his tongue like an annoying teenager who didn't get his way. "And did the times match up with what The Battlefords detachment provided us with?"

Adam nodded and closed the laptop. "They did. But enough about the case. How's your head feeling?"

"The dizziness is gone. Suppose that's a good sign." Then his stomach growled. "On the other hand, I could go for something to eat."

"You need food. I'll see if I can track down a nurse."

As he stood, Christian glanced at the nightstand and then back at Adam. "Where'd this cup come from?"

"A special delivery from your buddy. He dropped it off this morning while you caught up on your beauty rest. He said the coffee in this place isn't fit for human consumption."

"It's a damn shame, because I could use an energy boost right about now."

"Let me find a nurse and get you something to eat, hmm?"

Christian squinted his eyes. It was his way of simulating the tough guy act, but all it really did was make him look ridiculous.

"Don't give me that look."

"What look? I wasn't giving you a look."

"Yes, you were doing the macho guy thing. And to be honest, it doesn't suit you. Now, do you want me to find a nurse or smuggle in something unhealthy?"

Christian flashed his teeth and made a pouty face.

Adam stretched out his arms and groaned. "Say no more. You have a craving for anything in particular?"

"I could go for a juicy burger and fries."

As his grip on the guardrail loosened, a rapid knock at the door startled both of them. Seconds later, in strolled two nurses and a doctor. Adam stepped aside and hovered close.

"Ah, Mr. Anderson, you're awake. How are you feeling?" the doctor asked.

"Better—considering."

The doctor flipped through the chart. "Well, everything appears good. Your CT scan showed no irregularities. Your blood pressure and heart rate have returned to normal and have sustained at an appropriate level for more than a few hours now."

Christian leaned forward. "Does this mean I can get out of here? No offense, but this isn't the place I need to be right now."

"Do you have someone here who can look after you for a few days?"

Adam stepped forward. "I'll make sure he's well taken care of, Doctor."

"Well, then I can't find a reason why we can't get you out of here in under an hour. Hang tight, okay?"

"Yeah, I'll be right here."

The medical staff exited, and Adam returned to the chair. "Do you have anything to change into?"

"Yeah. In my suitcase."

"O-okay. Where is it?"

Christian cocked his head upward. "I left it in Gemma's bedroom."

Adam dropped his head into his hands. "Can your hunger wait an hour? I promise once you get discharged, I'll run you through any drive-thru you want."

Christian zoned out and his inattention frustrated Adam. "Christian. Can you wait for food?"

"I guess so."

"And your friend Gemma . . . does she have an address?"

He snapped out of his fog. "Sorry, yeah, it's 37 First Street."

"Does anyone else live there?"

"Her dad, Liam."

"Okay. I'll go grab your suitcase, that way you have something fresh to change into."

"But I have clothes here."

Adam's patience reached its limit and he tossed his hands in the air. "For fuck's sake, they're soaked in blood—your blood. In case you forgot, you lost enough to save six people's lives all while you nearly lost yours. I'm grateful Constable Pearson reached you when he did. Otherwise, I might be here to id—"

Christian reached out his hand. "Might be here to what? Identify my body? Babe, you got to chill out and take a breath. You're working yourself up for no reason."

"How can I, when all I do is worry about you. It's like once you get an idea stuck in your head, you run with it, and snub anything or anyone in your way."

Christian fumbled with the blanket. "Will you listen to yourself? Did I screw up and make a rookie mistake? You bet. And now I'm paying the consequences. I'm bruised, but I'm not knocked down."

"I need you to promise me that from this point forward, you'll stop and think about what might happen before you go off on another rouge mission."

Christian reached out and squeezed Adam's hand. "I promise I'll slow down and think about someone other than myself from now on. And, babe, there's no rush to run off to—"

Adam cut him off mid-sentence before he finished. "The answer's no."

"No?"

"Exactly. I know what you're going to say."

"What am I going to say?"

"You'll say the blood-soaked clothes are just fine."

"And? What's wrong with that?"

Adam scoffed, crossed his arms across his chest, and leaned his face into Christian's. "I never want to see you in those clothes ever again. In fact, I'm going to ask if they'll burn them when I see the doctor again."

Christian crossed his arms over his chest. "Fine. You win."

Adam leaned over the railing and planted a kiss on his cheek. "I always do. I'll be back shortly."

✸

A PLEASANT NURSE WHEELED CHRISTIAN ALONG the concrete pavers where a fresh dusting of snow blanketed everything in sight. Through the heavy snow, Adam's black Jeep stood out like a sore thumb amongst the sedans and hatchbacks that littered the parking lot. As Christian anticipated, the moment he was at the halfway point between the door and the end of the sidewalk, the driver's door flung open, and Adam hurdled over a snowbank stacked where the sidewalk connected with the asphalt.

He's trying too hard to flatter me.

Right before the nurse reached the end, the wheelchair stopped. "This is as far as the train goes."

"Thanks. I think I can manage the rest of the way."

Christian gripped his crutches and lifted himself from the wheelchair. The tops of each crutch slid below his armpit, and he hobbled along until Adam appeared at his side.

"You got this?"

"Yup. Where to now?"

"I was going to say a hotel, but the best I could get us was a motel. At least it's someplace quiet and safe where you can recuperate."

"What about the case?"

"Oh, trust me, we won't leave you out."

"Good. We've lost so much time because of this setback, now we need to hit the pavement running to catch up."

"Eh, about that. Pearson says no field work for you until you ditch those things." He pointed at the two metal sticks.

"I'll be back on my feet in a day—tops."

"I love how you find joy in lying to yourself."

"Whatever. Have you spoken with Pearson?"

"Hung up with him as I pulled in. He'll meet us at the motel as soon as he's done questioning some guys named Lee and Charles. But for now, how about we get something in your stomach other than lime Jell-O and orange juice?"

"Hell yes, best plan I've heard all day."

After traveling fifteen minutes out of the way, Christian got the coveted burger and fries and scarfed down the entire meal before the car even pulled up to the cleanest motel in town. The place certainly wasn't the best place he'd stayed in a while, but it wasn't the worst place either. Regardless, he was out of the hospital and all he needed now was a clean bed and Wi-Fi.

The car stopped outside the lobby of the Ridgeway Inn, a few short blocks from his childhood home. Adam left the motor running and dashed inside to snag a room for the two. Christian's heavy breaths fogged over the windows, and with the sleeve of his jacket, he wiped away the built-up condensation. His eyes scanned the exterior of the building, but slowly his mind drifted to the distant past.

A dramatic scene from twelve years ago replayed in his head. It was the night of junior prom, and he and Gemma loitered outside one of the rooms where Cassidy and a few of her friends hosted an after-hours party. As he took a shot of whatever liquor they had gotten their hands on, a brawl had spilled into the parking lot.

He and Gemma retreated and stood by helpless as two men threw punches and words around like neither meant anything. He remembered Cassidy forcing her way between them, but whatever she did or said, the one man slapped her across the face.

The car door opened, and he shook the memory away as he blankly stared at Adam.

"Everything okay?" Adam asked.

"Huh? Oh, I'm good. This parking lot brought back something from long ago."

"Happy memory?"

"Eh, wouldn't go so far as to say 'happy' . . . but also, no need to worry."

Christian reached his scratched, icy hand across the center console and squeezed Adam's. The brunette unwound and immediately the tension in his shoulders eased. He pulled back on the shifter and the car rolled forward. "Let's get you settled in, and we'll start on your first task—the video."

Christian hobbled along to the door, and once inside, he made a beeline for the bed. He glanced around the room. Two beds, a table, television, and an armchair filled the room. At some point over the last twelve years the owners had replaced the carpet, but the tired décor remained untouched.

He flopped onto the bed and tossed his crutches to the floor. "Not too bad. Any idea how long we'll stay?"

"As long as needed. I mean, we can't leave without finding Cassidy and Gemma, right?"

"When you're right, you're right."

Christian's attention faded again, and Adam sensed something was on his mind. However, leaving him to his own devices, he snatched the laptop from his bag and tossed it onto the bed next to Christian. He sat down next to him, and not once while he set everything up did Christian's eyes waver from the window.

"I wasn't going to ask, because, well, I'm sure being back here brings back a mix of emotions for you. But we're not watching this video until you tell me what's bothering you."

"I need a favor."

"Another one?"

Christian's jaw dropped at his bluntness.

"Relax. You know I'd do anything to help. So, what's this favor you need?"

"I need you to do some digging into my mother's disappearance. Times have changed, and technology has advanced so much in the last twenty-four years. Maybe . . . maybe there's something they missed all those years ago."

"Yeah. Of course. Whatever you need."

"The first thing I never got around to was following up on my father's side of the story."

"And his version is?"

"That she ran off to Calgary with someone she was having an affair with."

"Perhaps, but I'd think she'd have reached out to you by now to let you know where she is."

"Agreed. Still, can you run a search and see if any Sarah Andersons pop up in Calgary, or Alberta? Hell, check the entire country if you can."

"You have any idea how many names I'll get if I run that name for all of Canada? Way too many."

"Please, just do your best," Christian pleaded.

Adam stacked the flimsy pillows behind his back and turned toward Christian, who sat in a daze moving his lips, but nothing audible escaped.

"Something tells me, though, you already know I won't find her."

"I can't shake what my father said last night about how the letter he got wasn't in her handwriting."

"Perhaps whoever took her wrote the note to throw people off the fact she had been kidnapped."

"And that somebody might still be amongst these familiar faces I've known my entire life."

"Why don't I reach out to Pearson and ask him to drag her case file over here when he comes?"

Christian's lips wrinkled into a grin. "Yeah? You'd do that?"

"It's a long shot, at best. But we'll never know unless we try. Although, it's been so long ago, he may not have everything we need. I don't want to get your hopes up."

"Nah, it's there in that station house somewhere. The previous chief was a pack rat."

Adam reached across the bed and grabbed his cell phone from the top of the duvet cover. With a couple of clicks, he had the phone to his ear.

"Hey, it's Prescott. This may seem crazy, but hear me out."

Minutes passed by at a snail's pace, and all Christian could do was follow Adam with his eyes as he paced around the room. The discussion lingered on, with an occasional *uh-huh* and *right* amidst the silence. After five more minutes, Adam rushed to get off the phone and return his attention to Christian and the video they so desperately needed to make sense of.

"So?"

"No promises, but he'll have a look around and reach out to the retired chief if he can't find it."

"Better than nothing, I suppose."

"Anyway, let's get back to this video."

Adam returned to his warm spot next to Christian and plopped the laptop against his thighs. He queued up the video to an hour before Cassidy appeared, and slid the laptop over to Christian.

"Here's what we need to do. How good are you at makes and models of cars just by looking?"

"With nine years on the force, I had better be an expert."

"I need you to watch the end of the drive for any car that passes by. Make a note of the make and model until you see Gemma pull in."

Christian got to work, and with each vehicle he saw, he jotted down the information onto a notepad. If there was a duplicate, he noted it. Thirty minutes passed, and his eyes scanned the paper. Immediately, one particular vehicle jumped off the page.

He blurted out. "Chevy Silverado."

Adam gazed upward. "What's that?"

"There's a Chevy Silverado that passed six times between 7:30 and right before Cassidy wanders off."

"Good find. Anyone around town you know who owns one?"

"Nah. My dad has a junked-out Dodge, and Gemma's dad drives a Ford F-150."

"Well, it's a start. Anything distinct about the truck?"

Christian rested his head against Adam's shoulder. "Missing passenger-side mirror."

"Somebody knew she was getting out, and they waited for her."

"But who?" Christian asked.

"Who knew she was getting out?"

"As far as I know only Liam and Gemma . . . unless."

"Unless what?"

"There was someone on the inside feeding information."

"I'll buy that. But why would Cassidy leave knowing Gemma was picking her up?"

Christian rolled his shoulders. "I couldn't say."

"What does your *gut* tell you?"

"This was staged, and no one kidnapped her."

"I don't understand."

"What if she has been a willing participant in all of this?"

"Is Cassidy the type who could orchestrate something this detailed?"

169

Christian pondered Adam's question for a few minutes. "The girl I remember wasn't bright enough. Although, she did fool me with that cipher . . . so anything's possible."

Adam cocked his head.

"You and I have seen this sort of stuff before. We can't ignore a few red flags," Christian continued.

"I'm confused."

"Kids and cheating wives starved for attention. They disappear for a few days, the miraculously reappear and blame the entire thing on an imaginary perpetrator."

"You know, we need to pick an angle and stick with it. As an outsider, I'm going with kidnapping until I have something more concrete to suggest otherwise. Cool?"

Hesitant, Christian caved. "Fine, you win. We'll work worst-case scenario until we hit a dead end. Then all bets are off."

CHAPTER 16

MEANWHILE, AS CHRISTIAN AND ADAM
SCOURED through security footage, Constable Pearson
stood at the heart of the interrogation area. Two rooms
flanked each side of the space surrounded by two-way mirrors
and a heap of digital equipment. On a routine day, this was
the space where another constable would monitor the
questioning of a suspect. However, on this particular day,
things were anything but routine.

What Constable Pearson was about to conduct wasn't so
much an interrogation as it was a question-and-answer session
with the scum of Cedar Lake, Lee and Charles White. The
one question that burned on the tip of his tongue: Where had
Cassidy and Gemma Williams disappeared to?

To his left, Lee White slouched at the table, and in the other room, his son, Charles, drummed his fingers against the top of the metal table. Monitoring both rooms, Pearson analyzed how the anticipation influenced each of their personalities in different ways.

He wandered toward room one, where Lee rubbed his grimy hands across his face. His outward shell alone was enough to startle even the most toughened constable. The glass supported his shoulder as he watched the gray-haired man chomp away at his dirty fingernails. He pulled away and wrinkled his nose.

How can someone who handles meth all day do that?

Pearson shifted perspectives and checked in on Charles. His eyes widened as the disgusting hooligan leaned back, lifting two legs from the floor, and kicked not one, but both of his mud-covered boots onto the table.

That was the tipping point for Pearson. He grunted before he slammed his coffee cup down and scooped up Cassidy's file. With his blood boiling, he flung the door open and marched into the hallway. The time for games had passed, and so had the archaic techniques he'd stomached until now.

He turned the handle and flung open the door without a courtesy knock. Why give the parasite the consideration of a warning? When Pearson emerged, Charles lost his balance and the chair fell against the wall. Pearson laughed while Charles recomposed himself.

"Making yourself at home, I see."

"You can't keep me here. I know my rights."

"Ah, so you earned that law degree?"

"What?" Charles asked.

Pearson pulled out the chair opposite Charles. "Let's cut through the formalities, shall we?"

"Am I under arrest?"

Pearson shook his head wide from shoulder to shoulder, all while he stared at the folder on the table in front of him. "Nope."

Charles drew a long face. "So, that means I can go?"

"Nope."

"You gonna tell me why I'm here?"

Pearson clenched his jaw and allowed the silence to create enough tension that the addict's mind would spin to the point where he believed he was in the worst trouble. However, Charles was having none of Pearson's games. "Answer me, pig."

Pearson snickered under his breath. "Charming. The reason you're here is because I asked you to be."

"More like forced."

Pearson opened the thick folder in front of him. "Tell me a little about your girlfriend. You had any contact with her in the past week?"

"Nope."

"Do you remember the last time you spoke? A date would be great."

Charles folded his arms across his broad chest. "Can't say I do. Was before her father shipped her off down south."

"Uh-huh. I've heard you two broke up. Is that official, or mere rumors?"

Charles unfolded his arms and rested his elbows on the metal tabletop. "We never broke up. Who told you that? Gemma?"

"We'll get to her in a few minutes. Right now, let's talk a little more about Cassidy. Several sources report you two had a full-blown quarrel over at the A&W two nights before she overdosed. Is dating you so awful one must attempt to take their own life to escape the madness?"

Charles foamed at the mouth and slammed his back against the chair. "Screw you, man. I'm not answering anymore of your stupid questions."

"Oh, you're going to answer all of them. You know why?"

His icy stare didn't unnerve Pearson.

"Fine, let's skip Cassidy for a few and move on to Gemma. When was the last time you saw *her*?"

Charles kept his lips sealed, but Pearson had a trick up his sleeve. He walked to a small table situated in the corner of the room and grabbed a remote control. He aimed it at the television and immediately a photo of Gemma and Cassidy from a few months earlier filled the screen.

Charles glanced away. His apathetic reaction pissed off the rugged constable to his core. He stomped across the room and stood behind the wimpy wannabee. With both hands, he turned the heathen's head toward the image.

"These two are missing, and I've found one common denominator. And do you know what that is?"

Charles shook. "No."

"You and your merry gang of thugs. Now, I'll ask again. When was the last time you saw Gemma?"

Charles gritted his teeth but kept his cool. "I don't know."

With the click of a button, the screen changed, and a still from a surveillance camera at the local hardware store appeared.

"This jog your memory?"

He scoffed. "Maybe."

"Seems clear as day you must have done something to piss Gemma off."

Charles remained silent and kept his head turned away from the screen.

Pearson released his grip and returned to his chair. "What'd you say to warrant such a reaction? Hmm?"

"Nothing. She came at me out of nowhere."

"Right. Tell me about the conversation that led to her pointing her finger in your face."

"Basic shit."

"Doesn't look basic to me. She looks angry."

He muttered a few swear words under his breath. "I asked her about Cassidy."

"And? Asking her about her sister is harmless. Now, can we fast-forward to the point when Gemma asked you to get your ass out of town."

"She was calm, and for once I assumed everything was good. That was until—"

"Until what?"

"The skank flipped out and lost it right there in the middle of the store for everyone to see. She started spitting out gibberish about how my dad and I had brought nothing but unnecessary drama into her family and said I needed to stay away from Cassidy."

"And I suppose, like the caring boyfriend you are, you obeyed her demands?"

He shook his head and pounded his balled-up fist against the table. "Hell no. Cassidy's my girl. We've been together for over four years now. So, I was like, nobody tells me who I can and can't date. But then, well—she threatened me."

"With?"

"Said she had evidence, and if I came near Cassidy, she'd turn it over to you guys."

"What evidence?"

"Nah, we're not going there. Besides, it's nothing that involves either of them."

Pearson returned to his chair. "Okay. So, what, you let it go and agreed to leave town for a while?"

"Something like that."

"Okay, assuming all that is true, let me ask you this: Where were you last night around eight thirty?"

"With my dad out on the farm. I got there close to four in the afternoon and we sat around all day drinking. My dad mentioned something about Gemma and some guy dropping in to search the barn."

"Interesting. Continue."

"He was pissed and thought Gemma was up to something, like planting evidence, and he wanted to blow off some steam."

"And what does 'blowing off steam' look like to a bunch of drug dealers?"

"What we always do—target practice."

"In the pitch-black night?"

"Yeah. Why?"

"You weren't in town, say, near McGinty's Pub, were you?"

"McGinty's? Nah, even *I* don't go there. Too rough for my blood."

Pearson glanced down at the folder and flipped through the pages. He wasn't sure showing all of his cards *this* soon was the right move. Minutes ticked by, and they exchanged awkward glances at one other. Then the shriek of Pearson's cell phone broke the silence. He glanced down at the phone. *Adam Prescott.*

"Get comfortable . . . I'll be back." Pearson shoved everything back into the folder and excused himself into the hallway.

The door latched behind him, and he answered. "Pearson."

"Hey, it's Adam."

"What's going on? I'm sort of in the middle of speaking with Charles White."

"Ah, can't wait to get the full story on how that goes. Listen, two things: Christian and I found something interesting, and we also need a favor."

"You've piqued my interest."

"Is it possible to peel yourself away for twenty minutes so we can show you in person?"

Pearson wavered. He wasn't at all comfortable with the idea of leaving the father-son duo alone too long. "How out of the ordinary is this? I need to get through these interviews. You know as well as I do, if you leave a suspect to their own devices too long, they concoct stories in their heads."

Adam muttered. "So true. It can wait, but about that favor."

"Sure, go ahead."

"I need to know what model vehicles they drive?"

"Why?"

"Has to do with what I found. Can you just ask them?"

"Yeah, whatever either of you need. Whatever you found on that video is a good start."

Adam restrained his chortle. "It's a hunch. But it's an anomaly that deserves all of our attention."

"Good work. Well, let me get back with dumb and dumber here. I'll be back over your way shortly."

Pearson ended the call, and he hesitated to return to Charles. His head swiveled between both doors, and he made a split-second decision to reacquaint himself with Lee.

As with Charles, Pearson entered with no warning. Without as much as a hello, the constable pulled out the chair and slammed the folder against the metal tabletop.

"There a problem?" Lee asked.

"I don't know. Is there?"

"Don't think so. Why am I here?"

"We're investigating the disappearance of Cassidy Williams."

"And you think *I'm* involved?"

Pearson shrugged. "Are you?"

"Hell no. Like I told Gemma yesterday, girl ain't been around my place since she overdosed. You know, when Liam shipped her off to The Battlefords."

"Ah, so you know where she was?"

"Huh?" Lee asked.

"I mean, how would you know that. Patient information is confidential and we both know damn well you didn't ask Liam."

"Word on the street. It's a small town, constable. Shit like that spreads fast."

"Funny. I hadn't heard it. So, let me ask you flat out; you have someone working on the inside at the rehabilitation center?"

Lee scooted away from the table. "What? No. Listen, I heard it from a friend. That's all I'm going to say on the matter."

"Sure. Let's say for argument's sake, I believe you. You and your son know Cassidy better than anyone around. She's not at the rehab center anymore, so where should I start looking?"

Lee shrugged. "Hard to tell. Someone told me she disappeared from that rehab center. Maybe she is shacking up with someone in town?"

Pearson disagreed with a head shake. "Nah, we've questioned a few locals. No one has seen her. Any other theories?"

"Maybe she tried to walk back here?"

"A two-day walk with a windbreaker? Unlikely. What else you got?"

"Maybe she vanished to escape her possessive father?"

Pearson pulled out a screenshot of the time-stamped surveillance video, which showed Cassidy outside the rehab center, and tossed it in front of Lee. The old man turned his head away. Annoyed, Pearson slammed his fist against the table. "Pick it up!"

Lee scoffed but slid his filthy fingers under the picture and picked it up. He studied it for a moment and placed it on the table upside down. "And? She was alive at 8:30 AM on Thursday, so what?"

"Where were you between six and ten that morning?"

"Out on the reservation handling, uh, business."

"Does your 'business' have a name?"

Lee rubbed his jaw. "Do I need a lawyer?"

"If you've done nothing wrong, then no. We're merely having a friendly chat here. You're not under arrest and are free to leave whenever you like. What do you know about the vicious attack on a detective sergeant from Regina last evening outside of McGinty's?"

Lee folded his arms over his scrawny chest. "Not a damn thing. Who was it?"

"You know Matthias Anderson?"

Lee nodded.

"His son, Christian."

"Never met the boy."

"Ah, but you have. He paid a visit to the farm yesterday . . . with Gemma."

His eyes bulged, and he pressed his lips tightly together. "Wait. He's a copper?"

"He is."

"Well, I was with my boys last night out back shooting off our rifles. Man, I didn't ever think Matthias's offspring would be bright enough to become a copper."

Pearson overlooked the snide remark and continued. "Your boys? You mean Charles, Jason, and Thomas?"

"Nah, just me, Charles, and Thomas. Jason had this *thing* with his dad last night."

"Right. Also, DS Anderson mentioned he found what looked to be human blood in your barn. Care to explain?"

"Blood?"

Pearson stopped writing. "Yes, blood. You know, the red stuff in your veins."

"Well, it ain't human. Christ, I'm not a murderer . . . of people, at least."

"What is it, then?"

"Probably from the deer Charles brought home after his hunting trip a while back. I don't much care for all these intrusive questions."

"Well, you're free to leave whenever you choose."

With those words, Lee scooted out the chair and stood. "Well, then I'm out."

He walked toward the door, and Pearson turned, giving him one final stare-down. "One final question before you go: What make and model truck do you drive?"

"A Chevy S-10. Why?"

"No reason. Stay close in case I need to talk to you again."

CHAPTER 17

AN HOUR LATER, A LOUD BANG against the door interrupted their cuddle session, and Adam tossed his stuff onto the spare bed. He gave Christian a quick kiss before he raced for the door.

"Who is it?" he asked as he looked through the peephole.

"Who do you think?"

Adam detached the chain and opened the door. Pearson danced impatiently. His hands gripped the handles of a white banker box with writing along the side.

Anderson, S.

95-190

Pearson hurried inside. "Woof, it's cold out there."

"Well, well. Look at you, coming through like I had faith you would," Christian said.

Adam plopped back on the bed next to him.

"It was sent over to cold-case storage six years ago. And after sifting through aisles of dusty boxes, I found it. Everything you want to know about your mother's case is all in here."

Pearson dropped the box on the round table and swept his fingers through his hair to loosen the balls of ice, which clung to his spiky hair.

"Since we're all in for a long night of video enhancing and reading, can I make a dinner suggestion?" Pearson asked.

"You know the area better than we do," Adam said.

"There's this amazing Chinese place that does takeout. I mean, if your both hungry, I could place a call."

Adam and Christian swapped looks, and in unison, they responded with a simple, "Yes."

Pearson smiled, fetched the flyer from his jacket pocket, and tossed it onto the bed. "You guys take a look while I catch you up on how much of a train wreck the interviews were."

"Ah, right. You learn anything new?"

"To answer your question, Lee White drives a rust-bucket Chevy S-10, and Charles drives an El Camino."

"Damn."

Pearson rubbed the base of his neck. "Not the answer you wanted, huh?"

"I so hoped you'd say Chevy Silverado."

"Ah. So, that's what you found. Do tell."

Adam fiddled with his watchband. "Between 7:30 and 8:30, a Chevy Silverado passed on the main road nine times."

"You sure it was the same car?"

"Completely sure. The passenger-side mirror was missing. I can't imagine there are many of those in the area."

Pearson focused his gaze on the two. "That's a damn good find. Do you have access to SGI?"

A broad grin appeared across Adam's face. "Of course. I have access to anything we need to know. But before we start, there is one last thing."

"Yeah?"

"I've asked Christian to focus on the current case."

Pearson shifted his focus between the two. "Aren't we all working the current case?"

"That was the plan, but Christian has this vibe his mother's case is tied into this one. I've agreed to sift through her files in case it turns out he's right."

Christian chimed in. "My contribution would be influenced, not to mention a bit emotional."

"Totally. You're too close to that case, and no offense, but chances are good if you found something you didn't like, you might sweep it under the rug. You made the right call asking Adam to look into the possible connection."

Adam patted Pearson on the shoulder. "Exactly. So, if you want to help Christian, I'll get to reading."

"Wait."

All eyes in the room focused on Pearson. "Food first, then work. I don't know about you, but it's never a good idea to work on an empty stomach."

Christian grinned. "I couldn't have said it better myself."

THE FOOD ARRIVED AN HOUR EARLIER, and
Christian remained focused on the video. Twice now he'd
been through it, front to back and back to front, and his eyes
grew tired of watching the unchanged scenery over and over.
He stopped the video, slid the laptop aside, and massaged his
aching leg. He needed to tackle this from a different angle.
He closed his eyes and the answer came to him.

Search the vehicle registration database.

He logged into the SGI website and ran a search of
2005–2019 Chevy Silverados registered within a two-
hundred-kilometer radius of Cedar Lake. The wheel of the
mouse spun, and when the system returned the results,
Christian's jaw dropped. Six hundred results.

His stream of swear words caught the attention of
Pearson and Adam, and their eyes darted their focus on him.
Adam stopped skimming through the folder in his hand and
bolted to his boyfriend's side. He hovered over him and
placed the palm of his hand gently against Christian's
shoulder. "Everything all right?"

"Too many results. There's no way I can narrow this
down from six hundred."

Adam walked over and peeked at the screen, and out fell
a pronounced sigh. "Yeah, that's way too much to work
with."

His half smile curled downward into a frown. "Yeah.
This is hopeless. It's never going to work."

"Maybe it still can. Does the database allow you to
reduce the radius?"

"Maybe."

185

Christian replicated the search, and as he scanned the page, the box his weary eyes failed to catch earlier now stared back at him clear as day. Christian threw his hands in the air. "How'd I miss something so simple?"

Adam squatted at his side. "You've been through a rough few days. Could happen to any one of us."

"Suppose you're right."

"Listen, when you have a free minute, there's something I found in one of the witness statements I need to run past you."

"Yeah, give me two minutes."

"No rush. We got all night."

Christian wrinkled his nose while his finger rolled across the touchpad, and with one slight tap, he pressed "Search." Adam slid back into his seat and fetched the file he needed to show Christian. As he set the folder aside, Pearson had an ah-ha moment.

"Do either of you have access to check vehicle registrations in Alberta?"

"We don't. But you're a Mountie. Don't you have access to all the information countrywide?"

"You know what? Never had to search outside of Saskatchewan before, so to be honest, I'm not sure. Let me make a call."

Luke excused himself to the far corner of the room. Meanwhile, Adam slid the folder from the table and returned to Christian.

"Whatcha got?" Christian asked.

"There's a transcript of an interview they conducted with Lee White from 1995."

Christian raised his right eyebrow (an unintentional practice he acquired at some point during his time at the police academy). "Wait—hit the brakes. *That* was in the box?"

Adam crouched at his side. "Yeah. Alongside interviews they held with your dad, Gemma's mom and dad, and a few other names you'd recognize."

Christian's left eye spasmed. "You mentioned something shocking in the file."

"Yeah. First, do me a favor."

"Okay? What?"

"Take a deep breath. Hold it, and count to ten."

His eyes narrowed. "Why on earth would I do that?"

Adam gave a half shrug. "Due to the fact of what I'm about to say . . . you're not going to like it."

Christian took in a gulp of stale motel room air, closed his eyes, and after ten seconds he released. "Lay it on me."

Adam sat on the edge of the bed and flipped the folder open. "I'm giving this to you verbatim from the transcript. Whatever you do, don't punch, curse, or slap me."

Christian closed his eyes. "I won't—now read."

Constable Wilson: My name is Constable Cyrus Wilson, and the date is April 16 in the year 1995. I'm joined in the room today with Mr. Lee White. For the record, please state your name, date of birth, and where you were born.

Lee White: Lee Granger White. I was born August 3, 1962, in Swift Current.

Constable Wilson: Do you know why you are here today?

Lee White: I don't.

Constable Wilson: We're investigating the disappearance of Sarah Anderson. I received a tip you and Ms. Anderson are acquainted. Is this correct?

Lee White: Yes.

Constable Wilson: And how exactly are the two of you acquainted?

Lee White: Intimately. She and I have been involved in a (inaudible) relationship.

Constable Wilson: Can you repeat that? A what relationship?

Lee White: Sexual. We're having sex.

Constable Wilson: For the record, you and Sarah Anderson are having an affair?

Lee White: Yes.

Constable Wilson: For how long?

Lee White: Four months.

Constable Wilson: And her husband? Does he know?

Lee White: No. And I'd like to keep it that way.

Constable Wilson: I make no promises. When was the last time you saw her?

Lee White: Two nights ago. She had packed her bag, and we were planning to meet out at my place.

Constable Wilson: Was she moving in with you?

Lee White: No. We were leaving town—together.

Constable Wilson: What happened?

Lee White: She never showed. Ain't seen or heard from her since.

Near the middle of the transcript, Adam stopped. "Sorry to be the one to break the news. You deserve to know the truth, though."

Christian pursed his lips firmly together, and his face glowed red. "My own mother hooked up with that sleazeball?"

Adam stood. "Looks that way. You need a minute?"

"No. Stay."

Adam sank back into the depression in the bed and leaned in. "Keep it together, okay. I don't need you to 'out' yourself."

Christian released his firm grip on Adam's forearm. "Outing myself is the least of my worries right now."

"How so?"

"Do I have to spell it out?" Christian asked.

"Nah, we're good. Question, though: Had you ever met this Lee White character before?"

Christian dropped his head, and it shook from side to side. "Never. I didn't even know who any of these thugs were until two days ago."

"Well, then, we need to figure out where they came from and why they settled in Cedar Lake."

Christian's head steadily shook harder. "Nope. Lee White and my mother's affair isn't as important as finding Cassidy and Gemma. But, on the other hand, this information could be useful."

"How so?"

"What if Cassidy watched Lee do something to my mom?"

"Interesting angle. We'll fill Pearson in once he gets off the phone."

Adam returned and lounged back in the armless chair and raised the file closer to his face. The chatter from the corner stopped, but with Adam and Christian engrossed in other things, both of them failed to notice Constable Pearson had wrapped up the call.

The ripping of Velcro from Pearson's vest broke the silence and the outsiders' eyes peeked up. The golden glow of Pearson's skin had faded, and Adam made a comment to point it out. "Did you see a ghost or something?"

Luke blankly deflected his eye contact. "Worse than that. There's news."

CHAPTER 18

CHRISTIAN SLID THE LAPTOP ASIDE AND leaned forward. "Whatever it is, it can't be good."

Pearson bowed his head. "The station received an anonymous tip twenty minutes ago."

"What sort of tip?"

"The kind you never want."

Adam stood. "Well . . . spit it out already."

"A hiker found an arm sticking out from a shallow grave along the railroad tracks next to the abandoned sawmill outside town."

Christian's heart sank and his mouth fell open. "You don't think? Nah, it can't be."

"They've dispatched two constables and an ambulance to investigate. Let's not get ahead of ourselves here. It could be nothing."

"Of course," Christian replied while a flurry of worrying thoughts gathered in his head.

"I'm going to drive out and check on it. Do you mind doing me a favor?"

"Anything."

"Reach out to Liam."

"And say what?"

"Tell him you need him to stop by. Make something up. Whatever you do, don't mention anything about where I am, at least not until we're a hundred percent sure."

Christian and Adam swapped glances and mutually agreed. "Sure. Yeah, you got it."

Pearson squandered no time. He wrapped a scarf around his neck, patted himself down, and raced out the door. As the door thumped shut, Adam returned to an upset Christian's side.

"Maybe it's not her. For all we know it's a prank. Just someone having a good laugh."

An otherwise distracted Christian gazed out the window and, like someone on autopilot, replied, "Who would call in a dead body for a cheap laugh? No. It's gotta be either Cassidy or Gemma. Hell, what if it's both of them?"

"You heard Pearson. Don't get ahead of the evidence."

"Easy for him to say."

"He'll let us know something once he knows something. Okay?"

Christian hung his head. "I'm telling you, this is it."

Adam swept his smooth hand across Christian's bruised cheek. "Regardless if it is or isn't, we should reach out like he asked."

Christian returned his gaze inside the room and reached out his shaky hand toward Adam. "I suppose so. Truth is, this isn't the phone call I wanted to make."

Christian savored the kindhearted moment, but it did zilch to quell his overactive adrenaline, which sped through his veins like a runaway tractor trailer on a steep slope.

"I'll call as soon as my hands stop trembling."

Adam stretched out his hand and cupped Christian's hands in his. "Hey. It's going to be okay. I can always make the call if it'll be easier for you."

He shook his head. "No. I have to do this."

"You're not going to tell him over the phone, are you?"

"The man deserves more respect from someone he's known my entire life. I'll tell him in person."

"I'll give you a moment, then."

Adam retracted his hand and returned to the table scattered with files, and Christian reached across the bed for his phone. He dialed, and after two rings, Liam answered in his signature gruff tone.

"Hello?"

"Mr. Williams, it's Christian."

"Oh, Christian. Thank God you're all right. Your colleague stopped in earlier and told me you'd been attacked."

Christian's voice trembled. "Yeah, I'm a little bruised up, but I'm doing much better. Listen, I'm calling because I need to see you."

"Sure. You still in the hospital?"

"I'm out, thank God. I'm staying at the Ridgeway Inn. You have a few minutes to pop in?"

"I've got more time on my hands than I care to. You sound frazzled, is everything okay?"

"Ah, lack of sleep is all. Everything's fine. There's just something I need to show you."

"I'm on the way."

"Room 103."

Christian lobbed the phone to the side and exhaled forcefully. After nine years, he was no novice breaking tragic news to families; it was a part of the job. However, this time wasn't like all the other times. Strangers were easy, but a lifelong family friend—the pressure was on.

From afar, Adam sensed Christian's anxiety level rising and swooped in. He wrapped his arm around his back and pulled him in tighter. "What can I do to help? I hate seeing you all stressed out."

"If I choke, can you jump in for me?"

"You know I will. You're not in this alone. Remember, we're a team now."

His cheeks glowed like hot embers, and Christian pulled away from the embrace. "What now?"

"Now? We wait for confirmation from Pearson."

"I hate this."

⌘

ON THE HORIZON, THE LUMINESCENCE OF flashing blue lights against the gloomy, snow-covered backdrop caught Pearson's attention, and he reduced the pressure on the accelerator. The SUV drifted to the shoulder and he hung a hard right onto a desolate dirt access road.

He stopped behind a trove of emergency vehicles and propped the door open before he even slid the shifter into park. He reached for his mic but made no effort to move. Instead, his eyes scanned the barren land, and deep inside he hoped this was a false alarm.

Confirmation from dispatch came and he ripped the keys from the ignition and slammed the door closed. Racing along the curve in the road, he spotted his protégé, Constable Miller. "Whatcha got?"

"Deceased female. Ice cold to the touch."

"Go on."

"She's probably in her late thirties, long, brunette hair."

He lowered his voice and inched closer. "Is it her?"

Miller shuffled in place to keep warm. "Who, sir?"

"Who? Where have you been these past four days? Is it Cassidy Williams?"

The younger constable was a newbie and still more interested in doing stuff younger people did, and less involved in the job yet.

"She's been beaten pretty bad, so I can't confirm. Did she have a rose tattoo on her right forearm?"

Pearson's eyes widened and his head dropped. "That's exactly what I didn't want to hear."

He raised the police tape and swooped beneath. This wasn't the ending he'd hoped for, but it was the one the cruel universe doled out. With each step his boots sank into the puddles along the muddied pathway, and up ahead he spotted two medics moving at top speed.

He squinted to get a better look at their faces. One hung his head and it swayed from side to side, and the female glanced over at him, and her vacant stare sent a shiver up his spine.

"What's up with them?" he asked.

"I'd reckon they've never seen this level of mutilation before."

That word, *mutilation*, painted a gruesome image for Pearson, and guilt crept into his mind. Would things have been different had he acted quicker? Would she still be alive, if for once he'd considered she was in imminent danger?

The one-sided questions whipped back and forth, and the commotion of his inner voices drowned out everything around him. It wasn't until an icy touch against his hand sped up time, and he flinched.

"Whoa. Sorry, sir. You okay?" Miller asked.

"I'm good, my mind was someplace else. You were saying something?"

Constable Miller pointed his stubby finger off and to the right. "The gravesite is up past the fence post, if you want to have a look."

Pearson tapped against the DSLR camera around Miller's neck. "You've finished photos and collected the evidence already?"

"All done, sir."

"Christ, stop calling me sir. Do I look like a wrinkled old man?"

The constable cowered like a child whose father scolded him.

"Just call me Constable Pearson or Pearson. Either or."

"Of course, s—I mean, Constable Pearson."

Pearson scoffed under his breath before he sucked in a swallow of air and set off. With each footstep closer he took, the bleached-white sheet stood out amongst the soiled snow. He tossed his head back over his shoulder and forced a nervous grin as his colleagues looked on.

Maybe they're all wrong and it's not her.

Ten steps are all that stood between him and whoever lay beneath the sheet. He slipped a pair of latex gloves over his frozen hands, crouched, and said a quiet prayer to himself. The area was still and silent, except for a squawk or two from the ravens who flew in circles on the hunt for their next meal.

He forced in another deep breath, opened his eyes, and as he released his breath, it vaporized the moment it collided with the bitter cold. His hand trembled as it hung just above the sheet. Hesitant, he gathered his courage and peeled back the top corner. The swollen, bloodied, and lifeless face of the girl, who only yesterday he labeled a hopeless junkie, now was nothing more than an empty shell of a troubled soul. He swept his finger under her mud-caked brunette hair and swept the strands away from her face before he bowed his head in shame.

He retracted his hand, and a fierce gust of wind swept across the treeless landscape. A shiver skulked across his skin and he lost his hold on the sheet, which fluttered back to the earth. He retreated and as he went to stand, his wobbly legs gave out and he tumbled back against the freshly tilled soil.

He made no attempt to move. Instead, he remained fixed to the ground. He pulled his knees inward and crossed his arms over them. His head dropped, and he allowed despair to overwhelm his rigid personality.

I allowed this to happen. Me. Why? Why didn't I act sooner?

He pondered the questions he laid out for himself, taking more time than he expected. Just then a voice interrupted his concentration. "Everything all right, Constable?"

He tilted his head back and the two medics from earlier stood over him. "I'm fine, just thinking."

"Constable Miller said the chief medical examiner gave the green light to transport the decedent to the hospital until an investigator from Saskatoon can drive up. Do you need more time with the body?"

Pearson sunk his hand into the mud and hoisted himself to his feet. "That won't be necessary. Do me a favor, though."

"Sure," the female medic replied.

"Bag her hands and feet before you move her. If there's even a sliver of skin cells from her killer under her nails, I want it preserved."

The medic acknowledged his request with a simple nod and the two descended down the steep slope next to the railroad tracks.

Pearson gripped the young medic's forearm. "And, for the love of God, have some respect. Her name is Cassidy, not the decedent."

Pearson's hand dropped to his side as the medic hung his head. His nostrils flared as he focused his gaze on them as they began the task of retrieving the body. His boots sank into the soft soil of the embankment, and after a while he strolled down the gravel road to rejoin Constable Miller.

He stopped inches from the rookie and their eyes met. "Hope you didn't have anything special planned this evening."

"Nope."

"Good. I need you to keep her body in your sight at all times. No one in or out of the morgue unless I give the say-so. Are we clear?"

The young constable responded with a blank stare.

"Earth to Miller. Are we clear?"

He cleared his throat. "Yes, s—I mean, Constable Pearson."

"If you need me, I'll be available on my cell."

Pearson didn't wait for a reaction from his protégé and trekked along the rock-strewn access road toward his SUV. He slid behind the steering wheel and slammed the door closed behind him. He tugged the seat belt across his chest, but his shaky hand wouldn't let him insert the metal into the buckle. After a few failed attempts he stopped, and his head smashed against the headrest.

He'd strived his entire life to build a wall around his kindhearted soul. He never wanted to give off the impression he was a softy. Yet, as he squeezed his eyes closed tighter, her unrecognizable face was the only thing on his mind.

How could someone do this to another human?

He remained there for a few minutes, until the pent-up frustration came to a head. His eyes sprang open and he pounded the palms of his hands against the steering wheel. "Fuck."

⁂

MEANWHILE, BACK IN TOWN, THE ANTICIPATED knock against the motel room door arrived, and Adam stood from the bed.

"You ready?"

Christian clenched his jaw and grimaced. "As ready as I can be."

The door swung open, and there stood Liam, cracking his knuckles. "I'm looking for Christian."

Adam stepped aside, and Liam breezed through the door. Across the room, Christian rested in bed with his left leg supported on a heap of pillows.

Liam disregarded the formalities of making small talk and instead dashed across the room. "Jesus, Christian. They messed you up good."

"It looks worse than it is."

Liam crouched next to the bed. "Nah, it looks pretty bad. But I'm glad to see they haven't taken away your optimistic spirit. Where's Gemma?"

There it was. Another matter Christian had no idea how he'd answer. He swallowed hard a couple of times before the three words he hated using slipped out. "I don't know."

Liam rubbed the base of his neck as if the words hadn't registered in his brain. "Come again?"

"I have no idea where she is, Mr. Williams. She went down to the corner store last night around seven, and I haven't seen her since."

He stood over Christian's beaten body and rubbed at his beard. "How can this be? You two are like Siamese twins whenever you're around."

"I offered to run her to the store, but she's stubborn."

Liam's face lit up because he understood exactly what Christian was saying. "Yeah, it's one of the Williams family traits."

Christian turned his head away. "No offense, but I agree."

"Well . . . did you go out looking for her?"

Christian's mouth fell half-open, but he couldn't muster the words. Instead, his head bobbed up and down again.

"And this." He waved his hand up and down Christian's body. "How'd this happen?"

"The cashier suggested maybe she stopped off at McGinty's."

"That hovel? She'd never go there alone."

"It was a lead, and I had to check. Long story short, I ended up chatting with a not-so-reputable bartender."

"Let me take a wild guess . . . you met Linus?"

"Yeah . . . how'd you know?"

"Only two bartenders there. And given he's the only male and Gemma's ex-boyfriend, wasn't too hard to narrow down."

"Gemma and *that* guy? The same guy who drugged me in some sick attempt to render me helpless when his 'pals' beat my ass?"

"One in the same. Cedar Lake's a little scarier these days, huh?"

"Ya think? Tell me more about Linus."

"Gemma dumped him last year, when he began hanging out with Charles and the gang. Guy's a first-rate asshole, but I never expected he'd escalate to drugging patrons and then having them attacked."

"Man, I disregarded the red flags there. I'm closing in on the truth; otherwise, why would he call in his boys to attack me?"

"The further down the rabbit hole you go, the worse it's going to get. Speaking of worse, have you spoken with Constable Pearson lately?"

Christian's eyes shifted everywhere but directly at Liam. "Spoke to him this morning. He came to check on me at the hospital."

"Does he have any news?"

"None. We got our hands on the surveillance video from the rehab center."

"And?"

"She's on it. However, thirteen minutes before Gemma arrived, she wandered off and out of sight. Does she know anyone in the area?"

"Not that I know of."

"How about someone who drives a Chevy Silverado?"

Liam forced his lips tighter. "Silverado? Pretty common vehicle around these parts. But no. I don't know anyone personally who owns one. Why?"

Christian glanced away again. "A vehicle of interest. I've got nothing concrete—yet."

Liam walked around the bed to look Christian in the face. "There's something you're not telling me. It may have been ten years since I last saw you, but I could always see it in your eyes when you were holding something back."

Christian closed his eyes, and the voice of Pearson resonated. *Whatever you do, don't mention anything about this.* But how could he keep secret an important detail from the father who had not just one, but two missing daughters?

Liam leaned in and grabbed Christian with both hands. "What are you hiding from me."

The shaking forced Christian's eyes open and Adam darted from across the room to get the situation under control. He yanked Liam away and shoved him across to the other side of the room. "Take a seat."

Liam's anger boiled over and he charged the bed once more. Again, Adam blocked his passage and he repeated himself.

"Why?" Liam shouted.

"You don't know me, but trust me, you don't want to hurt Christian any more than he already is."

He paced and after a few minutes, the redness in his face dissipated and he pulled out a chair. "If he knows something, he should just say it. We're all adults here."

Christian stuttered. "I don't. How do I—"

Just then the door opened, and Constable Pearson appeared. Liam calmly rose from the edge of the bed, and his icy stare worried everyone in the room. Even though the words never passed across Christian's lips, Liam didn't need them to. It was clear what Christian was insinuating.

Liam crept closer to Pearson. The grieving father's nostrils flared, and the veins in his neck bulged. Then it happened. Liam's fists swung, missing Pearson by inches. Adam went in after him for the second time, except this time he wrapped his muscular arm around the man's neck and pulled tightly to subdue him.

Hateful words spewed from Liam's lips and Adam struggled to keep him back. "You sorry son of a bitch. You let them take my baby girl from me."

Pearson hung his head in shame. "You told him?"

While Adam fought to keep an unhinged Liam in line, he squeaked out a few words in between grunts. "No. We. Didn't."

The threats continued. "I'll kill you. I'll snuff out your life the same way they did hers. After I'm done with you, you'll be lucky to work in this town again."

From across the room, an immobile Christian watched as the drama unfolded. After tolerating as much as he could, he screamed out. "Mr. Williams, that's enough."

Christian's outburst caught everyone in the room off guard. The back-and-forth ground to a halt and soon all eyes focused on him.

"Constable Pearson is not the one responsible for taking her life. Some freak out there is. The way I see it, you have two choices. One, you can attack him, and perhaps you'll feel better for ten seconds. But you'll also go to jail. Or two, you can refocus your anger on finding who's responsible."

Liam collapsed in the chair.

"Well, what's it gonna be?" Christian asked.

CHAPTER 19

THE OLDER MAN STUMBLED TO THE bed and plopped down next to Christian. Instantly, the tears flowed, and he buried his face in his hands. For over ten minutes, Liam babbled on in incoherent bursts. Christian caught the meaning of a few, but many didn't make any sense.

If anyone ever asked Christian what his greatest weakness was, he'd freely admit his lack of empathy during a crisis situation. Even with all the preparation from the academy, not to mention the countless times he broke the news to loved ones, he could never allow himself to show his vulnerability to anyone.

And while his callousness may have shielded him from years of trauma, in this moment, more than anything, he wanted to wrap his arms around the man and offer a sense of comfort. Sadly, nothing came. And then it hit him: he'd turned into the person he swore he'd never become. And the realization gnawed away at his insides.

No one in the room spoke a word. They all sat by and waited for Liam to gather the strength to have a rational conversation. And soon, the sobbing and moaning subsided, and Liam pulled his hands away from his flushed face.

Liam glanced up and stared at Pearson. He wiped away the mucus that had accumulated on his mustache. "Where was she?"

Pearson cleared his throat. "Next to the railroad tracks out by the abandoned sawmill north of town."

"Did she suffer? God, please tell me she didn't suffer."

"I won't know for certain until I get the report back from the medical examiner. I can say, though, she's been out there for at least the past twenty-four hours."

"How did she die?" his voice grew angrier.

Pearson inhaled several times and chewed at his lower lip. "There's no nice way to say this, so I'll just say it. It looks like they beat, mutilated, and then strangled her."

Liam stared at the floor and in a hushed voice asked, "When can I see her?"

Christian ventured out of his comfort zone and rubbed his hand along Liam's back. "Soon, but not yet. Let's allow the ME to do his job, get her cleaned up a little, and then I'll personally take you there myself."

"Okay. I appreciate that, Christian," he said and turned his gaze to Pearson. "You have any suspects?"

"I'm looking hard at the White clan, but out of curiosity, does anyone else have a grudge against your family?"

He shook his head. "No. No one. I've said it all along: it's either Lee or Charles. One of them is responsible."

"What makes you so certain it's one of them?" Pearson asked.

"Because."

"Mr. Williams, I hate to say this, but we need a little more information than 'because' so we can focus our efforts in the right place. What aren't you telling us?"

The waterworks started up again, and this time around, Liam buried his head against Christian's chest. He glared at Adam, and pure awkwardness consumed his face.

The strapping French Canadian bit his lip before he moved his mouth. "Let the man cry."

Adam returned his attention to the evidence box positioned within arm's reach. With two folders left to search, he leaned over the box, but as he retrieved the next folder in line, his eyes homed in on the name written on the last folder. *Williams, Liam.*

His eyes fixated on Christian, who consoled Liam. When it was clear the tears weren't going to subside, he returned to the folder. Discreetly, he dropped the first folder and snatched Liam's folder. He scanned the first page, and then the second, but halfway through, one thing became clear: everyone with a connection to the current cases also had strong ties to Sarah Anderson back in 1995.

Adam slid the folder across the table for Pearson to read. After a minute, the two swapped quizzical grins, and Pearson rose from the chair.

"Liam, got a question for you."

The distraught father peeked his face out. "Yeah? What is it?"

"Do you care to share the nature of your relationship with Sarah Anderson with us?"

Liam gasped and pulled away from Christian. "Is *now* a fitting time? Cassidy is dead, and Gemma is missing. And you want to ask me questions from something that took place over twenty years ago?"

Pearson shifted from the sympathetic constable to a coldhearted asshole in the blink of an eye. "Just answer the question. What was your relationship with Sarah Anderson?"

He slid farther away from the boy he'd known forever, stood, and walked over to the spare bed. Christian's pupils overtook the whites of his eyes, and his mouth gaped ajar in slow motion.

"Mr. Williams? What are they talking about?" Christian asked.

"I should have known this day would come soon enough."

Intrigued, Christian dropped his leg and swung around so he could stare into Liam's eyes. But Liam refused to even give him that much. Instead, Christian turned his head toward Pearson for support. "What's he going on about?"

Liam placed his hand on Christian's knee. "This is not something you need to involve yourself in, Christian. This is water under the bridge stuff."

"Now who's the one hiding stuff?"

"I can't. I just can't do this."

Christian's face transformed to a deep shade of red from Liam's resistance to answer a simple question, and before things escalated any further, Pearson intercepted. "Perhaps we should continue this conversation over at the station?"

Christian interjected. "No. I want to hear what secrets he's been keeping from me all these years."

"Don't make me do this, Christian. This isn't fair to you."

Christian scoffed. "No, none of this is. Me returning to this hellhole isn't fair. Me trying to help your daughter isn't fair. Now either you tell me what in the hell is so hush-hush, or I'll—"

A folder waving in the air distracted Christian from completing whatever threat he was about to make. "Not to kill your flow, but I do have in my hand his own words from 1995. Perhaps we let those speak for themselves?"

"Please. Don't. You should be finding who hurt my daughters."

Pearson situated his hand on Liam's shoulder. "Oh, we neglected to tell you. We're exploring this from two angles. Let me paint you a scenario. Cassidy had information about Sarah Anderson's disappearance. Now we're not sure if she witnessed her murder or overheard later. It's likely whatever information Cassidy *did* have is what got her killed."

"What?"

Pearson pointed to an empty chair next to the window. "Take a seat. We can do this here or down at the station. Up to you."

Liam stared Pearson up and down, but then marched to the chair as instructed.

"Go ahead, DC Prescott."

Adam read aloud, word for word, from the transcript.

Constable Wilson: *My name is Constable Cyrus Wilson, and the date is April 18 in the year 1995. I'm joined in the room today*

with Mr. Liam Williams. For the record, please state your name,
date of birth, and where you were born.
Liam Williams: *Liam Scott Williams. I was born January 9,*
1960, in Cedar Lake.
Constable Wilson: *I'll cut to the chase. The RCMP are*
investigating the disappearance of Sarah Anderson. How are the
two of you acquainted?
Liam Williams: *Family friend. I've known her husband since*
elementary school.
Constable Wilson: *When was the last time you saw Sarah?*
Liam Williams: *A couple of days ago.*
Constable Wilson: *Where?*
Liam Williams: *At her house.*
Constable Wilson: *Was Matthias there?*
Liam Williams: *No. He was at work.*
Constable Wilson: *Sort of strange.*
Liam Williams: *How so?*

Liam shouted out. "Enough."

"Something you want to get off your chest?" Christian asked.

Liam buried his face in his hands. "I loved her."

Christian rested his elbows on his knees. "You loved who? My mom?"

Christian's foot bobbed up and down while he awaited an answer he wasn't sure he was ready to receive.

Liam stuttered. "It was never supposed to end this way."

"How was it supposed to end, then?"

Liam wiped his hands across his face. "We were going to leave town. That night. I had everything arranged for us down in Calgary."

"There was a letter sent to my father. You know anything about it?"

He nodded. "I sent it. Your mother didn't have the guts back in those days. But I did."

"You were going to run off with my mom and leave me here in Cedar Lake to rot away?"

"She struggled with leaving you behind, you have to believe me."

Christian's foot stopped bobbing and the sincerity of Liam's words drew him into his version of the story. "I don't know who or what to believe anymore. So, convince me. Why did she want to give it all up and leave her life behind?"

"Something happened."

"What?"

"I don't know, something serious. And whatever it was, it spooked her enough that we accelerated our plans."

Pearson chimed in. "Let me guess, she had information on someone and was going to come to the cops?"

Liam rubbed his beard. "Exactly."

"Would it shock you to know you weren't the only man involved with Sarah Anderson?"

He cocked his head to one side. "What? It was just me and Matthias."

Pearson dug through the evidence box and pulled out the file from Lee White.

"What's that?"

Pearson for once kept his mouth shut and sifted through the pages until he reached the passage he was looking for.

"Can I read something to you?"

"For Christ's sake, why the suspense?"

"'Two nights ago. She had packed her bags, and we were planning to meet out at my place,'" Pearson read from Lee White's statement.

Liam wrinkled his nose. "What is this?"

"This? Just a sworn statement from Lee White on April 16 in 1995."

"Who had their bags packed?"

"Wait—you're telling the truth. You didn't know."

"What? Can someone please fill me in on what the hell is going on."

"Your lover—"

Christian gagged.

"Sorry, Christian. Your *friend* was involved in another affair while she was sneaking around with you."

Christian snatched a pillow from next to him and wedged it between his arms and chest and buried his face into it. Two days ago, he was comfortable in his own bed, next to the man of his dreams, living the life he always wanted to live. Now, he'd learned more about the sordid deeds behind the scenes throughout his childhood, and every part of it made him want to climb back in his car and say screw it.

He took a quick breath and returned his focus to the chatter between Pearson and Liam.

"You must have misunderstood, or Lee's lying. I was the only other man in her life—well, besides Matthias."

Christian chimed in. "Liam—Lee wasn't lying. The two of you were having an affair with my mother and that's that. Why? Why would either of you do this to my father? Do you have any idea what your overactive sex drive turned him into?"

Liam hung his head. "I loved your mother and she deserved better."

"You loved her? Well, your cheap love destroyed my father's world. His entire world crashed and burned to the ground that April day when she vanished with no answer. How can I even begin to think about forgiving you?"

The broken man attempted to construct an answer, but his lips remained sealed as Christian's icy stare forced him to divert his eyes away.

"Pearson, get him outside and as far away from me before I do something I'll regret."

"With pleasure. I'll be here at eight thirty on the dot, so don't oversleep."

Constable Pearson jerked Liam by the collar from the chair, dragged him to the door, and pushed him out into the parking lot. The door slammed, and his gruff voice, pleading for Christian to listen, still echoed through the walls. Christian covered his ears and Adam quickly slid next to him.

"Wow, I didn't see any of that coming."

Christian rocked back and forth until he jumped to his feet and moved for the window. "I-I didn't come back here for all of this."

Adam crept up behind and wrapped his arm around Christian. As he squeezed tighter, Adam rested his head against his boyfriend's back. "I empathize. There are dark secrets coming to the surface, and yeah, it sucks. You undoubtedly want to tear out your hair. But, there's one thing you forgot."

Christian lowered his hand and interlocked his fingers with Adam's. "What's that?"

"I'm here, and together, we're going to weather this storm and get the answers you deserve to have."

Christian swung around and nuzzled his temple against Adam's shoulder. For the second time since he returned to Cedar Lake, he bawled as if all the anguish of his entire life came to a head. Adam held him tight until all of the emotions seeped from his ducts.

Christian pulled away and ran his palm across Adam's scruffy face. "Where could she be, Adam?"

At a loss for words, all Adam could muster in the spur of the moment was a shrug.

"She's out there, somewhere. Oh God, what if she's dead?"

"Hey. She's not dead. We'll find her. You have to keep your mind opened and your faith strong."

Christian lowered his head and it swayed from side to side. "I should have never agreed to come back to this vile place."

Adam reached out both hands and pressed them on Christian's cheeks. "We're going to find her. You trust me, don't you?"

"You know I do. I guess I just need some rest, babe."

Adam nodded and walked a step behind him towards the bed. Christian stopped and turned around. "I will pray that when I wake, everything over the last two days will have been an insane nightmare and I'm back in my apartment."

"It'll all work out soon."

He lowered his body against the mattress and pulled the duvet cover up to his chin. Adam leaned over and kissed him gently on the cheek. "Let me get the lights."

Adam rechained the door, flipped the lights off, and stumbled through the room to return to his partner's side. He slid under the covers and curled up behind Christian. With another kiss, he whispered in his ear. "Sweet dreams."

CHAPTER 20

A SOFT STROKE ALONG THE BACK of his neck awoke Christian from a deep sleep. His eyes flapped open and he rolled onto his back. He struggled to keep his eyelids from closing again, but through the dimness Adam's bright blue eyes grabbed his attention.

"Good morning," Adam said.

Christian smiled and snuggled closer. "It is; you're here. Although, I see I'm not in my bed, which means all of this isn't a nightmare."

"Indeed."

The couple basked in the affectionate moment, the first they'd enjoyed in a few weeks. Then Christian's determined mind awoke, and out came questions and doubts.

Christian pulled away. "I wish we could lounge here all day together."

"But?"

"I won't be able to fully enjoy your company until we find Gemma."

Adam ran his hand across Christian's chest. "Pearson will be here at eight thirty. We're going to find her."

"I know *we* will."

"Christian, I don't—"

"Think I'm ready?"

Adam tossed the covers from his body and one leg slipped out to the floor. "Exactly. Well, I suppose I better get ready."

Christian pulled Adam back into the bed. "I'm not a broken toy, and I hate that you keep treating me like one."

"I'm not."

"You are, but look at me, I'm feeling much better and my determination is stronger than ever."

"Still. You shouldn't overdo it."

"Look, either I can go alone, or you can come with me. It's your choice?"

"You don't have to be so nasty about it. If pounding the pavement is what you want, then who am I to stand in your way?"

Christian's lower lip curled down. "Sorry. I shouldn't take all my frustrations out on you."

"Yeah, you shouldn't. But, given everything you've been through, I'll overlook it *this* time. What d'you say we lay here until he gets here and make up for some lost time?"

Christian gave in and reburied his head. Then it came. A loud pounding at the door. They jumped, exchanged glances, and threw the covers back.

"Pearson," they said in unison.

Adam slipped on his wrinkled clothes from the floor, and glanced at the second bed, which neither of them had used. "Shit. The bed."

He tossed around the pillows and pulled back the duvet as to not draw any questions from the constable.

The door handle rattled and then another, harder knock came. Christian called out. "Just a minute. Not decent in here."

Adam stepped aside from the bed and asked, "Think it's convincing enough?"

Christian looked it over. "Good enough to me. Damn, I hate being in the closet sometimes."

Adam raced for the door so as to not keep Pearson hanging too long in the cold. He unfastened the chain and deadbolt, swung the door inward, and a chipper Pearson danced in place with a tray of coffees in one hand, and in the other an oversized Tim Horton's bag.

"You're early," Adam said.

"It's five till eight. How can you still be asleep?"

Christian pulled his head through his shirt. "How can we not? These past few days have been trying, to say the least."

"Anderson, I'm messing with you. I brought necessities to start our day off right," Pearson said. "Hope you love breakfast wraps and donuts."

"I love anything, as long as it's caffeinated and full of sugar," Christian joked.

Adam pulled the curtains back and flipped on the lights while Pearson offloaded the food onto the improvised dining table. His eyes roamed but soon Christian and Adam were back in the spotlight.

"Are you waiting for an invitation? Eat. Eat."

Breakfast was quick and simple. Now with a full stomach, Christian wiped the corner of his mouth, and got down to business.

"What's the plan?" he asked.

"I overlooked something yesterday when I interviewed Lee."

"Go on," Christian said.

"He provided everyone in their group with an alibi . . . except for one person."

Christian crumpled his napkin and dropped it onto the table. "Who?"

"Jason Nelson. But, eh, I don't know. The guy's a nobody."

"Well, the nobody is a somebody now. Why haven't you brought him in?"

"That's the plan."

"Why are we sitting here, then? Let's go get him."

Christian stood and Pearson held out his hand and stopped him. "Where's the fire? I drove by and his car was gone."

"Damn."

"Don't worry, we'll catch up with him at some point later."

"I got a question," Christian said.

"And I might have an answer."

"While you were out at the sawmill, did you do a thorough search?"

Pearson crinkled the burrito wrapper and chucked it into the empty bag. "Me personally, no. But I'm sure Miller or one of the others did. Why?"

"And I bet you found little to no evidence in the grave?"

Pearson slouched in the chair. "None. Where are you going with this?"

"The shallow grave isn't your primary scene. Now, I'm just thinking out loud, but maybe whoever snatched her held her captive in the sawmill and murdered her there?"

"Not possible."

Christian cocked his head. "Why not?"

"Have you been out to the sawmill since you returned?"

"Haven't had a reason to."

"Well, if you had, you'd see there are trees growing from the inside out. Full-on trees."

"So?"

Pearson's eye contact drifted away. "Let's say I entertain the notion and the sawmill is the primary. What evidence do you have to make you so certain?"

"No evidence, it's just homicide 101. If I were going to commit a murder, I'd do it someplace mundane. A place where no one would ever be suspicious about and go looking for details, where I could make the biggest mess and never worry about anyone hearing the screams."

"Dreadful picture."

"Listen, I'm willing to wager that when we arrive and bust through the door, then you'll come around to my side."

"Christian." The disdain in Adam's voice grew.

"What? I grew up here and anytime we had a tragedy, that damn sawmill was always involved. Even though he's new here, he's certainly heard the stories from years past."

Pearson reached into his jacket and pulled out his wallet. "Tell you what. Just for that, I'm in." He slapped a twenty-dollar bill onto the table. "I'm telling you, Christian, when we show up there, you'll see the entire place is dilapidated, just as it always has been since I stepped foot into this town five years ago."

Christian stood and walked to the nightstand. He sifted through his wallet and pulled out a twenty- and a ten-dollar bill. As he hovered over the table he slapped both atop Pearson's twenty. "I'll see you twenty and raise you ten."

Fifty dollars laid in the middle of the table and Adam shook his head at their childish behavior. "Come on, guys? This isn't productive."

"Sure, it is. There's fifty dollars at stake."

"Inappropriate."

"What? I'm trying to lighten the mood."

Adam clenched his jaw. "Cassidy is dead, and for all we know Gemma is too."

Christian fell into the chair. "Now who's being inappropriate?"

"I'm being realistic—big difference. We're no closer to connecting the dots on how your mother factors into all of this. Nothing personal, I just think our time is better spent out there searching instead of sitting here placing bets."

Pearson caved first. "He's right. Let's look into your hunch. None of us are perfect, and we could have overlooked something in the heat of the moment."

"Agree."

"Can you be ready in twenty minutes?"

"Make it thirty," Christian said.

"You bring your bulletproof vests?"

Adam scoffed. "Didn't think I'd need one."

"No problem, I have a few extra at the station."

"Is Kevlar necessary?" Adam asked.

Pearson glanced at his watch. "Better safe than sorry. Why don't you two get showered and I'll run by the station. Be back around nine, okay?"

Christian and Adam exchanged glances. "We'll make it work."

Pearson glanced at the trash accumulated on the table and began tidying up, but Adam interjected. "You were kind enough to bring us food, the least I can do is clean up the mess. Besides, don't you need to check in at the station and grab those vests?"

He dropped the bag onto the table. "I do. See you shortly."

As the door closed, Adam secured the deadbolt and Christian let out a sigh. "That was close."

"Nah, your paranoia is getting the better of you."

With a shrug, Christian dug through his suitcase and continued into the bathroom.

⌗

THE SUN HAD JUST CRESTED THE eastern horizon as they passed the final house along the empty two-lane highway that led to more remote places north of Cedar Lake. Pearson slowed and scanned the right for the gravel access road, which if you didn't pay attention was easy to blow past.

The unforgettable billboard up ahead signaled he was close, and Pearson veered onto the shoulder and hung a hard right. As he zoomed past the accumulation of tire tracks in the mud, a yellow piece of crime scene tape fluttered in the stiff breeze. And unlike yesterday, he barreled through and down the windy, bumpy road.

"This road is crap," Christian said.

"This is nothing; wait until you see the building."

As Constable Pearson foresaw, Christian did a double take as the car crept closer to the decrepit building. The overgrown garden nearly consumed the exterior, which years ago, would have never gotten this out of control.

Christian lapsed back to 1999. The summer when his father bought him his first bike. The sight of the place evoked a happier memory of racing with Gemma out here on those far and few warm, sunny summer days and playing childish games. Eventually, the sawmill gained in popularity with the kids from town as the make-out spot, and something even more.

Then along came a string of tragedies in his teens, and eventually the place closed its doors after the owner filed for bankruptcy to avoid paying out the various lawsuits that followed.

He smiled as his attention returned to the here and now.

"Man, this place brings back memories."

"Good ones, I hope."

"Eh, there was this one incident th—oh yeah, scratch that."

"Was it illegal?"

"What? No. Just not something I ever imagined I'd come across so early in my life."

The car stopped just shy of the rickety entrance. "I'll expect a full story later," Adam said.

Three doors opened and slammed closed in unison. Christian exhaled and a mist filled the air ahead of him. Pearson took the lead while they hung back. The stream of light from Pearson's flashlight illuminated the area, and with purpose he approached the door.

Pearson slinked in bursts, scanning the ground for any disruption to the area. A few yards from the door, he stumbled on fresh tread marks in the mud and two parallel lines traversing from the door to the tire impressions.

"Hold up."

Christian and Adam stopped. "What is it?"

"Got some recent activity here."

"I knew it," Christian boasted.

He wrinkled his nose and shined the light toward the door. The chain and padlock that secured the decrepit building sat in a heap on the ground. "Someone's been here recently."

Christian snubbed Pearson's order to stand down and bolted full speed ahead. He paused at the constable's side and clicked on his flashlight. "My instinct didn't fail me this time."

"Don't be overconfident."

"I'm not."

"You are. And cockiness precedes mistakes, and mistakes have consequences. Or, did you not learn your lesson the other night?"

Christian scowled at the reminder.

"At least let me clear the place before you enter."

Christian shifted his weight and planted his hands on his hips.

"I'm serious. For once can we not argue over something so trivial?"

Christian stepped back and Pearson pressed against the door. With his gun stretched out in front of him, he vanished into the abyss of darkness.

Minutes ticked by with no word from the inside. Christian danced in place while Adam stood with his arms crossed over his chest. Christian inched closer to the door as he contemplated disregarding another order, but then Pearson appeared at the threshold of the door.

"It's all clear."

"You sure?"

"Am I . . . come on."

Christian and Adam followed behind doing their best to not disturb any potential evidence scattered about the building. Once inside, they split up with Pearson going to the left and Christian and Adam off to the right.

Out of earshot, Adam leaned in and whispered, "Are you sure this is our primary?"

Christian only nodded and continued weaving the beam of his flashlight from side to side.

"What a creepy place. Speaking of, you want to tell me about what happened here?"

"Someday."

"Could *someday* be today?"

Christian shook his head. "I'll tell you about it when we're back in Regina and we've found my best friend."

"The breadth of your experiences never seems to amaze me."

Two steps forward and a faint moan bounced off the wooden beams. Christian stopped and extended his arm to block Adam from moving any farther.

"Hey. What the—"

Christian raised his index finger and pressed it against his lips. "Listen."

"To what?"

"You don't hear the moaning?"

"Nope. The only thing I hear is you being bossy, as usual."

Christian scoffed at his smartass remark before he yelled out. "Is someone there?"

He remained motionless and the moaning started again, except this time the moan accompanied a clanking of metal.

Adam exhaled from the shock. "There *is* someone here."

He smirked. "Told you so."

Adam ran back toward the door and shouted for Pearson. "We got something over here."

Christian chased the cries deeper into the building. Pearson and Adam rushed across the dusty floor, dodging fallen timber and rubble, and caught up with Christian. Near the rear of the main floor, they rounded a corner, and several hallways and doors threw a wrench in their plan for a quick rescue.

"Which one?" Adam asked.

With urgency in his voice, Christian said, "All of them. We have to check them all."

Each of them hurried down opposite, freezing corridors, lined with heaps of snow, and pounded on every door. The groans reached a feverish climax and Pearson stood outside the final door at the end of the hallway he chose. His eyes glanced down at the fresh chain and padlock crisscrossed through the door handle. He rushed back to a central point and cried out.

"Guys, I found something."

Pearson sped back to the door and jimmied with the handle. The chain rattled, but the door refused to budge. Whoever attached the lock meant business, and even if the hostage freed themselves from any shackles, there was no chance of escape.

Christian limped for the door and pressed his ear to it. The muffled cries increased his anxiety and he stepped back.

"It's her. I recognize that moan."

"I need something to break this damn chain," Pearson said.

"Just shoot it."

Pearson brandished his weapon. "This isn't the movies, Anderson. I got a better idea. You two wait here."

Pearson ran down the hall so fast he kicked his own ass. Christian pounded against the door, and through the muffled words, it was clear the voice was feminine.

His head rolled toward Adam. "It has to be her."

"For her sake, I hope you're right."

Christian cried out, "Gemma? Gemma, is that you?"

The clanking of metal escalated, and it was the sign Christian wanted. He brushed Adam aside and backed up. Without a word he charged and bashed against the door. What he'd deemed a good solution ended up with him falling to the ground. "Ow."

As Adam reached out his hand to help him up, Pearson rounded the corner at the end of the hallway and ran toward the door.

"What the hell happened?"

Adam shook his head. "Just smugness in action."

Pearson shook his head and raised the crowbar at his side. "I said I had a better idea, and you couldn't wait two minutes?"

"She might not have two minutes."

"You're the most impatient person I've ever met, and that's saying a lot."

Pearson swapped between banging the shoddy chunk of metal and prying at the doorjamb. As the sparks danced around, a final blow was all it took and the lock broke into several pieces as it fell to the ground. He loosened the chain on the door and cautiously pressed inward until the gap was wide enough for him to peek inside.

The room was barren, with the exception of a table, two wooden chairs, and Gemma tied and gagged.

Pearson pulled his face away from the crack. "It's her."

"How bad is it?"

"Think of how you looked and times that by two."

"What are we waiting for? Let's get her out of this dump."

The crowbar dropped to the filthy ground and Pearson ripped the chain away and tossed it aside. He crashed through the door and swept the room, while Christian and Adam eagerly waited outside.

"All clear."

Those were the only two words Christian needed to hear before he wasted no time rushing to his best friend's side. He slid the bloody gag away from her purplish-blue lips.

"Gemma. Thank God. Who did this to you?"

While Adam and Pearson worked to loosen the binds, she strained to utter the answer Christian sought. Sensing her discomfort, he eased off and turned her head. The sun peeked through a hole in the ceiling to reveal two black eyes, several deep lacerations across her pale face, and cigarette burns gouged into her forearms. In an instant, his face flushed, and he vowed revenge on whoever was responsible.

The last rope fell to the ground and she slowly rubbed her hands along her upper body. She shook from the cold, or hunger, perhaps even a combination of both. Without thinking, Christian removed his parka and draped it over her shoulder while Pearson stepped aside and radioed for assistance. She reached out her hand and pulled Christian closer.

One name crossed her lips. "Jason."

He pulled away. "Nelson? He did this to you?"

She nodded and a bead of blood splashed onto her stone-washed jeans. "This means war."

Pearson crouched at her side. "Help's on the way."

"It was Jason Nelson."

Pearson's eye broadened and his mouth remained ajar, but the news prevented him from uttering a word.

Gemma whispered again. "Where's Cassidy? She was here."

Christian held her tight, and always being the guy who got straight to the point, he laid bare the truth. "She's gone.

Her lip quivered and she choked back tears. Given the length of time without food or water, the steady stream Christian expected was nonexistent. The intensity of her moans grew stronger, and her grief pierced through his emotional barrier, and once it touched his blackened heart, there was no stopping the years of fear, heartbreak, and his own silent suffering from falling against her bloodied shirt.

Pearson and Adam kept their distance and neither interrupted the heart-wrenching reunion. Minutes dragged on and soon the faint screeching of sirens in the distance stole Christian's attention. He lifted his face, wiped away the wetness, and forced a half smile to give her hope.

"Help's on the way. Can you walk?" he asked.

She shook her head and in her raspy voice said, "No."

"I'll get her," Pearson said. "Gemma, I'm going to pick you up, okay?"

She nodded.

Pearson carefully hoisted her from the chair and cradled her in his arms. Her head leaned against his Kevlar vest and he scuttled out the door and along the hallway.

They escaped through the main entrance where two ambulances and Constables Miller and Whitlock stood in wait. Without hesitation, Pearson lifted her into the back of the ambulance closest to him and laid her down on the white sheet.

Christian dashed for the rear doors. "I'm going with her."

Pearson patted Christian's back. "Good. I'll borrow Adam and we'll get the scene secured."

"And Jason?"

"Don't worry about him right now. We'll find him. You just stick to her side."

Christian hoisted himself into the back of the rig and glanced over his shoulder at the place he once considered his fun hideaway from the realities of life as a kid. Now, after everything he'd endured, the place was nothing more than a carcass of a past life that, no matter how hard he tried, he'd never recapture.

Before the doors closed, Pearson poked his head in. "One more thing."

"Yeah?"

"No visitors."

"What about Liam? Surely he should be notified."

Pearson paused. "You're right. But only him. If any of the White clan show up you know what to do."

With nothing more than a head nod, Pearson slammed the rear door and the ambulance pulled away.

231

CHAPTER 21

GEMMA DOZED OFF THE MOMENT HER head thumped against the flimsy hospital bed pillow. And sitting in the room, with no outside distractions, Christian evaluated the life choices he'd made up to this point.

I'm a terrible friend. A terrible lover. But worst of all, I'm a terrible son.

Occasionally, when he tired of wallowing, his eyes drifted up. Each time they did, he caught a glimpse of Gemma's tattered body. She'd been to hell, tussled with the devil, and returned from his grip to tell her story.

He leaned forward and examined her body from head to toe. Patches of bald spots now replaced her tightly curled full head of hair. Her bloodied nailbeds told a story of a will to survive, but worst of all, Jason Nelson blemished her best asset: her radiant face.

He couldn't stop staring at the carnage he left behind. Three gashes lined her face. The biggest ran the length of her forehead. The wound was jagged and gapping. The other two less significant ran along each cheek.

Christian mumbled under his breath and hung his head. "Monster. That's who does shit like this. A monster."

When he raised his head, Gemma's eyes were wide open, and panic painted her face.

"Where am I?" she asked.

The words were eerily familiar. "You're at the hospital. You don't remember us rescuing you from the sawmill?"

She turned her head to the side but cringed in pain.

"Hey, hey. Just keep still."

Her chapped lips flaked, and her mouth was drier than a raisin in the blazing sun. He glanced over at the pitcher of water on the nightstand. "You thirsty?"

She didn't speak. Instead, she reverted to their secret code from their childhood. Blink once for no and twice for yes.

Two blinks.

Without hesitation, Christian poured a glass and lifted the plastic cup to her lips. She took a few slow sips and closed her eyes.

Gemma shoved the glass away and Christian slouched back in the uncomfortable chair. "We don't have to talk. I'm here, though, if you need anything."

She wiggled her arm through the guardrail and reached out for him. He quickly interlocked his hand with hers and smiled.

Her raspy voice trembled as she mustered out one word. "Christian?"

"Yeah?"

"Thank—you."

"For what?"

"You saved me."

"You don't need to thank me. I'm just happy we found you in time."

When it came to Gemma, he'd never held back his emotions. He squeezed her hand tighter, and to keep up the pretense everything was fine, he choked back his tears.

They sat in silence and Christian gazed out the window, watching the snowflakes grow larger and thicker. A squeeze at his hand drew his attention back to her.

"Water," she whispered.

Christian fetched another glass of water; however, this time she took bigger sips than before. She took a few deep breaths. "My dad?"

"I tried him an hour ago, but I got voicemail. Should I try again?"

His question stirred a perkiness in her eyes.

"Say no more, I'll be right outside the door."

Christian excused himself to the hallway and sifted through his recent calls for Liam's number. He pressed the phone to his ear and two rings later, a familiar husky voice answered. "Tell me you have good news."

"We found her. She's alive."

"Thank God. Where was she?"

"At the abandoned sawmill."

"Where they found Cassidy?"

The calmness in the man's voice surprised Christian, but he pressed on. "Yeah."

"Where are you now?"

Christian paced in circles outside the door to the room. He glanced at the placard on the wall. "Room 211 at Cedar Lake Memorial."

Without a goodbye Liam hung up and left Christian holding the phone shaking his head.

He stopped shy of the door and propped his forearm against the wall. His eyes twitched as he held back the imminent flow of tears, and as much as he wanted to allow himself to break down, this was neither the time nor the place for him to lose it.

His face was warm, and his eyes stung from the saltiness that backed up in his ducts. Again, he rubbed his eyes and took a deep breath. He glanced through the window and forced a smile. It wasn't a beam of utter joy, but instead, it was one of gratitude.

Had things taken a different twist, how would he ever bounce back from the guilt? Yet while he stared at her from afar, there she was, full of life and breathing. Nothing else in that very moment mattered.

He pushed the door inward and shook the phone in his hand. "He's on the way."

She made no effort to speak, only a subtle nod of acknowledgement.

He walked back across the dimmed room to her bedside, scooted the chair closer, and lowered his body into it. Her gaze drifted to the snow falling outside and Christian grunted.

She turned her head his direction. He stared her directly in the eyes. "Gemma?"

In her sassy fashion, she responded with, "Christian?"

He released a nervous laugh. "I'm relieved sitting on death's doorstep didn't strip away your feistiness."

"Never. Any word on Cassidy yet?"

His Adam's apple quivered. He assumed this entire time she remembered him breaking the news in her makeshift prison cell. He stuttered. "I, um, we'll get to Cassidy in a few minutes. Do you remember back in 2009, a few weeks after prom?"

"You mean, what happened at the sawmill?"

His eyes shifted. "Yeah."

"You're talking about when we found Lindsay Ross hanging from the rafter?"

Christian fidgeted in the chair. "Yeah."

"What about it?"

His words hitched in the back of his throat, and immediately he scrambled to stall telling her again as long as possible.

"It's just the other day, when you said we all have secrets, and some of us share secrets. It just has been stuck in the back of my mind."

"Christian, we've talked about this before. You can't keep going through life blaming yourself. You have nothing to feel guilty about. She took her own life—end of story."

He leaned forward. "But what if I could have done more to prevent it from happening?"

"Yeah, well, what if that person who distributed her diary to the entire school had never done it. Then you and I wouldn't be sitting here rehashing this. And do you know why?"

She paused and took another gulp of water.

"Because she'd still be alive and probably sitting right here with you."

He held in a deep breath and after a few seconds, released. "I guess."

"You have to stop with the 'what-ifs' and get on your life. Fact is, you've never been happy since that day."

"I'll try. Sorry I brought it up."

"Why did you?"

"Suppose being there triggered something. I mean, after all, we fled like cowards and phoned in an anonymous call."

"We were young. And all you wanted in life was to become a cop. It's not like either of us strung her up there and murdered her."

"I know. I know. Anyway, it has just bothered me all these years, that's all."

Gemma's patience expired and she blurted out. "What about my sister?"

"I need to ask you a few questions before we talk about Cassidy. Think you can do that?"

Another gulp of water. "Depends. What about?"

"What you remember after you were kidnapped."

She closed her eyes and nestled the back of her head deeper into the pillow. After a few seconds of pause, she scooched into an upright position.

Christian clicked the voice recorder on. "You don't mind if I record our conversation? I may need your words later on."

"It's fine."

"Okay. Let's begin."

"Wait."

His finger pressed against the pause button. "What's up?"

"I need more water."

"Yeah. Of course." The tepid liquid sloshed in the glass and he handed it over. In one gulp, she downed half the glass and wiped her mouth with her hospital gown.

Christian's jaw dropped. "You all good now?"

"Yup."

"All right," he pressed record once more. "My name is DS Christian Anderson, with the Regina Police Service, and I am joined in the room by Gemma Williams. The date is February 3, 2020, and the time is four fifteen in the afternoon. Can you please state the date and place of your birth for the record?"

"July 29, 1987. I was born in Cedar Lake."

"I'd like to revisit the second of February. This would be the evening of your abduction."

"You know it was."

"Gemma, please. I need to keep this interview formal. It's necessary if and when we go to court."

She rolled her yes.

"You were at the market on First Street buying cigarettes, right?"

"I was."

"And as you left, that's when someone abducted you?"

"Yes."

"Do you have any recollection of who your kidnapper is?"

The roughness in her voice continued to die down the more she spoke. "At the time, no. I wasn't sure who it was.

All I remember is someone grabbing me, and I tried to fight them off. Then they covered my face with a cloth."

"And what do you remember about when you came to?"

"I was shivering and it was dark."

"Did you know you were at the sawmill?"

"I did. I recognized the smell and the room."

"You mentioned earlier something about seeing Cassidy."

She nodded. "She was there with me, but not for long. He took her away."

"How did she look when you saw her?"

"She was good. We talked a little, trying to figure out how to get ourselves out of there. But then the door flew open and he yanked her from the chair. I screamed out for him to stop, but he didn't care. He held the knife to her back and marched her outside the door."

"For the record, who barged through the door?"

Her eyes narrowed and the pupils expanded. "It was Jason. Jason Nelson."

"Did he say anything?"

"No. I carried on screaming. If he was going to slit my throat, I wanted to die knowing I did everything I could. Instead, he kept his distance when he returned."

"I see. Do you remember how you got the cuts, bruises, or cigarette burns?"

She gasped. "I . . . yes. Someone wearing a mask and hood arrived and Jason launched into a lightning round of questions. I refused to answer, and each time I responded with something other than the right answer, I got either hit, burned, or cut as my punishment."

"Then what?"

"Then it all stopped, and the mystery guest left. Jason hung by the door with that oversized knife at his side. I'm telling you, something was off about him."

"Off? How so?"

"Of all of Lee White's thugs, Jason was the sweet one. For a low-life drug pusher, he had a heart of gold. But, the more I watched him. . . I don't know. It was as if something sucked out his soul and left behind a broken man."

"At any time did he say why he took you?"

"No. He had some heated discussions over the phone, though."

"With who?"

"Couldn't say."

She fell back against the pillow and covered her face. A soft knock at the door interrupted and Christian clicked pause on the recorder.

In walked the same gray-haired doctor who treated him not even a day earlier. He looked up from the chart in his hand and jumped back.

With confusion in his eyes, he asked, "Wait? Weren't you just here yesterday?"

"Yup. And destiny brought me back."

"I see. Just came to check on Gemma. How are you feeling?"

"Sore and dehydrated. But it beats the alternative."

The doctor half-smiled. "He's not bothering you, is he? Because, if so, I can have security escort him out."

Her eyes widened and she glanced over his way. "What? No. Christian's my best friend."

"I remember. I'm only teasing. Got to make your own fun around this place. And after the traumas you two have been through, I assumed you needed a good laugh."

"Wait. Have we met before?" Christian asked.

"A long time ago. Doubt you'd remember me, but I played poker with your father on Saturday nights at your house. Man, those were some fun times."

Christian wagged his finger. "Wait a minute. I do remember you. Rogers," Christian scanned through the names in his head. "Simon. Simon Rogers. Right?"

He chuckled. "I see there's been no permanent damage to your memory. I didn't mention anything yesterday, seeing as you were in bad shape, and then we had 'Prying Pearson' loitering a few feet away at all times."

"I understand. Wow, I'm amazed you remember me after all these years," Christian said.

"How could I forget? You may not remember, but back in the day your father and I were thick as thieves. We were always into something. My wife and your mother spent most days joined at the hip too."

Christian's head drooped. "What was she like? My mother."

"Captivating. Complicated. Cedar Lake was too restrictive for her. She was meant for bigger and better things."

Gemma smiled and pulled the blanket closer. "It's crazy how everyone in this small town is connected."

"Oh, you have no idea," he said as he approached her and shined a penlight into each of her eyes.

"This may be an odd question, but what was my father like back then? I've seen what he's become, but I've always imagined he wasn't a hopeless drunk his entire life."

"Not back then. Your father had what the kids today call swag. And he madly idolized your mother. When she vanished, it shattered his heart." The doctor continued on. "I struggled to keep him involved, you know, take him out and help keep his mind off her leaving. I tried, but the bottle was stronger than my efforts. Once it got its claw into him, there was no getting him back."

"I've replayed it in my head a million times—what could have been."

The doctor jotted down a few notes and locked eyes with Christian. "Fate is not ours to decide."

Those few words jolted Christian and he reached out for Gemma's hand.

Christian's eyes narrowed. "Suppose you're right. I hate to cut our reunion short, but . . ."

Sensing he'd stumbled into a serious conversation, Dr. Rogers smiled. "Listen, I didn't mean to interrupt. I'll give you two a little privacy for a while. And Gemma . . . if you need anything, I'm a call away."

Dr. Rogers tapped his hand against the railing and proceeded toward the door, but as his hand gripped the handle, he glanced over his shoulder. "Christian, great running into you. I can't believe how much you've grown up. If you have more questions about anything, my door is always open."

"Thanks, Dr. Rogers, I may take you up on your offer."

The door closed and Christian turned his attention to Gemma, who hadn't taken her eyes off him since the mention of ominous news.

"You had news to share?"

He squeezed her hand. "A couple of things."

"What? Tell me."

"You sure you're ready for all this?"

"Christian. I've known you damn near all my life. I can handle anything."

"Okay. First, your father and my mother were shacking up."

Her vacant eyes stared directly at him, but nothing evacuated her mouth.

"Gemma? Did you hear what I said?"

"I—" she stuttered. "Wow. Never in a million years would I expect to hear the words *shacking up* and *father* in the same sentence. How'd you find out? Did my dad tell you?"

"He didn't have to. We found it while digging through the witness statements from when my mom disappeared. Naturally, I confronted him."

"Christian, damn. How are you taking it?"

His shoulders curled upward. "What's done is done. Am I upset? Sure. Am I going to dwell? No."

"Keeping those feelings pushed down, as usual, I see. Props to you. Well, seems you've uncovered more than the two of us would have."

"Not so fast. There's more."

"More?"

"You remember your frenemy—Lee White?"

She rolled her eyes. "How could I forget his ugly mug?"

Christian's eyes darted away from hers.

She gasped. "No. For the love of God, tell me she wasn't banging him too."

He bit his lower lip and offered a nervous laugh. "She was."

She flung her hands about and stuck out her tongue. "No offense, Christian, but that's not the image I want fried into my brain."

"And you think I do?"

"I'm so sorry, this is all my fault."

"How so?"

She took a deep breath. "For calling you to come back here. You could have gone the rest of your life without knowing *any* of this. But then Cassidy had to go missing—again—and I dragged you back into this saga we call Cedar Lake."

"Could be a blessing."

She coughed. "I'm sorry, did you say *a blessing?*"

"Yup. Think about it. I always wanted to reveal what happened to her and we're teetering on the edge. But, there's just one more thing, and it's regarding what you asked me earlier."

She perked up and then the dreaded question came out of her mouth once again. "What about Cassidy? You keep stalling. Did you find her?"

Unable to stall any further, Christian clenched her hand and released an audible sigh. "We did. And it's not the happy ending you hoped for."

CHAPTER 22

PEARSON SLAMMED ON THE BRAKES AS the one stop light in town changed from green to yellow. The sun hovered above the horizon and the ambient clatter of police gibberish emitting from the radio soothed Adam's nerves.

They had finished securing the scene an hour earlier and left Miller and Whitlock in charge of evidence collection. Right now, the most important thing was finding their suspect and getting him into custody before he could do any more damage.

The conversation trailed off and Adam glanced out the window at the boarded-up buildings which littered the downtown landscape. Soon his mind drifted back to the morning the text from Christian came in.

There he stood in the kitchen of a rundown shack where he and his partner struggled to keep two hyped-up addicts separated.

A quick glance at the message and he frowned. Adam didn't know much about Christian's past, but one thing he'd learned early on in the relationship was his bitterness towards Cedar Lake.

He pecked back a quick reply, *be safe*, and returned to the situation at hand. The rest of the morning Adam mulled over the message and after a few more calls, the worry about Christian took a back seat.

Then came silence and Adam's instincts kicked in. He just never anticipated he'd have to traverse across Saskatchewan just to be by Christian's side again.

Pearson made a move for the radio and Adam jolted back to reality.

"You okay?"

"Yeah. Fine. Just tired."

Pearson grinned and transmitted his message to the dispatcher awaiting a reply. The light changed and Pearson squashed the pedal to the floor. Smoke billowed from the tailpipe and Adam clutched the handle above the door.

"You always drive like this?"

"Only when I'm hunting down psychopaths."

"Where do you think he could be?"

"He could be anywhere. I do know one thing, though."

"What's that?"

"This damn judge needs to hurry and sign this warrant."

"So, while we wait, should we check his usual spots? Surely he has a favorite hangout."

"Nope. Those boys tend to shake it up every other week. Typical for drug dealers around these parts."

"Same back home."

Pearson nodded and grinned. "I want to ask you something. Something personal."

Adam's hands clammed up. *Please don't be what I think he's going to ask.*

"Okay?" he asked in a drawn-out fashion.

"You and Christian. I get a sense there's something going on between you two, something you don't want anyone to know. Isn't there?"

Adam wrung his hands together and closed his eyes tight.

He tried to stall but Pearson asked the question more direct.

"Are you two, like, a couple?"

He exhaled and unleased their secret into the world with two words. "We are."

The car went silent and Adam refused to glance in his direction. What had he done? Pearson noticed the tension building and spoke his mind. "Hey, man, between you and me, be yourself. However, I can understand why you'd want to keep it a secret."

An appreciative reply caught in the back of his throat. He took in a deep breath and mustered up one simple question. "How so?"

"Are you kidding? It takes courage to want to thrive in law enforcement *and* be out of the closet. Sure, views have changed for the better since I joined the force, but on the downside, there's some people out there who will never come around."

"You're not appalled?"

"Nah. Frankly, I'm honored you trusted me enough to be honest to not only me—but also to yourself."

Adam's eyes lit up. For the first time in his life, he'd allowed the authentic him to shine through, and an immense weight receded. "Thanks, Luke. Thanks for being so understanding."

"Can I let you in on a little secret of my own?"

Adam leaned in. "Sure."

"My brother's gay."

"For real?"

Pearson nodded and spun the steering wheel to the right. "At first, it upset me. He's my only brother and I worried stupid things, like would I ever have a niece or nephew to spoil? Would I ever be best man at his wedding? So asinine when I consider how selfish I'd been."

"What changed your mind?"

"Life carried on. And, as the years passed, he brought around a few of his boyfriends, and after a while it all felt like it was the way it should be. You know what I mean?"

"All too well."

"For once in his life he was happy—authentically happy. That's all it took for me to accept things."

"Sort of like, if he's happy, then I'm happy, huh?"

"Exactly."

"A good approach to have for anything in life."

The voice of the dispatcher squawked across the radio. "Pearson?"

He reached for the mic. "Go ahead."

"Have reports of a gunshot at the residence of Gary Nelson. 119 King Street. Can you respond?"

"En route. Stand by for an update."

Pearson flipped on the lights and siren and raced across town along the deserted streets of Cedar Lake.

✤

THREE MINUTES LATER, THE CHEVY TAHOE skidded to a stop outside the one-story house at the end of King Street. In the driveway sat two vehicles: A Dodge Charger and a gray Chevy Silverado with a missing passenger-side mirror. Pearson typed the license plate information for the Silverado into the computer, and after a few seconds, the owner's information populated.

Gary Nelson.

Pearson rolled his head toward Adam. "Well, well. What do we have here?"

Adam remained silent.

"It's your mysterious vehicle from the rehab surveillance camera."

Adam glanced at the screen. "Who's Gary Nelson?"

"Jason Nelson's father," he said as he grabbed the mic. "Dispatch."

"Go ahead."

"I've arrived on scene. I've also located the suspicious vehicle from the rehab surveillance video. Saskatchewan license plate number zero-one-one, Delta, Lima, Echo."

"Copy that."

"Any update on the warrant to search the property I put in earlier?"

"Standby."

A few moments passed and the dispatcher returned to the airwaves. "Pearson, that's an affirmative on the warrant. Do not enter until backup arrives."

"10-4."

Pearson dropped the mic and glanced at Adam whose mouth remained agape.

"How'd we overlook something so simple?"

Pearson cracked open the door. "We had no reason to suspect it. Listen, you wait here."

"But—"

"Backup is on the way. If anything happens, there's a gun in the glove box."

Adam unbuckled his seat belt and grabbed Pearson by the forearm. "But she said not to enter . . ."

"There's what she said and what I have to do. Warrant is secured."

"My gut says you should rethink going this alone."

Pearson smirked. "Tell your gut I can handle this guy. Just watch my back. Okay?"

Adam rolled his eyes. "Now who sounds like Christian?"

Pearson ignored the comment and proceeded into the blustery world as snow crystals whooshed past his head. He loomed closer to the vehicles and his hand never left his side piece.

He edged alongside the truck, running his fingers across the coating of undisturbed snow. He reached the driver's side and peeked inside.

Empty.

He continued up the driveway and along the front of the house. The blinds in each window blocked the view of what awaited him inside. He felt a lump in his throat, which only grew with each step forward he took towards the front door.

His right foot touched down on the front porch and awaiting him was an ajar front door.

Something wasn't right.

Pearson twisted his head and shot a glance at Adam who waited in the passenger seat. As much as he wanted to holler out, his damn pride wouldn't allow him to renege on his stubbornness.

He lingered at the edge of the porch for several minutes before he jerked his gun from the holster. Two more steps forward all while his heart pounded against his rib cage. He reached out for the wooden door, but fear overcame him. He paused. He released the built-up air which vaporized into a fine, white cloud of air, and in his head he counted down from three.

Three, two, one.

He pivoted his left foot outward, gripped the gun in front of his body, and as the lone cloud in the sky floated away, the rays from the last bit of sunlight gleamed across the large picture window.

He pressed hard against the door, but something on the other side obstructed his entry. He shoved harder. A few inches were all he needed to squeeze his body through. And once inside he squinted to adjust to the darkness.

"Police. Jason you can come out."

The house sat eerily calm and he took another step deeper inside. His left foot went to move and something slippery underneath his foot forced him back to the door.

He reached for his flashlight and shone the beam towards the floor. Then he realized why there was no answer to him.

Lying in a pool of blood with a bullet to his head was Gary Nelson, Jason's father. His head faced the door, and it made Pearson believe the man was fleeing something or someone.

He lost.

He backed out the door and bent forward to catch his breath he'd held. His head jerked back at Adam, who sat with a blank expression across his face. He held up a finger but remained adamant he wouldn't ask for his help.

Just as he was about to re-enter, two cruisers swooped in with their lights flashing. Pearson remained at the door while Constables Miller and Whitlock rushed through the front yard.

⁂

ADAM GREW TIRED OF SITTING IDLY by watching as the three men talked on the front porch. He tugged at the door handle and lifted his hood over his head.

As he approached, their conversation tapered off. "So? Backup's here, so why aren't you inside?" Adam asked.

Pearson shooed his junior constables inside and pulled Adam aside. "Listen. I don't know how things work in Regina, but here, we have a plan before we conduct searches."

"Yeah, sorry, I was out of line there. I apologize."

"Don't apologize, just don't be like your boyfriend and get quick tempered."

Adam sensed something in his eyes. "What's wrong? There's something going on . . . isn't there?"

Pearson hung his head. "I'll level with you. Gary Nelson—he's dead. Found his body right there next to the front door."

"And Jason?"

"Not sure yet. Tell you what, you can come inside. But you are not to touch anything. Deal?"

"Deal."

Pearson entered first and Adam tailed a few steps behind. Either Miller or Whitlock had managed to flip on the lights, and Adam stood a few inches from the pool of blood which covered the tile floor.

Chaos.

That's what greeted him as he glanced around at the flipped over end tables, broken picture frames strewn across the carpet. Whatever happened, Gary Nelson put up a fight for his life.

Ultimately, it was a battle he lost.

From a back bedroom, Miller yelled out. "Pearson, you might want to see this."

Adam and Pearson sidestepped through the litter of debris and down the hallway, where the destructive path continued. At the end of the hall, the two constables stood outside the door.

"Whatcha got?" Pearson asked.

Without a word, they cleared a path and Pearson stopped just outside the room. Propped against the bed sat Jason. His legs spread out in a 'V' formation, blood spatter covered his shirt, jeans, and the grey comforter. Sitting on the floor, next to his lifeless hand, sat a nine-millimeter.

"Shit," Pearson said.

Miller cleared his throat. "What are you thinking? Suicide?"

"Appears so. This is not the ending I wanted."

Adam peered over Pearson's broad shoulder at the ghastly scene. Not able to contain himself, he spoke up. "We can't rule out foul play either."

"Meaning?"

"Meaning, since I arrived here I've quickly realized that not everything is always a simple as we want to believe. This seems too convenient. Your suspect in Gemma and Cassidy's kidnapping just decides to end it all?"

"Could be he didn't want to go to prison. People take their own lives all the time," Miller replied.

"All I'm saying is let's not get ahead of ourselves just yet."

Everyone stood outside the room, quiet. Until a chime from a cell phone cut through the tense air. Everyone patted themselves for their phones.

No of their phones made the noise.

Pearson glanced across the room and then the illumination from Jason's cell phone caught his eye. He took a deep breath and walked towards the desk while the other three waited outside.

Now, with an unobstructed view, Adam noticed Jason clutching something in his hand. He didn't ask for permission before he moved closer and knelt at Jason's side.

A necklace.

He pulled a pen from his Kevlar vest and flipped over the emerald and diamond crusted pendant.

To my Sarah. Love, Liam.

He returned to his feet and paced. "We got a problem."

As Pearson slipped on a glove, he drowned out Adam's message, and reached for the phone. As he lifted it, the screen came to life, and the text message sent a shiver down his spine.

"Pearson, did you hear me? You might want to see this," Adam repeated himself.

Pearson snapped back to reality. "Actually, we have a bigger worry at the moment."

Adam moved closer to the desk and Pearson held the phone up for him to read the message. The senders name was a familiar one and Adam gasped.

In large caps he read the message. Is our little problem taken care of yet?

Adam covered his mouth and his eyes widened. "Christian."

Without exchanging another word with each other, they raced past Miller and Whitlock and out the front door.

CHAPTER 23

BY THE TIME PEARSON AND ADAM discovered Jason's body, the news about her sister was fresh in Gemma's mind. Christian leaned forward, unsure why she hadn't fallen apart at the seams. Instead, her vacant eyes told more than any tears ever could. He squeezed her hand.

"Gemma?"

She eyeballed him but said nothing.

"Is everything . . . okay? You heard me when I said we found Cassidy, right?"

Her head bobbed a little, yet the words remained hitched in the back of her throat.

"This isn't the outcome either of us expected, but I can tell you Pearson and Adam are out hunting Jason down as we speak. I'm here for you, and if you need anything, *anything*, you can talk to me."

Her eyes closed and her breaths slowed before her chin drooped forward. He squeezed her hand and, out of respect, he bowed his head. The beeping heart rate monitor sitting at his side ruined what could have been a beautiful moment.

Then her soft voice cut through the tense air. "What did she ever do to anyone to deserve this?"

His head raised and he opened his eyes to find hers glaring at him. He scoured his mind for something reassuring, but instead he blurted out from the script he'd repeated a hundred times in the last decade. "You can't let your mind go there, Gemma. Nothing Cassidy did or didn't do got her to this point."

And he was right. Given all of her problems, most were self-destructive. And even if she had done something to someone, murder should have never been the first choice. Whoever she referred to in her journal must have been the culprit behind the heinous act.

"I'm scared," she admitted.

"Of what?"

A shimmering tear rolled down her cheek. "What if this is just the beginning? What if the moment I get out of here and go home, they come back and do the same to me?"

"Then you'll come stay with me in Regina for a while. You know, until things cool down."

She sighed. "It's a thoughtful offer, but I can't . . ."

Christian's forehead furrowed. "Can't what? Leave . . . here? From my experience these past few days, I can't fathom what has its claws dug into you so bad."

She retracted her hand and crossed her arms across her chest. "I have plenty going for me here, thank you very much."

"Let's not argue about this. Not right now. And especially not after everything we've been through. I'm not talking to you as a cop, I'm talking to you as a friend. The only way I can keep you safe and alive is to bring you back with me. It's that simple."

"Can't you just stay here?"

He scoffed. "Here? No thanks. I spent the better part of adolescence doing everything in my power to escape. Nothing you say will ever bring me back here longer than I need."

"You can stay, Christian. Ask for more time."

"Maybe I should be clearer: hell no. I finally have a decent life, one I always dreamed of. Nah, as much as I love you, I love me too. And I'm not about to give up everything I've worked my ass off for because you insist on being stubborn."

She pouted her lips.

"And no, your guilt trip won't work this time. You have two options: you can stay here and take your chances with whoever has it out for your family, *or* you can come with me and be looked after 24-7."

Her nostrils flared. "The hospital is safe, and I'm never leaving."

As Christian prepared his rebuttal, the door smashed inward. In raced Liam with tears streaming down his face.

He swept across the room and kneeled at her side. "Oh, thank God your alive. Who did this to you?"

"Jason Nelson."

The middle-aged man collapsed onto the bed and wrapped his muscular arms around her. She winced in pain. "Ow, ow."

Liam pulled back and planted his lips on her cheek. "I'm sorry, baby, I can't help myself. I'm just happy you're back." Liam's eyes shifted their attention toward Christian. "Where the hell is he?"

"Who?"

"Nelson. Is he in custody?"

Christian diverted his eyes away from his icy stare. "They're looking for him. He wasn't there when we found her."

"He best hope Pearson gets to him before I do."

Gemma gasped. "Dad."

"What? Trust me, that boy doesn't want any of this right now. First, he murders your sister and then does this to you. It's not right."

"For Christ's sake, dad, violence doesn't solve anything. I'm sore, but alive, and trust me, I'm going to come back stronger."

"We'll both survive, still doesn't make it okay. You have no idea how these past couple days have been an emotional roller coaster for me."

"I do, trust me"

He kissed her forehead. "But none of it matters. God answered my prayers and I got you back."

Christian tilted his head and rested the palm of his hand against his face. Watching their interaction made him miss the closeness he and his father once had. One thing was evident: Liam loved his kids.

A buzzing from his pocket interrupted Christian's musing about the way things used to be. He dug into his jeans for his phone, and with it in hand, he glanced at the screen.

Adam Prescott.

With a quick tap he ignored the call and slid the phone beneath his thigh. "Mr. Williams," Christian interjected. "I was telling Gemma I think for her own safety she should come stay with me in Regina for a few weeks, just until the RCMP wraps up their investigation."

"Really, Christian? You're throwing me under the bus like that?"

Liam wiped away the wetness from his face and the corner of his mouth twitched. He turned toward Gemma, taking a moment to scan her body, and then reestablished his attention back on Christian.

"Say no more. As soon as the doctor releases her, get her as far away from Cedar Lake as you can."

Assuming her father would take her side, his response blindsided Gemma and she immediately interjected. "You two talk about what I want like it's your choice. It's not. Dad, you'll keep me safe, won't you?"

He reached out both hands and planted them on each side of her face. "Baby, this is bigger than both of us combined. You're going with Christian . . . and that's final."

Gemma's pleading with her father continued on for over ten minutes. And no matter how many times Christian interrupted to try to talk some sense into her, she shot down every logical argument he put forth.

A loud commotion in the hallway snatched Christian's attention away from the family feud and his eyes wandered for the door. Then in a millisecond, it swung open and in scuttled Pearson and Adam.

A determination burned in their eyes, and Christian leaped from the chair. "Whoa, guys, where's the fire?"

Adam motioned with his hands. "Christian, back away toward the door."

Christian stayed glued to Gemma's side and smiled. It was obvious there had been some sort of mistake. "What are you talking about?"

Adam's faced lit up with concern, an unease Christian had not yet experienced. "Just do it."

Christian took baby steps backward from the edge of the hospital bed, and Pearson focused his attention on Liam.

He slid the gun from its holster and spoke calmly with a hint of dour behind his words. "Liam Williams, place your hands atop your head, and interlock your fingers."

Gemma scooted away from her father to the opposite side of the bed. "Holy shit. Dad, what's going on? What did you do?"

Liam ignored Pearson's instructions.

Gemma's hands trembled as her eyes swept across every serious face in the room. She returned her attention to her father, whose tears she once wiped away with her fingers had dried up. And the frown he'd sported since he arrived had curled into a smirk.

"I'm sorry. I'm so sorry I have to do this." He reached into his waistband and clutched a .357.

With Liam distracted, Christian's strides grew larger, but not enough to get enough space between him and Liam. The desperate father reached out with his free hand and yanked Christian back into a headlock.

261

Christian squirmed, but something evil consumed Liam's soul, and no matter how hard he fought to break away, there was no getting out of this one on his own.

"What the hell has gotten into you?" Christian asked.

"Shut up and hold still."

Across the room, Pearson stood with the gun extended and his finger hovered over the trigger. "You don't want it to go down this way. Let Christian go, drop your weapon, and let's talk this over."

Liam pulled Christian back toward the corner. "If you shoot me, I shoot him. Why would we want anyone else to suffer?"

"None of us want more suffering, Liam. What'd you say you lay your weapon down and I'll do the same. There has to be a way we can talk this out rationally."

"The time for talking passed a long time ago. From what I can see, you have two options. You can let me walk out of here, or we have more bloodshed. What's it going to be?"

Gemma clutched the blanket closer to her body and froze, unsure if any sudden move she made would add a gunshot wound to the list of other ailments. The color drained from Christian's face and Gemma knew she had to intervene.

She mustered up the courage to shake away the anxiety. "Dad? I want you to look at me."

His eyes rolled her way. "Not now, Gemma. Can't you see I'm up to my neck in a heap of shit right now?"

"Why are you doing this? What have you done?"

"What I should have a long time ago," he said as he began waving the gun around the room. "Now, everybody just shut up and let me think of a way to make this work."

Hell-bent on neutralizing the situation, Pearson took a bold move. "Hey, look, I'm putting my weapon down. Can you do the same? No one else has to lose their life today. All right?"

As promised, Pearson lowered his weapon and disconnected his finger from the trigger. When the magnitude of the situation settled in, beads of sweat bubbled up along Liam's forehead.

"Liam. It's all over. We found Jason and his father."

"Who?"

"Don't act dumb. You're well aware they're both dead. But, lucky for us, he left us clues which brought us to you."

"What are you blabbering on about?"

"You see, there was a text message from you. Funny thing about criminals is, they really should have a passcode on their phones."

Liam's vacant face never wavered.

"Come on, Liam. Do you really want to do this here? In front of Gemma?"

"Do what? You got nothing on me."

"I have your text messages and not to mention Sarah Anderson's necklace. To my Sarah. Love, Liam. Ring any bells?"

The heart rate monitor beeped in quicker intervals. "Will one of you please tell me what the hell is going on?"

"Gemma, not here," Christian said as Liam tightened his grip around his neck.

Liam turned Christian at just the right angle to where he locked eyes with Gemma, and they exchanged fearful glances. Pearson and Liam exchanged shouts a few more times, each attempt resulting in failed negotiations. Out of nowhere, the door smashed in and in rushed Charles White.

"You son of a bitch. It was you. You took her away from me."

Taken off guard, Liam twitched, and with one simple slip his finger tightened on the trigger. A lone shot exploded next to Christian's head and the recoil jolted Liam back and loosened his grip. Christian seized the opportunity and slithered from his arms. The world before his eyes slowed and all his senses cranked into overdrive.

The burnt gunpowder smothered Christian's nostrils and he collapsed to the floor. He covered his head with both hands, and from across the room Pearson ran at full throttle and his barrel chest crashed against Liam's small frame. The two men tumbled to the floor and Christian didn't move.

A tug at his jacket and everything sped up. As he glanced upward, Adam's face hovered over him. "Christian, we got to move."

Adam gripped Christian's collar tighter and dragged him toward the door. Amidst the chaos, another shot rang out. The second blast snapped Christian out of his fog and he staggered to his feet and out the door.

Once out of harm's way, a few inches on the other side of the door, Adam propped Christian against the wall and patted him down.

"Are you hit?"

Dazed, Christian stuttered. "Um, no, I'm okay. Get Gemma the hell out of there."

Without hesitation, Adam raced back inside. Seconds later, he dragged another body from the chaos, except it wasn't the person Christian expected to see. A crimson-red streak of blood smeared the floor and Adam propped Charles against the wall.

A few drops of blood spatter dotted Adam's face, and before Christian could reach him to wipe it away, Adam shook him. "Don't worry about me, go get him help."

Adam crawled along the floor out of sight. Christian remained frozen next to the guy he had assumed all along was responsible, and just before Adam returned for a third time to the chaos, Christian belted out, "Where are you going?"

"To save Pearson and Gemma before he takes them out too."

He waved his arms. "Go. And Adam?"

He stopped. "Yeah?"

"Be safe."

Adam inched on all fours and disappeared back into the brawl. Charles groaned in agony and Christian skidded across the floor on his knees to his side.

"What the hell are you doing here? This isn't how this was supposed to happen."

More shouting and another scream distracted Christian from the crisis laid out on the floor in front of him.

Charles grabbed Christian's shirt and pulled him down until their faces nearly touched. "He killed her. He killed the love of my life."

"Liam?"

"Yes."

"Okay, they'll take him down. I need to get you help. Just hang in there, all right?"

Charles groaned.

Christian drowned out the background noise and centered his attention on the one thing in his control in that moment: saving Charles White. He hurried to his feet and raced down the hall. As he rounded the corner, two nurses huddled together, waiting for whatever was happening to stop.

"Hey, you," he pointed at an older nurse. "I need a stretcher. Can you help?"

The nurse sobbed but moved her head up and down through the bouts of tears.

"Okay. Go. If he doesn't get help now, he'll die."

She scampered off in a hurry while the younger nurse clung to the wall. Christian approached cautiously and crouched to her level. "I get it, you're scared. I am too. I need help controlling the bleeding. Do you think you can help?"

Through her rapid breaths she managed to squeak out the words Christian needed. "I—I can."

"Okay. Come with me."

Christian grabbed her by the hand, and they raced back around the corner just as Pearson tossed Liam against the wall while Adam placed the handcuffs around his wrists.

"Liam Williams, you are detained with respect to: attempt to commit murder."

The nurse rushed to Charles side and Christian breezed past the commotion and paced outside the door. As his hand pressed against the door, he overheard Pearson continue the speech he recognized all too well.

". . . not influence you or make you feel compelled to say anything to me for any reason, but anything you do say may be used in evidence."

He didn't wait for permission and busted through the door. Gemma remained in the bed with her legs pressed against her chest. She trembled and buried her face between her legs.

He made a beeline for the edge of the bed. He cautiously sat on the edge of the bed and she jerked away.

"Gemma. It's me—Christian. You're safe now."

He pulled her as delicately as possible against his chest, and she lifted her face while choking back tears.

Tears streamed down her face. "Oh my God, what the hell?"

"Your dad, well, he's absolutely lost his mind."

Christian slid closer to his best friend and she wrapped her arms around him. Her grip was strong, and she dug her fingers into his back.

"I thought my dad shot you."

He held her tight against his body. "I'm okay. It's all over. You can breathe now."

The wailing continued on as Adam rushed into the room. Christian had his back to him as he called out. "Christian, you okay?"

His head bobbed and he locked eyes with Gemma. "Gemma, you okay? You're not hit or anything?"

She shook her head and his question only drove her tears to gush harder.

A few minutes passed and Christian's grip never loosened. Eventually, her adrenaline subsided, and she pulled away. "Charles? Is he . . ."?

Christian glanced up at Adam.

"Dead? No. But he's in bad shape."

"Will he make it?" she asked.

Adam nodded. "More than likely, yeah, he'll pull through."

"I can't believe this whole time I fingered him as the guilty one. Now I feel like such an idiot that I couldn't see what was right in front of me."

"What do you mean?"

"My dad. After Cassidy overdosed, he changed. Now everything is making sense."

"Care to share, because I'm lost."

"My dad must have killed your mother, and somehow Cassidy knew about it all this time. She didn't have to die because of it, you know."

"Hey! We aren't even sure my mother is dead."

Gemma glanced up at Adam. "You said Jason had her necklace. Why would he have that?"

"We don't know yet. Like Christian said, let's not jump to conclusions without evidence."

As the conversation between Adam and Gemma continued, something dawned on Christian: Gemma was speaking to a stranger. "I should probably introduce you two, huh?"

Gemma bit her lower lip and Adam reached out his hand. "I'm Adam. Adam Prescott, Christian's . . ."

Christian chimed in. "This is my boyfriend."

Her eyes lit up and for a moment, the chaos from moments earlier faded away. She gave him a once over and extended her hand. "Nice to meet you."

"You too. Listen, I'm going to go check on Pearson and see if he needs any help. You two okay?"

"We've got each other," Christian said.

Adam stepped for the door and with the two of them alone, Gemma gripped his hand. "Does your offer still stand?"

"Yeah. Of course."

She wiped her face. "Good. I can't, no, I won't stay here."

C. L. BREES

PART 4

TUESDAY

"One of the happiest moments in life is when you find the courage to let go of what you can't change."
Unknown

CHAPTER 24

THE AMBIENT BLUSH OF DAWN PEEKED through the sheer drapes of the motel room and Christian's eyes sprung open. With a groan, he rolled onto his side and his hand fumbled across the nightstand for his phone. He tapped the screen and the soft glow illuminated enough for him to catch the time.

Eight forty-five.

The sandpaper sheets scratched at his skin as he pushed himself upward and stretched his arms over his head. His eyes scanned the room for signs of life. But everyone else remained fast asleep.

In typical fashion, Adam sprawled out across the bed, stealing most of the covers and real estate. Christian let out a small chuckle when he noticed Adam's hand pressed against his forehead like a damsel in distress.

He grabbed his phone from the nightstand and snapped a quick photo.

If there's no photo, it didn't happen.

A few feet away, Gemma's head faced away, and if she wasn't snorting, she gasped for air, and the scene took him back to the many nights the two snuck out and sometimes fell asleep in some shady places.

He slid what little covers he had covering his body and the hairs on his arms stood on end. With stealth, he planted his feet onto the plush carpet and his first order of business was caffeine.

Coffee. Must get coffee.

The moment he got upright, though, the chance of the first mouthful splashing against his tongue withered when a hand grasped his forearm and pulled him back into bed.

"Where are you off to?"

"Coffee."

"The coffee can wait a second." Adam nestled his head into Christian's lap and let out a moan of fulfilment.

His craving for coffee increased, but how could he disappoint the man who saved not only his life, but Gemma's too? He gave into the affection and slid his arm around his boyfriend's upper body and pulled him against his chest.

"What a night," he whispered.

Adam's eyes arched up, and he grinned. "Man, was a wild ride. Let's be real, though, it could have ended a lot worse."

Christian nodded and darted his eyes at Gemma. "Thank God he's locked up and can't do any more damage."

He bent forward and pressed his lips against Adam's forehead. "Babe, come on. My body is craving coffee, and unless I get it soon I'll get a headache."

Adam released his grip and playfully pushed him out of the bed. "And we both know how you get when your head hurts."

"Bitchy."

"You said it. Hey, while you're up, would you be so kind as to pour me one too?"

Minutes passed and an earthy aroma filled the air and Christian watched Gemma flop over and snort. Given every twist and turn over the last few days, seeing her relaxed was a welcome sight.

He returned to the bed, a mug in each hand, and Adam reached out and snatched one. Christian slowly sat at the edge of the bed and took a sip of the liquid sunshine his body screamed for.

"So, what's next on our Cedar Lake agenda?" Adam asked.

"Our part here is done. Gemma *might* need another day of rest, two tops. After that, we're out of here."

"And your dad? How are you going to leave things?"

The notion unnerved Christian. A part of him accepted clearing the air was the best course of action. How he wanted to repair their fractured relationship and reconstruct it to the way it was before his mother disappeared. Then again, there was a piece of him that wanted nothing more than to zip up his suitcase, chuck it into the trunk, and turn his back on this cursed place once and for all.

Christian grunted.

Adam swept his hand in a circular motion across his back. "Well? What's it going to be?"

"Let's play it by ear, okay?"

"Christian, you gotta let go of the past so you can move forward."

"But I've gotten so good at keeping everything about me buried inside. What's another forty, eh, fifty years going to hurt?"

"Well, I have a confession to make."

"Yeah?"

"I may have let it slip to Pearson we are a couple."

"You what?" Christian raised his voice.

"Shh. It's all good. He's okay with it."

"Okay, and? We're talking about my father here and I don't know how he'll take the news."

"Why would you torture yourself like that? It's obvious you want to make amends with your father, but for some reason doing so scares you. And don't roll your eyes at me."

Christian huffed. "Of course it does. It scares the crap out of me to admit I spent the better part of the last twenty years blaming my father for everything bad I assumed he had a hand in."

"Then why don't you tell him how you feel?"

"My pride gets in the way. Every. Single. Time. I'll say this, just once: you're right."

"I'm right? About what?"

"I can't allow this to fester. I want to reconnect with him and the only way I can ever do that is to rip off the Band-Aid and dive right in."

A knock at the door broke up the somber mood. Christian jumped to his feet, spilling the hot coffee against his bare leg. "Who is it?"

"Christian? Hey, it's Dad."

He stuttered. "Pop? Uh, hang on—let me throw my clothes on."

The commotion aroused Gemma from her deep sleep and she rolled onto her stomach. In a fury, she grabbed the pillow, hid her face, and groaned. "What time is it?"

"Early. Adam, get dressed and sit at the table or something," he ordered.

Adam threw his hands up. "Yeah, yeah. Don't keep him waiting too long."

Yanking the last clean pair of clothes from the suitcase, Christian slipped on his jeans and V neck over his head. Next to the bed lay the bloodied jeans from the previous evening, and the nauseating mix of disinfectant and iron filled his nostrils and he gagged. He gave the room a final approval, ensuring everyone was where they should be to not arouse suspicion. Satisfied, he raced for the door.

With one quick jerk he unchained the door, clicked the deadbolt, and pulled the door inward. Standing opposite him was Matthias, with a leather-bound notebook in his hand and an expression of concern written blatantly across his face, Christian grew concerned. "Wait. What's wrong?"

Matthias wrapped his arms around Christian's neck and pulled back after a second. "Scare the shit out of me, why don't you."

"What? How?"

Matthias sighed at his dimwitted question.

"What has you out of bed so early, Pop?"

"Why do you think?"

He shot him a quizzical glance. "You tell me."

"Boy, you can't be *that* stupid. In case you've forgotten, this is a small town and word travels fast."

Christian hung his head, and with a hint of sarcasm mumbled under his breath. "Oh, how I've missed living here."

"You gonna invite me in?"

Christian stepped aside and Matthias proceed into the warmth of the motel room. The bearded man stood at the door, brushed off the accumulated snow from his shoulders, and scanned the room. "They've remodeled."

Christian shook his head and returned to his spot on the bed. Adam's eyes peered over the top of the case file in his hand but made no effort to introduce himself to Matthias.

Gemma remained swaddled in the comforter on her bed. The tension in the room built and she did her usual actress bit and squealed. "Ooh, look at you, all cleaned up and looking sharp."

Matthias stood speechless in the doorframe as the cold air snuck inside.

"Well, don't be shy. After everything I've been through, I could sure use a hug."

Matthias stepped forward as he unzipped his jacket. He tossed it on the back of the chair and continued on his march toward the girl he'd treated like a daughter since as long as he could remember. He leaned forward and extended his arms, wrapping them tenderly around her neck. He pulled her close and his trimmed beard brushed against her swollen face.

"You've certainly had better days, my dear."

She loosened her hold and he pulled away. "Yeah, haven't we all. But guess what?"

He plopped down next to her. "What?"

"I might be bruised and down for a few days, but my heart's beating and I have those two to thank for it."

Matthias's head swung around, and he stared back at Christian until the unfamiliar face caught his eye. "Christian . . . who's this?"

Crap.

"Oh, sorry, Pop, this is Adam. He's a colleague of mine whose been helping on the case, err, cases."

Adam dropped the folder onto the table and made his way to formally introduce himself.

"Adam Prescott, sir. I just have to tell you what an honor working with your son the last three years has been."

Matthias gripped Adam's brawny hand and smiled. "He's a special kid, ya know."

Adam grinned. "Oh. I couldn't agree more."

With a timid laugh, Christian glanced down at the book in his father's hand and quickly found an excuse to change the subject before things derailed. "Say, what'd you bring?"

His eyes lit up and he shifted the book between his hands. "It's something your mother held near and dear to her heart."

"Don't keep me in suspense."

Matthias stopped fidgeting and extended the book outward. "Her journal."

Christian's jaw dropped. "Wait. How long have you had this?"

"Since last night."

"How'd you just now find it?"

277

"She came to me."

Taken aback, Christian jumped to his feet. "Who came to you?"

"Your mother."

"Wait? She physically came to you?"

He shook his head. "Her spirit came to me. Let me explain. I sat on the floor of our bedroom, staring down a bottle of Jack Daniels. I wanted to drink away the pain so much, but as I got the cap off, there she stood. She said the time had come."

Hanging on his father's every word, Christian leaned in. "The time had come for what?"

"To let her go."

Christian's eyes widened. "That's deep, Pop. Then what happened?"

"Well, then she walked towards the closet and when I blinked, she was gone. I tore out all the clothes and tossed them aside. I believed I'd find her inside, but instead, I uncovered her secret cubbyhole."

"Are you okay?"

The older man smiled. "I will be. You see, I've wasted so much of my life, holding out hope she'd waltz through the door and back into my life. But after twenty-four years, I think the ship sailed a long time ago."

Christian's lips hovered open and he inched closer. "Did you read it?"

Matthias bobbed his head.

Christian lowered himself onto the edge of the bed next to his father. "You must have found something important to have you over here so early."

"The last few entries should give you a better perspective on what may have happened."

Matthias held the book out with one hand and Christian glanced down, unsure if what he was about to read held answers he sought. His hand trembled as it fell into his palm.

With his eyes closed, the encouraging voice of his father set his nerves at ease.

"Son, can I say something before you dive in?" Christian kept his eyes tightly closed and jerked his head up and down.

"None of this will be easy to digest. However, I believe you'll get a better understanding of her state of mind before she vanished."

Christian inhaled and his eyes sprang open. He released the pent-up breath he held.

"Near the back, the entry dated the twelfth of April."

Christian flipped open the book and turned the pages until he reached the entry.

April 12, 1995

I need an escape from this hellhole town I once portrayed as home. Matthias and I had another fight this morning and those vile words that spew from his mouth is a clear indicator I allowed my life to spin out of control. And at this point, there's no apologies, no actions, which could ever bring things back from the brink of extinction.

I know I shouldn't leave. What will become of my beautiful son? I'd give my last breath to steal him away, but would doing so be fair to Matthias, let alone Christian? Believe me, I tried so hard to make things work, but no matter what I do, the man I vowed to love, honor, and cherish until death do us part, can't break himself away from McGinty's long enough to be the loving husband he promised me he would.

So here I sit, with the picture from our wedding next to me. How I miss those days when we believed we could take on the world, when we had big dreams. But those dreams faded eons ago, and now I have no other choice other than to take Liam up on his offer. Oh, how I yearn for a simpler time.

This will be my last entry before I venture off to Calgary to begin a new life. A better one with the man who has given me so much love, comforted me when I was on the verge of breaking down. This man has the guts Matthias never had nor ever will.

I deserve better than Matthias.

Christian stopped halfway through and his head turned toward his father who sat patiently.

"I can't read any more. This is too much."

Matthias placed his hand on his son's shoulder and smiled. "I told you it wouldn't be easy. But you have to keep going."

I've run into one small hiccup in our plan. Last night, as I tried my best to sneak out of Liam's place without his kids noticing, Cassidy confronted me in the living room. Of the countless times I'd come and gone as I pleased, this of all nights had to be the one where I questioned what I was doing.

She told me she knew about me and her father. She got right up in my face and the smoldering hatred in her eyes sent shivers down my spine. I'm worried now. Worried she may do something to break this up. Worse, I'm scared she might do something to me.

As of now, the plan is for Liam to pick me up after Matthias leaves for work on Friday. I can't wait to get away from here and work on the life I've always deserved.

Christian released his grip on the page and the book closed with a soft thud. He bowed his head and set it on the bed between him and his father.

His nostrils flared, not out of irritation, but from sadness. His entire childhood he believed everything was perfect, when it wasn't. His breaths grew shorter and deeper, and Matthias wrapped his arms around his son's neck and pulled him tighter.

Matthias rested his head atop of Christian's and broke down. "I'm sorry. I'm sorry for being a lousy husband and father all those years. If I had tried harder, she'd still be with us."

Christian's face reddened and he relinquished the shame that had tormented him for so many years and collapsed into his father's chest. There were no remarks either of them could say that would make reading her final words any less heartbreaking. However, Christian accepted this was the first step toward the healing process, and with all of his emotions bubbling to the surface, there was one other secret he couldn't keep classified any longer.

Lies and secrets were what brought everyone to this point. Right there, with everyone watching, he made the decision to break the endless cycle of poor life choices and be honest about who he was. It was the only way he'd ever be able to move forward with his life.

He pulled away, and by this point Gemma flanked him on the other side and held his hand.

"Pop," he said as he sucked back his tears.

"Yeah?"

"I have to tell you something that's been on my mind for the last twenty years. It's just . . . it's so hard to look you in the eyes and tell you I've kept a secret from you."

Matthias raised an eyebrow. "More secrets?"

"If you and I are ever going to mend our broken relationship, there's something you need to know about me."

"Well, boy, what are you waiting for? Spit it out already."

Christian shook and Gemma squeezed his hand tighter since she recognized what was about to drop from his mouth. "I never told you this, well, given I didn't think you'd understand, or approve."

"Why wouldn't I understand?"

He sucked in a deep breath, closed his eyes, and, while breathing out, in one fell swoop spewed the words he'd waited so long to say from his mouth. "Pop—I'm gay. And Adam . . ."

Matthias's eyes widened.

"And Adam, well, he's more than just my colleague. He's also the guy I've been dating the last six months."

Matthias immediately tensed, and his sympathetic veneer swung from compassionate to disconnected. Still reeling from what had happened in the blink of an eye, Adam scooted the chair back and rushed toward his devastated boyfriend, who had turned his head away from his father.

His secret was out, and there was no getting it back.

Adam squatted in front of his boyfriend, and he reached out his hands and gripped them. That touch was all it took for the restrained waterworks to kick into full force. The hush increased and by now the only thing heard between soft gasps for air was the relief in Christian's voice.

Gemma and Adam turned their focus to Matthias who kept his eyes facing forward. Never once did they shift during the entire uncomfortable moment.

Eventually, after several minutes of weeping, Christian whisked away his tears and turned his gaze back upon his father.

"Pop. Say something. Anything. Tell me you love me. Hell, tell me you hate me. Just say something."

With a long drawn-out breath, Matthias sighed and turned his head toward his son. "Christian. You're my son, and there's nothing you could ever say or do to make me hate you."

Christian let out a semi-laugh and snort in the same breath. "I'm sorry, Pop. I didn't want to tell you this way, but I think you deserve the truth."

"I can't say there wasn't always a part of me that knew. I was raised to never speak of such things, but times have changed."

"I understand. And I get it—this will take some time to adjust to."

"It will. And somehow every day I surprise myself even more with how far I've come."

Christian smiled through his bloodshot eyes.

"And, son."

"Yes?"

"I do love you. And you're right, this is exactly what we needed in order to rebuild our relationship."

Speechless, Christian leaned over and wrapped his arms around his father's neck. "Pop. Thank you."

Matthias squeezed him tight and rubbed at his eyes. "You're not going to get all sappy on me . . . are you?"

"Maybe. Pop, I love you and I've missed you."

"I love you too."

CHAPTER 25

THE THUMPING OF A PEN AGAINST the metal desk passed the time for Constable Pearson as he sat, pondering his next move.

The dark black rings below his eyes gave away exactly how tired he was, even though the dedicated constable would tell anyone otherwise. He'd spent all evening glued to his chair, hunting through file after file, hoping to find something to help him make sense of everything.

Still, no matter how many times he reread the same passages, there was nothing to indicate he'd end up where he was now—with Liam in a holding cell, Charles in intensive care, and Lee White still running the streets.

His heavy eyelids shut but sprang open the moment Constable Miller walked into the office.

"Good morning," the young constable said.

"What's good about it?"

"You'll probably bite my ass for saying this, but someone has to—you look like shit."

"Thanks for stating the obvious, Miller. What can I do for you?"

"We finished searching the Williams house."

"And?"

"Clean. No weapons, no drugs, nothing to give us any more clues as to why Liam did it."

The tapping stopped and Pearson dropped the pen. "You're telling me there weren't any more journals anywhere hidden in that house? No trophies from his alleged crimes?"

"Umm."

"You didn't look for that stuff. Did you?"

Miller hung his head.

"We're not holding Liam on drug or weapons charges; we're holding him on attempted murder and suspicion of murder. I don't give two shits about more weapons or drugs. None of that will explain why he murdered his own daughter."

"You're right, sir."

Pearson squeezed the bridge of his nose, as he usually did when he was annoyed. "Dammit, man, I've asked you to stop calling me sir more times than I care to count."

"I can't help it."

"Just," he began and gritted his teeth. "Go back and search again. Check air vents, under mattresses, hell, check the bookcases and closets for hidey-holes. There's evidence there, and I don't want to see any of you back at this station until you've ripped the entire house apart. Are we clear?"

Miller trembled at the outburst and timidly nodded before Pearson released him. As he burst out the door, Pearson's cell phone rang, practically on cue. Through his hazy vision he picked up the phone without even checking who it was.

"Pearson."

"Morning. It's Christian."

"Hey, buddy. How's Gemma holding up?"

"As good as one might expect. She's seen better days, though."

"I bet. So, what's up?"

"Why does something need to be up? Can't I just call to say hi and check on you?"

"Anderson, you call for two reasons: when you find something or need something."

"Clearly we've spent too much time together the past few days. But, I might have something you want to see. Have you interviewed Liam?"

"Nope. Was hoping my team would have found something in the house to shed more light on his motives, and so far they've returned with jack."

"I see. My dad stopped by the motel and brought me a gift you might find interesting."

"I like gifts. Whatcha got?"

"My mother's journal. There's an entry the night before she vanished."

Pearson fell back in his chair. "Will this help me?"

"Might. Gave me a little more insight into the situation."

"I'll bite. How quick can you be here?"

"Fifteen minutes, maybe less."

"Perfect."

The call ended and Pearson leaned forward and lowered his face into his hands. "Please, please, have something useful."

⌘

AS EXPECTED, FIFTEEN MINUTES PASSED AND Christian arrived at the detachment, his messenger bag slung over his shoulder. As he breezed through the front door, Pearson leaned against the doorframe, with the identical stance from the morning the two met. Except something had changed over the last two days. His handsome face had faded and now an exhausted man stood before him.

Christian glanced up and jerked back. "Damn. Not to come across rude, but I think you need sleep more than you need the answers in this book."

Pearson yawned. "I'll sleep when I know we've got the right guy. You got that journal?"

He patted the side of the bag. "Right here."

"Good. Where's Adam and Gemma?"

"Back at the motel. This isn't the place she needs to be right now."

"Ah, right. She's recovering *and* a loose cannon."

"Something to that effect."

"Well, come, have a seat."

As Christian passed through the inner door, an unpleasant stench crept into his nostrils and he choked.

"Um. When was the last time you slept? Or took a shower, for that matter?"

Pearson lifted an armpit and even his own stench made him gag. "What? Only been a day, err, maybe two. The days are blurring together."

"Jesus. And you think you'll extract a confession out of Liam looking like a big ball of hell?"

"Christian, I don't have time for your judgmental comments."

He paused and turned around as Pearson shut the door. "Yes, you do. How about we come to a compromise?"

"A compromise? Starting to sound like my ex-wife now."

Christian sneered at the comment but carried on. "I'll show you what I found if you promise me you'll go home, take a nap, grab a shower, and come back later this afternoon."

"Why are you so concerned with how I look? Or smell? I'm not sure how you all do things in Regina, but up here when you're working a major crime, appearances go out the window."

Christian tossed his hands up and backed away. "I wasn't going to say this, but you've left me no choice. Look in the mirror. You're exhausted, and when people push themselves beyond a certain point, well . . ."

"Well, what?"

"They screw everything up."

"Ah, so you're more worried about the case than me."

"I'm worried about both. Look, can we stop this pissing match and shake already?"

Pearson clenched his jaw and diverted his eyes away from Christian.

Maybe he's not as naïve as I once assumed. Now I understand why everyone in Regina spoke so highly of him.

289

Pearson returned his stare back at Christian who by now had crossed his arms over his chest and tapped his foot waiting for an answer.

"Do we have a deal, or not?"

Pearson scoffed and extended his hand. "Yeah, we got a deal. Man, this entry better hand me an answer on a silver platter."

"Might even do you one better. Believe me, what she wrote will explain more than Liam probably knew back then."

Christian rifled through his messenger bag as Pearson paced in anticipation. But then, the moment Pearson waited for came as Christian clutched the journal in his hand and stood.

"Near the end, last entry." He handed the book over.

Pearson flipped slowly though the book's yellowed edges, and then his fingers stopped.

His eyes scanned the lines of text, and with every new paragraph he read, the width of his eyes ballooned. He closed the book and glanced up at the smirk written across Christian's face.

"Top-notch shit, huh?"

"Better than top-notch. Still, nothing in here answers my questions."

"And those are?"

"What happened to your mother? What motive did Liam have to murder Cassidy? And let's not forget to ask ourselves: How is Gemma wrapped up in this?"

Christian cocked his head. "Are you blind?"

"Huh?"

"My mother flat out said she was scared of Cassidy, not Liam. What if we got this all wrong and Liam isn't responsible, but Cassidy is?"

"Nah. How could a little girl take on your mother? I'm telling you, we have the culprit sitting in a cell."

"So, you've made up your mind: he's guilty."

"He shot Charles last night and took you hostage. And you want to sit here and tell me he's not a monster?"

"That's not what I'm saying at all. There's more under the surface, but you're too tired and cranky to even see it."

"So . . . what are you saying then?"

"I'm saying you need to go home, take a nap, and, for the love of God, take a shower. You'll think more rationally and put things together better with a rested mind."

Pearson rubbed his burning eyes while Christian herded him toward the door. "Fine. You win. I'll catch a little shut-eye—but only for an hour or two."

"An hour or two is better than none."

"After, you can't let me waste any more time."

"I won't because I wanted to ask about the interrogation. I—" Christian said.

Pearson stopped dead in his tracks. "What about it?"

"I hope you'll let me observe."

Pearson cocked his head. "Why?"

"Context, mainly. If Liam hurt my mother, I want to gaze into his eyes when he admits it."

"Christian, I just ca—"

"Yes, you can. I promise, I won't make a scene, or disrupt you at all." Christian held up three fingers like he did during his three years as a Venturer Scout.

291

Pearson's condescending smile sent a mixed signal, but then he went serious again. "I'll take your request into consideration. For now, go and get back to Gemma. There's no telling who else is involved in this sordid mess."

Christian smiled, extended his hand, and gripped the constable's. At last, he'd gained Pearson's confidence after a rocky beginning. "Thanks. And don't forget to call me when you've made up your mind."

Pearson released his grip. "Yeah, yeah. Go, otherwise I'll change my mind on the spot."

Christian snatched the bag from the floor and marched for the door. With a quick head turn he glanced over his shoulder as Pearson returned to his desk to grab his jacket and keys. Christian walked through the door and muttered under his breath, "Damn him."

CHAPTER 26

THE DOOR TO THE INTERROGATION ROOM
swung open and Pearson stood face-to-face with the monster
who hours ago he'd fingered as the man who slaughtered his
own flesh and blood. After a hot shower and an hour of sleep,
he walked in with a different attitude. Their eyes locked, and
Liam glared at the constable.

Pearson released his grip, and the door creaked until the
metal latch clanked against the jamb. He lingered near the
doorway, and his eyes fixated on the empty shell of a man
who was once full of soul, except now he more resembled
someone who just lost everything.

With a smirk written across his face, Pearson strolled
toward the table, pulled out the metal chair, and plopped

down. Even though Pearson would never admit it, Christian was right about telling him to take a few hours to worry about himself.

With the stench of rotted sweat replaced with the aroma of lemongrass and rosemary, the dark bags beneath his eyes all but a memory, and an alert mind, there was nothing preventing him from confronting Liam. Not only was he determined to get to the truth surrounding what happened to Cassidy, but with the new evidence Christian retrieved, he was certain he had enough to tie Sarah Anderson and Gemma into everything.

They exchanged no words, only an array of facial expressions and plenty of deep breaths, which in a silent room became amplified. Pearson slid the stack of files and the journal aside and plucked the top folder, making it obvious which folder he had. In bold letters on the label affixed to the tab at the top was a familiar name: *Liam Williams.*

Pearson flicked open the file and cleared the tickle in the back of his throat.

"Good morning," he said.

Liam turned his gaze away.

"How'd you sleep last night? Those are fresh mattresses donated just last month," Pearson continued.

The silence persisted.

Pearson shut the cover of the folder and folded his hands out in front of him. "You don't have to talk; that's your right. But I am required to ask if you've obtained legal counsel."

Liam resumed his glare and shook his head.

"Okay. Do you need legal counsel?"

Again, Liam signaled he did not.

"Then let's begin. And a heads-up: by law I must record our conversation both visually and audibly. Do you have any objections?"

Liam grunted and stroked his beard.

"Is that a yes or no, Mr. Williams?"

"Start the damn recorder."

Pearson pressed the record button on the tape recorder. "My name is Constable Lucas Pearson. The time is 2:40 in the afternoon on Tuesday, the fourth of February, 2020. I'm joined today, in interrogation room B of the Cedar Lake RCMP detachment, by the accused, Liam Williams. For the record, please state your full name, address, and date of birth."

A boisterous sigh vacated Liam's mouth. "Liam Scott Williams. I live at 105 First Street West." He paused.

"And your date of birth, Mr. Williams?"

"January 9, 1960."

"Again, I advise you I am questioning you under caution. I have given you an opportunity to obtain legal counsel; however, you have declined to do so. Is this correct?"

Liam nodded.

"For the record, I will need a yes or no."

"Yes."

"And you fully understand your rights under the Charter of Rights and Freedoms as I have explained them to you?"

"I understand."

"Perfect. Liam Williams, I am charging you with attempted murder in connection with the shooting of Charles White on the evening of the third of February. Do you recall this incident?"

"Yes."

"I'll get straight to the point. Why? Why'd you shoot him?"

Liam pursed his lips tighter together.

"And what makes that entire situation sadder, is the fact you shot an innocent man as your daughter lay a few feet away recovering."

Liam crossed his arms over his chest. "You know perfectly well why I did it."

"I do, but I need to hear your version."

"I assumed when you found Jason and his father that was the end for me."

"Did you have anything to do with their deaths?"

"No. I swear I didn't. I went by the house because Jason wasn't responding. When I walked in I found them both dead. I got the hell out of there as fast as I could."

Pearson twirled the pen. "And you shot Charles White . . . because?"

Liam shrugged. "It was an accident. The gun just went off. I wasn't going to shoot anyone, that wasn't my intention. I just wanted to get away."

Pearson tapped his pen against the table. "I see. Well, let me lay out what I have on you. First, we have enough evidence to finger you as an accomplice in the kidnapping of Gemma. Second, the attempted murder of Charles White. Anything else you want to own up to?"

"I—" Liam said as his voice trailed off.

"Oh, and before I forget: We're also charging you in the murder of your daughter. Care to tell me how a loving father goes off the rails so much that he'd murder his own flesh and blood?"

Liam leaned forward and lowered his face into his hands. He kept his mouth shut, except for the audible rapid breaths he exhaled. Pearson shuffled the folder but his razor-sharp eyes never wavered away from Liam.

Eventually, he pulled his hands away and tears streamed down his flushed face. Whether those tears were genuine or not, Pearson had yet to determine.

"Why are you so emotional over this? Can I assume it's a sign of remorse? Or is it because you got caught?"

Liam squeezed his eyes closed to avoid having to stare at Constable Pearson directly in the eyes.

"Liam. Unless you tell me something, I have no choice other than to tack on the murder charge. Now is your time to explain what happened."

Liam's mouth twitched, but nothing came out. Pearson wrinkled his forehead. *Is he talking to me, or himself?*

Then his lips stopped moving and he opened his eyes. He took a deep breath, and as he wiped away the wetness from his cheeks, he blurted out one of the answers Pearson waited to hear. "I did it."

Stunned, Pearson delved further. "You did *what?*"

"I killed her. I strangled her and buried her alongside the railroad tracks."

"And Gemma?"

His head bobbed. "I set it all up with Jason Nelson's help."

The pen dropped from the constable's hand, his eyes widened, and he rested his elbows against the cold metal table. There was still one question left unanswered. "Why?"

Liam turned away. "You wouldn't understand. You probably think I'm a monster, but I'm not. I'm truly not."

"Don't assume I won't understand. And no, I don't think you're a monster. In fact, I think it takes a special sort of person to murder one of his own. Man, I can't imagine the pent-up rage that flowed through your head when you snuffed her life."

"I didn't want to. But that ungrateful tramp left me no other choice."

Pearson sifted through the files and pulled out Sarah Anderson's case file from 1995 and flipped open the cover. Pinned inside to the first page was a five-by-seven photo of the breathtaking woman Liam wanted to spend the rest of his life with, or at least those were the desires he'd expressed during his interview.

Liam squirmed in his seat, occasionally glancing over at the photo laid out in front of him. A haunting reminder of the life he missed out on so many years ago. The tears that had subsided minutes earlier flowed again like a geyser, and for the first time since everything began, empathy filled Pearson's heart.

"Tell me more about you and Sarah. How long had your affair lasted?"

"Only a few months. We weren't supposed to fall in love. But you can't stop things from happening, no matter how hard you try."

"I understand. I do. Believe me if you want, but I was married once," Pearson said.

"You? I thought you were a habitual bachelor, from talk around town."

"That's what I want people to believe. Nowadays, I stay focused more on work than anything else."

The tears stopped again. "So, what happened?"

"I found myself in a local bar in Moose Jaw one night. Same depressing story you hear from everyone. I went to drink away my depressing life. Then, out of nowhere, this pretty, younger version of my wife nestles up at the barstool next to me. She made small talk, then upped the ante. Two more drinks and next thing I know we're back at her place."

"And? Did you seal the deal?"

Pearson nodded. "Biggest regret of my life. And you know why?"

Liam shrugged.

"Consequently, this girl and my wife were friends. And the next day, my wife confronted me with pictures and details. Not a chance in hell I could lie my way out of that one."

"So, what you're saying is you understand what I endured?"

"I do. But I have one final question I need an answer to."

"Okay."

"Did you have anything to do with Sarah's disappearance?"

He forcefully shook his head. "Wasn't me. I swear."

"You have no idea what happened to the woman you had been sleeping with for months? Well, lucky for you, I got my hands on her journal from around the time the two of you were carrying on."

"Proves nothing."

"Proves plenty. What happened? Did she tell your wife about your affair?"

"No," Liam shouted.

"Oh, right. Perhaps Cassidy blabbed your secret?"

C. L. BREES

Guilt crept into Liam's mind and he glanced away from Constable Pearson.

Pearson, growing tired of the disrespect, returned to his forceful self and slammed his hand on the table. "Look at me when I'm talking to you."

"I don't know what happened to her. I swear."

"If that were true, then Cassidy would still be alive, and Gemma wouldn't be holed up in some cheap motel recovering from what you allowed that goon, Jason, to do to her."

"You don't know what you're talking about."

"I think I do. Let me tell you a tale. A tale about romance, greed, jealousy, and revenge."

"Jesus, so dramatic," Liam replied.

"Here's what I think happened. On the evening of the twelfth of April, back in 1995, your wife was at work, so you had your sweetheart over for a bit of fun after you tucked the kids into bed."

Liam slouched in the chair. "If you say so."

"There was one little problem, though: Cassidy. She woke up and found Sarah sneaking out the door and she saw red. She confronted her at the door, they exchanged words. Did you know about that?"

"No."

Pearson grabbed the journal and flipped to the last entry. "Says here, and I quote, 'She told me she knew about me and her father. She got right up in my face and the smoldering in her eyes sent shivers down my spine. I'm worried now. Worried she may do something to break this up. Worse, I'm scared she might do something to me.'"

300

"So? Are you saying you think Cassidy did something to her?"

"What I'm saying is, you were well aware Cassidy had insider information into your affair all along. Here's the interesting thing about traumatic memories: kids do anything and everything to bury those memories as far down as possible. Probably why people always say kids are resilient. But years went by, and then came the drinking, then drugs, until one day all of those unpleasant recollections found their way to the surface."

"You're crazy."

"No, far from it. Cassidy murdered Sarah, and you either helped her cover it up or—" He stopped. Something wasn't adding up.

"I didn't help her cover up anything. I didn't know. I *really* didn't know."

Pearson fell back in his chair. "You're right. You didn't know—back then—but then Cassidy overdosed, and you sent her away. And for once she got the help she needed. She was free of all those vile toxins and she remembered the thing she did twenty-four years ago. She called you and wanted to come clean about all the wrongs she had done in her past. Yeah, now everything makes sense."

"Care to enlighten me?"

"There was an entry in Cassidy's journal, near the time before her overdose. She keeps saying she can't get the image of that woman's face out of her mind. She remembered what happened and must have told you when you stopped in to visit her at the rehab center."

"Where's your proof?"

"Oh, I have enough to hold you here until a judge arraigns you. And as far as proof about Cassidy, that's as easy as getting a subpoena of her visitation records. What are the chances your name will be there on multiple occasions in the last few weeks?"

Liam crossed his arms over his chest.

"Did she tell you what she did with the body?"

Liam refused to give him the satisfaction of knowing he'd figured everything out.

Pearson smirked and scooted the chair away from the table. "Make yourself comfortable. We're not through. The time is 3:20 PM and we are taking a quick break."

He pressed stop on the recorder and walked toward the door. Once he was outside in the hallway, Christian exited the observation room.

"Impressive interrogation skills."

"Years of practice, I suppose," Pearson said as he placed his hand on Christian's shoulder. "Let's chat in the other room."

CHAPTER 27

AS PEARSON AND CHRISTIAN RETURNED TO the office to calculate their next move, the door swung open, and in burst Constable Miller, swinging a plastic evidence bag with a DVD case inside.

"Miller, what the hell?" Pearson asked.

"You were right."

"About?"

"We found this mixed in with the DVD collection at the house."

"Better not just be some illegal copy of *The Little Mermaid* or something," he joked.

"No, it's serious. Just take a look at what is written on the back."

Miller handed over the bag and Pearson lifted it toward the light. He studied every corner from the front to the back, and written in a crude fashion was one word: *Confession.*

Pearson pushed Christian aside, ran for his desk, and scooted the chair away so hard his rear end nearly missed the seat when he flopped down. Everyone huddled behind him as he reached for the scissors tucked away in his messy drawer, and Christian spoke up.

"Wait, stop."

Every eye in the room stared him up and down.

"Are you an expert in digital forensics?"

Then all eyes shifted to Pearson, who clutched the bag. "No."

"If you break the seal, Liam's lawyer can easily claim you manipulated the video."

"He hasn't requested one."

"Doesn't matter. He may later on, right?"

Pearson huffed. "Anderson, take a hard look around. Do you see a resident forensics person on staff?"

Christian scanned the room to appease Pearson. "Nope. But lucky for you there is one right down the road. So, drop the scissors before you do something we can't undo."

The bag and scissors crashed onto the desktop. "So, get him here. Time's running out and I need something other than theories to coerce a confession out of him."

❖

ADAM SITUATED HIMSELF IN THE LUMPY chair in the observation room. Pearson, Christian, and Constable Miller flanked each side of the table and watched as he signed the evidence bag and cut open the seal. He slid out the case and inserted the DVD into the computer.

Adam clicked a few keys and rested his back against the chair. "Better grab some coffee and check on Gemma. This may take a while before the copy is finished."

While Pearson and Miller left, Christian pulled out a chair and sat next to him. "Thanks for taking care of Gemma."

"Yeah, she's been filling me in on your life."

"I'm sure she has. And another thing—"

A long pause ensued. "What?"

"Thanks for helping me realize I don't have to live in the shadows anymore and for coming to handle this computer stuff."

"I mean, if we're going to continue dating, it's better if we're both honest about who we are with everyone."

"True."

"And this computer stuff is outside Pearson's realm."

"And we can't afford any mistakes."

Adam glanced up from the keyboard. "Don't get all holier than thou, this stuff is outside your comprehension too."

"Touché."

Ten minutes passed and the door opened. "So, you make any progress?"

"Ready when you guys are."

Adam had the video queued, and when everyone was in place, he pressed play. The lighting was dim, but with some manipulation, Adam tweaked the contrast and the picture brightened. There was no audio and Christian crinkled his eyes.

"Check the speakers."

A few adjustments later, a feminine sob blasted through the speakers. The video autofocused, and the bloodied face of Cassidy entered the frame. Christian gasped and both of his hands reached up to cover his mouth.

"What the—" Pearson began.

"Shh."

The camera shook, then stabilized as a shadowy figure walked toward her and squatted at the petrified girl's feet. With their back toward the camera, it wasn't clear who the masked individual was, but given the height and build, it was safe to say it was a man.

Seconds later, the person spoke, which confirmed everyone's suspicion.

"You're an unruly girl," the man said. His gloved hand extended, and he brushed the leather along her cheekbone.

"Let me go," she blurted.

"You know what you did, don't you?"

Her sobs grew louder. "No. Why are you doing this?"

Then the shadow figure pulled a necklace from his pocket and dangled it in front of her face. "You took my love away—the woman I was meant to spend the remainder of my life with."

"Who? Who are you talking about?"

"Sarah."

Adam paused the video and glanced up at Christian.

"Why'd you stop?"

"That necklace. Jason had the same one clutched in his hand when we found him in his bedroom."

"Good eye," Pearson said.

"As if the text messages weren't enough, this certainly ties Jason and whoever this guy is."

He pressed play and the video resumed. The sobbing quickly stopped the moment the name from the past crossed the man's lips. Then her fear subsided, and a smirk graced her face. "Sarah Anderson?"

The man peeled away his mask. Even from the back, the distinctive beard and nose gave away his identity.

Under his breath, Christian mumbled, "Liam."

"You murdered the only woman I ever loved."

A mix of sheer terror and evilness painted Cassidy's face and she struggled to get her words out. "D-dad?"

Liam made no other comments. He stood, whipped out a hemp rope from his jacket pocket, and with patience strolled behind his daughter.

Adam's hand shook as he clicked pause. His head whipped over his shoulders, and he took in the range of facial expressions staring at the monitor. "It's pretty clear what's about to happen. Do we keep going?"

Christian pried his lips apart and stuttered. "I. We have enough. We don't need to sit here and watch this man murder his daughter. No, you can turn it off."

Pearson interjected. "Christian. The word written on the back of the case said 'confession.' I haven't heard a confession . . . have you?"

"He has a valid point," Adam replied.

With a huff, Christian turned around. "Well, go on, then. Press play."

Christian faced the two-way mirror that looked in on interrogation room B, where Liam's head rested on the metal tabletop. As the screaming, choking, and gasping for help continued, Christian closed his eyes and hummed in his head to drown out the morbid howls. Then the screaming subsided, and as Cassidy gasped for air, he swung around and faced the monitor once again.

"Now that you know I mean business, you're going to give me details," Liam said.

"Okay, I'll tell you what you want to hear," she began. "I did it. I killed your beloved Sarah."

Liam raised his hand and smacked her across the face. "Worthless junkie. What'd you do to her?"

Her head cocked around. "I'll tell you if you promise to let me go."

Over the years, Christian had witnessed countless domestic assaults, parent-child issues, and stood face-to-face with pure evil itself. But this? This was viler than anything he'd ever experienced. The showdown resumed. "You'll tell me regardless."

Liam kept the rope tight against her neck and turned her face toward the camera. "Now . . . what did you do to her?"

"What do you think?"

The power in his voice strengthened as he gave another tug on the rope. "Tell me what you did, or I swear to God."

Her legs flailed and her gasps for air sent Christian's pacing into overdrive. Again, Liam loosened the makeshift garrote, and she blurted out. "Okay. Okay. I caught her leaving the house one night and I confronted her."

"When?"

"The night before she vanished."

"Where is she?"

"I didn't mean to, but when she came back the next morning with her car packed, she tried to fight me. I grabbed a knife from the kitchen and she just walked into it."

He didn't let up and repeated his previous question. "Where is she?"

"Does it matter?"

He yanked again. "It matters because I loved her."

"Did you think I was about to let your sleazy affair break up our family?"

Liam turned away from the camera and whipped the rope away from her neck. With the rope dangling at his side, he paced behind her, trying to process how an innocent affair got so out of hand.

She caught her breath and continued on. "It's all your fault I turned out the way I did. You. You never loved Mom, or me, or Gemma. You only loved yourself and *that* bitch."

Liam gritted his teeth together and snapped back. "You know that's a straight-out lie. I love you all. How can you justify murdering a woman because we had an affair?"

She remained quiet.

"No, you only have yourself to blame for the poor life choices you made, Cassidy. You. And you alone."

"If you had stayed faithful to Mom, I wouldn't have had to kill her. And if I hadn't killed her, then I wouldn't have needed to turn to drugs to numb my pain away."

Christian mumbled under his breath and Adam paused the video. "What was that?"

"It's just—all these years I speculated about what happened. And in the course of four days we've gone from searching for a victim, to linking my mom in on this, to exposing our victim as not the sweet, innocent girl we all thought she was. This is . . . this is—"

"Upsetting?" Adam asked.

Pearson threw in his two cents. "A sense of relief?"

"I—I can't explain. But this video, this back-and-forth. It makes my skin crawl."

Pearson patted him on the back. "You're ghost white, my friend. Maybe you could use a break, you know, check on Gemma."

Christian nodded. "Yeah, I think some fresh air would do me good." He wandered toward the door and turned his head over his shoulder. "If she reveals where she buried my mom's body . . ."

"You'll be the first to know, Christian," Adam said.

"Thanks."

He pulled the door closed and scanned both ends of the deserted hallway. With his hand still firmly gripping the door handle, his back fell against the wall. Even though the investigation took a different course down a dark path, one Christian never expected, there was some truth to what Pearson said.

After four days of nonstop twists and turns, a sense of relief was an understatement. The truth about every repressed secret had simmered to the surface, and for the first time, he had answers to all of his one-sided questions. And they were the first step in allowing him to make peace with the past.

Now came the duty of catching Gemma up on where things stood. He sighed and released his hand from the handle. He took two steps and stopped.

How am I going to put this? Screw it, I'll just wing it.

He marched full speed ahead, and as he rounded the corner, there sat Gemma at Pearson's desk with her nose in her phone. She glanced up and gave him a half smile.

"So? Any news?"

Christian didn't say a word. Instead, he walked around the desk and reached out his arms, pulling her in close to him. His lack of a response was plenty of response, and it was all Gemma needed to fly off the handle.

"He murdered my sister—his own daughter—didn't he?"

Christian kept her held tight, mainly to keep her from bolting down the hallway.

"Answer me. Did he kill her? Or not?" she asked, this time with a touch of hostility.

"I couldn't stomach to watch the entire video. But, yeah, he had his hand in everything. He murdered her and arranged your kidnapping."

"I . . . wow. How can this be? Why? Why would he do this?"

Christian loosened his grip and planted his backside on the edge of the desk. "Why does *anyone* murder?"

She shrugged. "Love? Greed? Money? Aren't those the biggest culprits?"

He nodded. "Well, in this case, all three of those with a dash of heartbreak are to blame."

When what Christian insinuated sank in, her eyes widened. "This has to do with what happened to your mom. Huh?"

He turned his head away and nibbled at his lower lip.

"For the love of God, Christian, tell me."

His head swung back, and their eyes met. He swallowed hard. "Cassidy murdered my mother. She made a full confession on video."

"Damn. And now all of those journal entries make perfect sense. The whole time we assumed Cassidy *saw* her murder, when in fact she did it."

Christian nodded.

"I don't know what to say. I wish there was something I could do other than say I'm sorry."

"None of this is your fault, nor is it mine. For Christ's sake, we were four when she murdered her. What on earth could we have done to stop it?"

"I know, I know. Knowing it doesn't make this any easier to process, though."

Christian wiped his hands across his tired face and looked up at his best friend. Her eyes met his and she reached out her hand and grabbed his.

"What happens now?"

"Pearson will go back in with the evidence. Your dad will more than likely make a full confession to her murder and your kidnapping. Then he'll be arraigned. After that, either he'll go to trial or straight to sentencing."

"And me? What happens to me?"

"What do you want to happen? Do you want to stay here in Cedar Lake? Or, perhaps this is a sign you're destined for bigger and better things."

"Like what?"

"Like, maybe for once, just once in your life, you can stop worrying about what could go wrong and trust everything will go right. And nothing is going to go right until you get the hell out this town."

She bowed her head. "I don't know, Christian. This is the only place I've ever known. Where would I go? What would I do?"

Christian stood from the edge of the desk and squatted to her level. He gripped her hands in his and lifted her chin. "You can come with me. I have a spare room you can rent until you get on your feet."

"No, I can't—rent is too much and I have no money."

"Yes, you can. I think you can afford to pay a dollar a month until you get a job. Then, if you want to stay longer, we'll renegotiate."

"You'd do that? For me?"

"Why wouldn't I? You're only my closest friend. And I know what you're thinking: 'I'll only be in your way.' Well, you won't. Besides, there's more opportunity for you in Regina than there ever will be if you stay here."

"Doing what? I have no degree, no professional work history. Who'd hire someone like me?"

"We'll figure things out. Gemma, believe me, leaving this place back then was the best things I ever did."

She hesitated, and just as she was about to reply to his proposal, a commotion erupted down the hallway. Christian released her hand and raced over.

"What's going on?" he asked.

Constable Miller led Liam down the corridor, and Pearson turned his head. "We know where she is."

"My mother?"

Pearson nodded as Christian's jaw dropped. Was it possible, after twenty-four years of wondering, that Christian would have his long-awaited opportunity to say goodbye?

"Where is she?"

"Closer than you think."

Gemma appeared out of the shadows, and the first thing she saw wasn't Christian, or Pearson. It was her father. She screamed. Nothing coherent, just an earsplitting scream, and she charged down the hallway, past the four constables huddled together.

If it wasn't for Pearson and his catlike reflexes, things could have been much worse. His muscular arm blocked her from getting any farther, and he pulled her toward him. Her hands flailed, and she kicked and dropped the f-bomb like a noun, verb, and everything in between.

Through her bouts of tears, she cried out. "I hope you rot in hell. How could you murder her? And then try to murder me? You're not a father, you're a monster."

Pearson kept her held tight against his chest while Christian stroked her hair in an attempt to quell the rage that exploded from the petite girl. "Gemma, get ahold of yourself," Christian said.

His pleas fell on deaf ears. She carried on, all while Constable Miller stood in front of Liam to block him in the event she broke loose from Pearson's grip.

Liam shouted back. "I should have finished the job while I had the chance."

Pearson had heard enough and he unleashed his anger on Miller. "Get this scum out of here."

Being an obedient novice constable, Miller shoved Liam through a door that led to the holding cells and Christian yanked her arm and dragged her back into the office.

Christian shook her. Whatever demon had possessed her body, he had to break her free from it. In spite his attempts,

314

the repressed rage controlled her unlike anything he had ever witnessed. Two more shakes and she snapped to.

"I hate him. How could that asshole do this to our family?"

Christian held her in his arms, and soon the adrenaline subsided, and a stream of tears replaced her fury.

"I know you hate him. I hate him too. But right now, I need you to chill out for two minutes. Can you do that for me?"

She whimpered but bobbed her head as he led her to Pearson's desk. She lowered herself into the chair and wiped away the salty moisture from her cheeks. Constable Pearson and Adam approached.

"Forensics team will arrive in about ninety minutes, give or take. You don't mind if I commandeer Adam to assist me with securing the scene while we wait, do you?"

"He's all yours. I'll get her back to the motel and give my dad a call. If there's one person who can settle her down, for some unknown reason, it's my father."

"You positive everything's under control?" Pearson asked.

He glanced down at Gemma, whose face remained buried in her hands and the sobbing intensified. "Yeah, I can take things from here. You two go but keep me updated on what's going on."

"Aye aye, captain."

"Ah, by the way, you never mentioned where she buried her."

They exchanged glances, and Adam gave his approval with a head nod. "Might as well tell him. We both know if we don't, he'll follow us anyway."

"Yup. He will," Pearson agreed.

"Cassidy buried her in their backyard under the shed and then drove her car out to the lake and pushed it in."

Gemma raised her head and choked back the tears. "Excuse me?"

Pearson threw his hands in the air at her brunt tone. "Gemma, I'm only the messenger. If Cassidy says she buried her under the shed, then we have to check it out."

"There has to be some sort of mistake."

Christian planted his hand on her shoulder. "Gemma, please. Why would Constable Pearson or Adam lie about something this serious?"

"I don't know."

"Exactly. Maybe Cassidy just said it in hopes they'd let her go. There's no guarantee she's even there."

He glanced at his watch.

"All right, it's quarter to one. Still a few good hours of daylight left."

Christian waved his hand. "Go. Miller can hold down the fort."

With a smirk, Pearson opened the door. "We'll be in touch."

CHAPTER 28

ADAM TIED OFF THE LAST BIT of police tape around a fence post and rejoined Pearson as he studied the shed.

"Whatcha thinking?" Adam asked.

"How happy I am I never allowed my affair to ever go beyond one night. This is the shit you read about but never expect to happen in a small town like Cedar Lake."

"Have you ever come across something so twisted over the years you've been doing this?" Adam asked.

He shook his head. "Not this twisted."

"Me neither. I suppose real love drives you to do some weird things. How do you think I ended up here?"

Pearson grinned. "You *really* do love him—don't you?"

Adam ran his fingers through his hair and pinched his thumb and index finger closely together. "Maybe just a little. Can I tell you something and know it'll stay between you and me?"

Pearson nodded and pulled his jacket closer to the scruff of his neck. "More secrets, huh?"

"Not a secret, per se, more like an omission. If Christian knew, it would break his heart."

"Gotcha. Your omission is safe with me."

"Before I arrived here, my intention was to keep our relationship casual. You know, low-key with no demands on one another, but now—after seeing him in the hospital bed. I knew I was in this for the long haul."

Pearson interrupted. "Your feelings got the better of you?"

"So, you get what I'm saying?"

"I do. Believe me when I tell you this. Christian, he's a respectable guy. A bit stubborn, but regardless, you won't find another guy like him anywhere."

"How can you be so sure?"

"Hard to explain. I just *feel* it."

"So, since you have him all mapped out, explain this one: If we find his mother's remains tonight, how's he going to react?"

"Let's flip the script. How would you react if someone admitted to murdering and burying your mother in their backyard?" Pearson asked.

Adam shrugged. "I can't say. But Christian, he's been without her since he was four years old. And now that I have the backstory on his father, it seems like he had no one and raised himself."

"Prescott, you're avoiding the main question."

"How do I think I'd be? My whole world would stop. However, if something *did* happen to my family, it would be unexpected. Christian, well, he's had more than two decades to prepare for this day. But I don't want to compare my life to his."

"Yeah, pretty hard to compare."

"Even so, he's resilient. A fighter. And I'll be there for him through all of this."

Pearson's grin broadened. "That's what I like to hear. On the positive side, he'll mentally get the closure he needs, but there's a long road ahead. Even though he'll never admit it, he's not fully healed physically. He'll need time."

Adam smacked his lips. "You got that right. I know he'll be right back at it the day after we get back. But I'm going to make him take a week or two."

"You guys will survive."

"We will."

"All right, enough with the depressing talk. Where the hell is this forensics team?"

"Beats me. Should be here any minute, though."

They waited, with only the howling wind blasting through the trees to give them something other than their voices to listen to for a change. Adam checked his phone, hoping to see a message from Christian, but nothing.

As he slipped the iPhone back into his jacket pocket, the first van appeared followed by another towing a backhoe. The doors opened in sync, like something you'd see in an action movie, and six bodies exited dressed from head to toe in white Tyvek suits.

Pearson leaned closer to Adam and whispered over the wind. "And so it begins."

The leader of the pack, an older gentleman with a hint of gray along his temples, advanced as they shivered in the cold.

"Constable Pearson?" he asked, unsure of who was who.

Pearson half-raised his hand. "Yup, that's me."

"DS Clark with the Saskatoon Police Service." He extended his hand and the two men shook.

"Thanks for getting here so quick."

"Not a problem. We're always happy to assist the RCMP when we can. I've been read in on the situation. You believe a body to be buried beneath a shed and a car to be at the bottom of Cedar Lake?"

He nodded. "We have a video confession in which the suspect stated she buried the victim here twenty-four years ago."

"Right," he began as his head tilted upward at the sky. "Well, given the weather and the fact we need to dismantle the shed, no promises on this being quick."

Pearson glanced over at Adam, who had scampered off to sign the investigators into the crime scene. "Take your time. We've got all night if need be."

"All right, they're eager to get started. Why don't you two get warm. My team can handle things from here."

"Thanks. If you need us, you know where we'll be."

With the last person signed in, Pearson and Adam scurried through the heavy snow back to the shelter of the SUV. The doors slammed closed and Pearson cranked over the engine. Adam stared at the picture of him and Christian on the home screen of his iPhone.

A raspy sigh leaked from his mouth, and Adam raised the million-dollar question. "You think they'll find her?"

"Only time will tell."

Adam unlocked his phone and flipped through the photo album from their trip to Banff only two months earlier. With each swipe Pearson's eyes shifted.

"If you miss him, you should call him."

"Nah. I said I'd call when we had some information."

He cut off the screen and slipped the phone back into his jacket. Then a knock at the frosted-over driver's-side window startled them.

Pearson cracked the window, and an older lady wrapped in a heavy parka with a wool scarf wrapped over her head stepped back.

"Can I help you, ma'am?" he asked.

"You the police?" she asked.

"We are. Is something wrong?"

"Not wrong. Just curious what's going on? Been lots of you in and out of Liam's place all day. He in some sort of trouble?"

"It's an active investigation, ma'am, so I'm not at liberty to say. Are you a neighbor?"

She nodded.

"Mind if we ask you a few questions?"

"Sure."

Pearson unlocked the doors. "Hop in."

The elderly woman yanked open the door and slid into the seat. With a quick brush, a clump of snow fell to the floor. "Whatcha want to know?"

"How long have you known the Williams family?"

"Oh my, as far back as I can remember. At least thirty years."

"That's a long time. In those years, have you ever seen anything suspicious?"

"How so?"

"For instance, ever see anybody coming and going who didn't belong?"

She scoffed. "I've seen more than one should over the last thirty years. These past five I have to say were the worst. That daughter of theirs, oh, what is her name—"

"Cassidy?" Adam asked.

Her eyes lit up. "Yes. Cassidy. She had a great deal of shady characters here. And her worthless boyfriend, Charles. Don't even get me started on him."

"Yeah, he's a piece of work. I'm curious about someone else from longer ago. Say, twenty-four years."

Without missing a beat, the elderly woman cut in. "Sarah. You're talking about Sarah Anderson, aren't you?"

"And why would you ask that?"

"Come on, I knew about their affair. Hell, the whole block knew."

"And Liam's wife—did she have any idea?"

She scanned the floorboard. "No. We never said anything."

"Why not?"

She pushed her black-rimmed cat-eyed glasses up the bridge of her nose and scrunched her face. "Young man, back in those days you minded your own business. Not like today where everywhere you look someone is airing their dirty laundry for the entire world to see."

"True. Do you ever wonder what became of her?"

"Of course. I remember the day the whole town combed the fields and forests around for days. But then Matthias came forward and said he got a letter from her. She wrote she was safe in Calgary. I mean, we didn't have no reason to question his honesty."

"Of course not, Miss . . . ?"

"Ms. Thompson."

Adam spoke up. "Ms. Thompson, did you ever by chance see anything strange in the Williamses' backyard?"

Her eyes scanned up. "Can't say I did. The only thing they ever did back there was build that blasted shed. Come to think of it, it was about the time Sarah disappeared."

"Had they already broken ground before Sarah vanished, or after?"

"Oh, before. I remember plain as day since they knocked part of my fence over. Liam was apologetic about the mishap, and I let it go. He even went as far as to pay to replace my whole fence, not just the part he knocked over."

Pearson exchanged a glance with Adam—he was more certain now than before they arrived they would find Sarah's body this evening. Pearson returned his attention to the backseat, where Ms. Thompson's eyes scanned the floorboard once more.

"Ms. Thompson, you've been a great source of information. Is there anything else you think we should know?"

She took a moment to ponder. "No, I've said too much already."

"No, ma'am, quite the opposite. You provided us with an important fact. Listen, you get on home now and try to keep warm, okay?"

Her eyes narrowed as she reached for the door handle. "You sure you can't tell me why there's people dressed like astronauts in his backyard?"

Pearson's brows drew together, but he maintained his pleasant tone. "No, ma'am. I'm certain you'll read all about this on the front page of the newspaper in a few days. Can one of us offer you an escort back home?"

The nosy woman sighed. "I can manage on my own, thank you very much."

The door swung open for less than three seconds as Ms. Thompson exited, but in that miniscule amount of time, a blast of bitterly cold air made its way inside the vehicle. Adam rubbed his hands together in an attempt to warm himself.

"Well, isn't she, um, interesting."

A broad grin adorned Pearson's face. "The nosy old crow did prove a point, though."

"What? That elderly people have nothing better to do with their time than snoop on their neighbors?"

"You're a funny guy. No. She confirmed why no one ever questioned why Liam had a fresh hole in the ground. The entire block knew he was about to build a shed."

"Ahh," Adam said. "So, you think Cassidy had the murder planned out the entire time?"

"I hate to say this, but, yeah, I do. No way this was a heat-of-the-moment sort of thing."

⌗

TWO HOURS PASSED AND STILL NO word from DS Clark or anyone from his team. The clouds cleared an hour earlier, and now the sun hovered in the horizon. Daylight was fading, and Pearson nibbled at his fingernails while Adam responded to a growing list of unread messages from concerned colleagues.

A brisk movement from the driveway caught Pearson's attention and he slapped Adam against the shoulder. "Hey, maybe he's bringing news?"

Adam pressed send and tossed his phone onto the dashboard.

"He doesn't seem happy."

Pearson turned off the engine and opened the door. "Only one way to find out. Let's go."

They exited the vehicle and the flash-frozen snow crunched beneath their feet as they approached DS Clark.

"What's the word?" Pearson shouted.

"You were right. Along with some bones, we found a purse," DS Clark said as he dangled an evidence bag in front of him. "Also found this."

Pearson fetched a fresh pair of latex gloves from his pocket and slipped them over his hands.

"That can't be what I think it is, can it?"

Clark nodded. "If your victim was a Mrs. Sarah Anderson of Cedar Lake, then, yeah, it's what you think."

"My God," Adam blurted.

Pearson's jaw remained ajar as he reached out and seized the plastic bag. He swung it around until his eyes fixated on the image on the front of the identification card. "It's her. It's *really* her."

Adam leaned in to get a closer look and he pulled away when he read the name. "I'll be damned."

"We're still sifting through the purse, but after decades of abuse, I'm not sure if anything in there will be helpful. I'll keep you posted."

Pearson handed the bag over. "I understand."

"Listen, the sun's setting, and we got a long way to go. You two should grab a coffee or something."

"I think we have another place to visit first."

"You have a number I can reach you at, Constable Pearson?"

He dug into his pocket and pulled out a business card. "Cell number is on the back."

DS Clark tapped the card in his hand before he turned and walked away.

Once the forensic investigator was far enough away, Adam released his breath and choked on his words.

"Yeah, exactly. Now, do you want to deliver the news, or shall I?"

CHAPTER 29

A RAP AT THE DOOR AROUSED Christian just as his heavy eyelids closed and his head fell forward. He shook himself awake and scampered to the door, where two familiar faces stood on the opposite side of the peephole.

He unbolted the door faster than he ever had, and when the door swung inward, the first words out of Christian's mouth weren't hello. Instead, he blurted out, "Did they find her?"

Adam crossed over the threshold first, and Pearson followed behind. "Before I say anything, you better sit for this."

"I don't want to sit. I want to know if you found my mother."

Adam's lower lip quivered. "I can't say with one-hundred-percent certainty, but a body has been found. The team also found a purse and an identification card."

Christian's knees buckled and he dropped to the ground. Matthias raced to his son's side and wrapped his arm around him.

"It was Sarah's ID, wasn't it?" Matthias asked.

Pearson supplied a simple nod while Christian gasped for air from the shock. Matthias rubbed his hand in a circular motion against his son's back, and after a moment, Christian turned his gaze upward.

"It's over. The twenty-four-year mystery is over. Isn't it?" Christian asked between breaths.

Pearson stepped in. "I imagine so. But let's not get ahead of the evidence. We still need to wait for the DNA results to be sure."

While everyone anticipated a long, drawn-out crying episode, to their shock, not a single tear shed from Christian. Instead, when the shock receded, he relaxed his face, and for the first time since they'd met, Adam saw the wheels of the healing process in motion.

Matthias planted his rear on the ground next to his son. "So, where do we go from here?"

"Liam's arraignment is scheduled for tomorrow morning. Then, we'll wait and see. I can guarantee you one thing—he won't be going anywhere any time soon."

"And the White clan? What'll happen to them?"

Pearson's lips slumped into a frown. "Well, with no real evidence of any wrongdoing and the fact Charles is still on a respirator, my hands are tied. But, believe me, I'll have my eyes on them. There's one thing drug dealers miscalculate, and that's their grandiose delusion they hold all the power."

"Their time is coming, Pop. I have complete confidence in Pearson. With him around, things around here are on the upswing."

"When will we be able to give her a proper burial?"

Pearson stared the gray-haired man straight in the eyes. "In a few weeks. There will be an autopsy, more evidence collection, and we have to await the DNA confirmation."

Christian squeezed his father's hand. "These things take time, Pop."

Matthias lifted his glasses and wiped away the tears that bubbled in his eyes. "And you'll come back for the funeral?"

"Pop, of course I will. I miss her every day."

Pearson crouched in front of Matthias. "Mr. Anderson, is there anything else I can answer for you?"

Matthias adjusted his glasses and glanced at Gemma, who sat on the edge of the bed, quiet and despondent. "There is one more thing. What happens to Gemma now? Surely you can't expect her to stay here with no family."

All eyes shifted toward the bed. She cleared her throat. "I told you, I can take care of myself."

Christian released his grip on his father, stood to his feet, and limped to the bed. He squeezed in as close to her as he could and grabbed her hand. "Even amongst this distorted thing we call humanity, the fate gods had intention when they brought you and me together. If you think, after all we've been through since elementary school, I'd leave you behind in this shithole to rot away, you're sorely mistaken."

"But, Christian, we've—"

His pitch raised an octave. "No buts. And I'm serious. Once Pearson releases the house, we'll go and gather your things."

She folded her arms across her chest and rolled her eyes like an annoyed teenager. "And then what?"

"And then, my friend, you're coming with me and Adam back to Regina so you can get started on your new life."

Her cheeks flushed, and she ousted her standoffish attitude. After a deep breath, she flung her arms around his neck. "You promise, no matter what, you'll be there for me through this?"

"Are you joking? Won't just be me," he said, and his eyes scanned the faces in the room. "We'll *all* be there for you."

Everyone in the room formed a semicircle around the bed, and one by one, each of them gave her words of encouragement and blessed the decision as the right one.

"Now, you better check on me occasionally. I see what happens when one frees themselves from the clutch of Cedar Lake," Matthias joked.

"Yeah, I mean, who's going to bring you those fresh pizzas a few nights a week now?"

He smiled. "Oh, Gemma. I'm in a better place now, and it's time I take care of me, and it's time you focus more on you for a change."

She glanced around at the friendly faces and her face lit up with genuine happiness. "You're right. To hell with Cedar Lake. I need to find myself."

Soon the celebration of moving forward faded and the reality of the challenges that awaited each of them sunk in. The banker box of evidence and witness statements still sat on the table, and Christian tapped at the top of the box.

"I suppose we've finished up with this."

"You want to do the honors?" Pearson asked, removing a black Sharpie marker from the breast pocket of his parka.

"I thought you'd never ask."

Christian uncapped the thick marker and across the front of the box, in oversized letters, he wrote the word most investigators long for: *CLOSED.*

PART 5

SIX MONTHS LATER

"When you bring peace to your past, you can move forward to your future."
Anonymous

CHAPTER 30

GEMMA ADJUSTED THE STRAP OF HER navy-blue cocktail dress as she slid into the front pew next to Matthias. She ran her fingers down the front to smooth out the wrinkles and glanced at her neighbor.

"Lovely day for a wedding, huh, Mr. Anderson?"

His eyes shimmered with happiness. "Sure is. You look amazing. I guess city life agrees with you."

"Eh, it's been an adjustment. But, as with anything worthwhile in life, it'll take time."

"And the new job? Still loving it?"

"Yeah. You know, pays the bills. And I received some news that's even more exciting than the job."

He leaned in as the organ music began playing. "Oh? Do tell."

"I got my acceptance letter in the mail yesterday."

"To college?"

She nodded. "I start classes in the fall. I'm going to follow through with my lifetime aspiration."

Matthias scratched his head. "I don't think I ever asked you what you wanted to be when you grew up."

"A nurse. I always wanted to go to nursing school since I was still in my training pants."

"Nursing school is a good fit for you. You're good with people. I'll say, Gemma, I'm impressed. Let this show you one thing."

"What's that?"

"You're never too old for a new start."

She clutched the older man's hand. "After everything I went through in Cedar Lake, Christian and Adam took me in. So I'm taking a page out of their playbook as a way to repay them for their compassion."

"What d'you mean?"

"They saved me from myself, and if I can save just one person, then Cassidy didn't die in vain."

Matthias grinned. "And this whole time you worried leaving was the end of the world."

"At the time, yeah, I did."

"But now? Now you see coming here was the better choice?"

A smile stretched across her face. "With my father's impending trial, this is the safest place I can be—as far away from him as possible."

Matthias pulled her in. The soothing instrumental music stopped, and all heads turned toward the rear of the sanctuary. A stream of sunlight filled the room, and the metal latch of the door clanked. Immediately, a hush fell over the audience.

Anticipation built and Gemma bounced up and down like a fangirl waiting on her favorite celebrity to make a grand entrance. Her hands quietly slapped together, and her lips stretched to the point that made her face hurt. "This is it. The moment we've all been waiting for."

The heavy door slammed closed and the thud echoed through the rafters. The suspense accumulated as a few minutes passed with no sign of either of them. The once silent room grew into a mix of low murmurs, head shakes, and panic-stricken faces.

The intro to "Somewhere Only We Know" commenced and the roars of chatter waned. Then, on opposite aisles of the chapel, Christian and Adam emerged. Outfitted from head to toe in matching black tuxes, they strolled in rhythm along the short path to the alter.

Sniffles behind her head diverted Gemma's attention away from her best friend. She rolled her head to the side and saw the man who only months earlier could barely find the strength to get out of bed, with his black-rimmed glasses in his hand. He quickly wiped away a tear and shoved his glasses back onto the bridge of his nose. He shot Gemma a smile, and she returned one. He reached out his hand and gripped hers.

The music faded and Christian and Adam stood at the front of the church, their hands interlocked in one another's. The pastor opened a book and his booming voice filled the room.

"Please be seated. On behalf of Christian and Adam, I welcome each of you on this special day."

The pastor carried on with the reading the couple chose, the same one Gemma warned against, and as she tuned out the boring passage, she leaned over and whispered in Matthias' ear. "I'm glad you made the trip. I know this isn't what you dreamed of for Christian, but I've never seen him so happy. And you can bet he appreciates your support."

"Yeah, not what I pictured years ago, but I like Adam and I'm happy if he's happy. I've had time to adapt, and while I'm not fully there yet, it's all worth it to have him back in my life."

She patted his hand. "That it is. I have faith you'll find the only thing that's changed is the person he's chosen to spend the rest of his life with."

The reading finished and Gemma pulled away.

"Christian, do you take Adam to be your life partner? Will you be honest with him and will you stand with him through whatever may come?"

Christian released a nervous laugh. "I will."

"And you, Adam, do you take Christian to be your life partner? Will you be honest with him and will you stand with him through whatever may come?"

"I will."

"Do you both promise to make the necessary adjustments in your lives so you may live in a harmonious commitment together?"

They exchanged smiles and turned toward the friends and family who eagerly awaited their response. They turned back toward each other.

"We do."

"Ladies and gentlemen, Christian and Adam have written their own vows, and at this time, I'll ask Christian to begin."

The pastor closed the book and stepped back to give the floor to the couple.

Christian's hand trembled and his face reddened. Public speaking had never been his strong suit. "Adam, from the moment we met my life has never been the same. Throughout all the years of feeling like I failed at finding my chance at love, you came along and showed me all I needed was to allow love to break through my impenetrable wall. And the moment you broke the barrier down, all those feelings didn't matter anymore."

Christian paused and a took a deep breath.

"You have no idea how happy I am for this opportunity to spend the rest of my life by your side. The day I realized it was true love was when you rescued me from Cedar Lake, during one of many rogue adventures."

The room filled with laughter and an adorning smile graced Adam's face as he rocked back and forth on the heels of his glossy black dress shoes.

"Christian. The moment you walked into my life I wasn't sure how things would turn out for us in the end. But the day I realized you were the one I wanted to marry was when I saw you laid up in the hospital. I never want to do things separate from here on out. My vow to you is to devote every moment, of every day, to caring about you more than myself, working hand in hand to build the life we both deserve, but best of all—we get to take on the world . . . together."

As the ceremony continued, Christian and Adam exchanged their rings. A thunderous ovation interrupted for a brief moment, and after the ruckus diminished, the pastor returned to his book.

"Christian and Adam, we have heard your promise to share your lives in marriage. By the power vested in me by the province of Saskatchewan, I now declare you married. You may seal your vows with a kiss."

The happy couple leaned into one another and their lips touched in a heartfelt moment. They interlocked fingers and lifted their hands into the air. The crowd jumped to their feet and the happy couple dashed down the stairs from the alter and down the aisle for the exit.

※

GEMMA SAT ALONE WITH HER HEELS dangling from her finger. She gazed around the room at the picturesque embellishments. Her foot bounced up and down waiting for her best friend and his new husband to arrive at the reception, which she imagined would be any moment. Out of the corner of her eye, a familiar face stood out amongst the strangers faces.

Pearson?

Their eyes met, and her shaky leg froze. She dropped her shoes to the ground and jumped from her seat. A few people stood in her way and she politely shoved them to the side.

Gemma spread out her arms as she grew closer. "You made it."

They embraced. "I said I would. How was the ceremony?"

"As beautiful as you'd expect. I know they'll both be surprised to see you here."

He smiled. "Thanks for inviting me down. I can't wait to see the expression on their faces."

And as the clock struck five, Christian and Adam swept through the double doors of the reception hall. Everyone broke out into cheers, shouts, and even a few ear-piercing whistles sprinkled in. They moved forward, and everyone created a path for the smiling couple to stroll toward the front of the room. As they approached the final few well-wishers, standing at the end were Pearson and Gemma with broad grins across their faces.

With his attention still focused on shaking hands, Christian failed to notice the constable or his best friend waiting. Adam tapped him on the shoulder and leaned in while pointing toward them.

Christian followed Adam's finger, and when their faces registered, he blinked twice to make sure he wasn't dreaming. He stuttered before he covered his mouth and doubled over while tears of gratitude streamed down his face.

Pearson stepped forward and in an instant, everyone in the room stood silent. All he had was one word. "Congratulations."

Adam charged toward the towering man and first gave him a big hug, then they shook hands. "What in the world are you doing here? You said you had to work."

"Surprise . . . I lied."

"No, don't say it's so," Christian joked.

"This is why I did it—to see the priceless reaction on your face."

When the shock wore off, Christian stepped closer. His hand dropped from his face and his voice shook from the adrenaline. "I can't tell you how much this means to us to have you here."

They embraced, and not until the DJ blasted an upbeat song did they released their hold on one another. Christian leaned in to whisper in Pearson's ear. "You mingle and enjoy yourself. We'll catch up with you as soon as we can. I can only assume you have news to share."

Pearson nodded and patted Christian on the back. "Yup, but it can wait. You should enjoy your day and we'll talk shop later."

An hour passed. The waitstaff cleared the plates from the tables, Gemma and Adam's best friend, Kevin, managed to embarrass each of them with his speech, and not once did the energy in the room drag. With a free moment, Christian grabbed Adam and they made their way to the table where those closest to the couple sat.

Adam hovered over Pearson and rested his hand on the man's shoulder. "You guys having a good time?"

"The best," Pearson replied. "And Gemma stole the show with her walk down memory lane."

Her ears turned cherry red and she playfully swatted at him. "Stop. You're just saying that."

Adam smiled and glanced at his parents. "And the two of you look like you're ready to bust a move and show us those dance moves you've been practicing."

Adam's father smiled and scooted out his chair, and the couple strutted in the direction of the dance floor. With them out of earshot, Christian wasted no time getting down to business.

"So, you brought news?" Christian asked.

"Indeed. Liam changed his plea on Friday and admitted everything in open court."

Adam crouched between the constable and Gemma. "So, there won't be a trial, then?"

"Nope. The judge handed down her sentencing yesterday morning."

All heads leaned in.

"So? How much time did he get?" Gemma asked.

Pearson fiddled with his tie and glanced at the eager faces. "Life sentence."

"Life sentence? I-I don't know what to say."

Christian scooted out the empty chair next to Gemma and pulled her close to him. "We got what we wanted, justice for your sister. Justice for you."

Matthias cut in. "Your father *was* a good man. I couldn't say when things went south."

"I wish we had the answers, but I believe we'll never know," Pearson replied.

Matthias mumbled to himself but loud enough for the table to hear. "Perhaps his love for Sarah was stronger than the love for his kids."

"What was that, Pop?"

"Just saying I'm relieved. For once he did the right thing and thought about Gemma and didn't want to put her through the torture of a trial."

Her jaw gaped open at the old man's callus comments. "How can you be so cruel? In the span of eight years I've lost my mother and my sister, and now the only anchor that kept me motivated to wake up every day is him going to prison for the rest of his life. How is any of this justice?"

Not even the plastic at the bottom of the chair legs could prevent the screech it made as Gemma scooched away from the table and bolted for the hallway.

"Pop, are you for real?"

"What?"

"You implied her father never loved her or Cassidy. We both know that's not true, and it's unfair for you to suggest so."

Matthias shrugged his shoulders. "I call 'em as I see 'em, son. Good riddance to him."

Christian stood from the seat and walked behind his father. With a firm grip on the old man's shoulder, he leaned down. "I'm going to check on Gemma. You and me, we'll discuss your crassness later."

Without as much as a goodbye, Christian sprinted across the packed room toward the door. If there was one place he knew she'd be, it was the ladies' room, the one place he always found her.

He paced outside the bathroom door. It was the last place he wanted to spend the evening of his wedding, yet given the circumstances, it was the one place he needed to be.

He covered his eyes, pushed against the door, and immediately the fragrant whiff of lavender tickled his nose. He shouted, "Police, if anyone other than Gemma Williams is in here, please leave within the next fifteen seconds. Otherwise, when I uncover my eyes you cannot say I didn't give you fair warning."

There was no mass exodus, only a soft, continuous sob from the stall closest to the window. He kept to his word and waited fifteen seconds, and with his sight restored, he moved in her direction. The heels of his shoes clacked with each step he took, until finally he stopped at the pastel-blue door and reached out his hand and pressed it inward.

In her beautiful dress, Gemma sat on the toilet seat cover with her face buried in her hands.

"For the love of God, Gemma. Can we please not have a repeat of prom night 2009?"

She unburied her face and a small chuckle brought a forced smile to her face. "Oh, Christian, you always know how to cheer a girl up."

"I'm sorry about my dad. I know he's still grieving in his own way, but regardless, it doesn't excuse his piggish behavior."

She sucked back the wetness. "It's not only what he said. Although, that didn't help matters."

Christian crouched to eye level with her. "Then if not just him, what else?"

"I'm alone for the first time in my entire life. Thirty years old, and what do I have to show? Don't you see . . . I'm an orphan abandoned in this shitty world."

"You do remember I sort of know what it feels like to feel alone."

"You do?"

"I mean, yeah. The day I packed all my belongings, loaded my car, and fled Cedar Lake. You think I had anyone there to help me?"

Her eyes rolled to the side and she thought over his question. "Now that you mention it, no, you had yourself."

"Exactly. You're upset not because you have to start over. You're upset because you are holding on to anger toward your father. The only way to fully heal is to forgive."

"You make it sound so easy to just say, 'Eh, so he cheated on my mother, killed my sister, and tried to kill me. But, hey, life goes on.' Is that what you're getting at?"

He shook his head. "No. Not even close."

"Then how? How do I forgive him when he's left my life a mess?"

"It'll take time. Look at my father and me. Ten years it took for me to forgive him. Ten years of my life wasted being angry, blaming him for every problem in my life. The problem was never him; it was me and my lack of moving forward."

Gemma's head hung and she broke eye contact.

"I know you're upset, but could you look at me?"

The sobbing resumed.

"You'll move past this. You're a strong woman, stronger than anyone I've ever known. If I can move forward and find happiness, so can you."

"But I literally have no one."

Christian scoffed. With both hands he reached out and gently shook her from her pity party. "And how can you say you have no one? Gemma, you have me. And my father has always been there for you even when I wasn't. Hell, now you have Adam to antagonize whenever you want."

Her mascara-stained eyes met his and she gently nodded.

Christian reached over and tore a long ribbon of toilet paper, wadded it up, and handed it over. "We're your family now and none of us will ever abandon you. We're in this together from this moment forward."

She reached out her hand and Christian hoisted her from the toilet seat. With a quick dab under her eyes, she breezed past him toward the mirror. Her hand gripped the edge of the sink, and she leaned in closer to get a better glimpse of herself. The bathroom door swung open and the distinct intro to "Time After Time" crept in. Without hesitation both of their heads turned.

An unsuspecting woman at the door took one look at them and jumped back. "Christian? Why on earth are you in the ladies' room?"

"Nicole!" he exclaimed. "Yeah, there's no need for alarm, we were just leaving."

Gemma wiped her face one final time and chucked the soiled tissue into the wastebasket. He grabbed her hand and pulled her closer to his face as they whizzed by. "It's my wedding day, so what d'you say we get back and make new memories instead of living with our old ones?"

She extended her hand. "May I have this dance?"

He lowered his head in embarrassment. "I suppose I owe you for ruining prom, huh?"

"Yeah, something like that."

He pulled her into a hug, and they rushed through the bathroom door to rejoin the party, which hadn't even reached its high point.

While the road ahead was long and unpredictable for them, right now they had each other, and that's all either of them needed in that moment.

ABOUT THE AUTHOR

C.L. Brees, the author of An Unsettled Past, Dark Ending, and Among the Ashes, was born and raised in rural northeast Indiana, a place where sometimes he found the environment a bit too restrictive for his overactive imagination. He had bigger plans and set his sights on exploring the world for inspiration. Currently, he lives in Germany.

C.L. Brees gained extensive knowledge in the world of criminal justice and forensics from the University of Baltimore, where he earned a Certificate in Crime Scene Investigation, a B.S. in Forensic Science, Magna Cum Laude, and an M.S. in Cyber Forensics in 2014 and 2015, respectively.

Before accepting his current assignment, he worked as a criminal justice researcher, a forensic analyst for a Baltimore law firm, and spent several years as a project manager on a major study for the National Institutes for Health.

HTTPS://WWW.CLBREESAUTHOR.COM

HTTPS://WWW.TWITTER.COM/CLBREESAUTHOR

HTTPS://WWW.FACEBOOK.COM/CLBREES

ALSO BY C. L. BREES

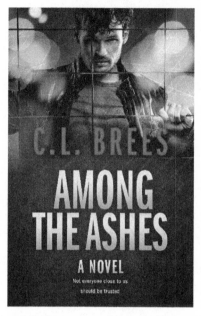

As one of the most up-and-coming criminal defense attorneys in St. John's, Newfound, Caleb Winters has virtually everything anybody could hope for: incredible friends, a new lover, and nearly perfect record of crushing his foe, Crown Prosecutor Andrew Murphy, in court.

An early morning phone call on the day of his closing submissions dredges up faded memories. Skeletal remains were found north of town and the constabulary believes them to be of his missing husband, Sebastian.

After losing his case in court, Caleb's new lover disappears. He suspects his angry client is responsible for his disappearance, but his pleas with the constabulary only drive them to put Caleb at the top of their suspect list. As the days go by, and the bodies pile up, the constabulary must consider the possibility someone else is behind the mayhem.

With a handful of suspects, all with a motive for wanting to ruin Caleb's life, will the constables assigned figure out who's accountable for the chaos? Or will Caleb find himself like his friends; departed too soon?

Made in the USA
Coppell, TX
08 March 2021